The City of the Jugglers

The City of the Jugglers; or, Free-Trade in Souls

A Romance of the "Golden" Age

William North

THE UNIVERSITY OF SOUTH CAROLINA PRESS

An AccessAble Book, Published in Cooperation with University Libraries, University of South Carolina

New material © 2008 University of South Carolina

Cloth edition published by H. J. Gibbs, London, 1850
Paperback edition published by the University of South
Carolina Press,
Columbia, South Carolina 29208

www.sc.edu/uscpress

Manufactured in the United States of America

17 16 15 14 13 12 11 10 09 08   10 9 8 7 6 5 4 3 2 1

Library of Congress Cataloging-in-Publication data is available.

ISBN 978-1-57003- 811-2 (pbk)

About This Book and Its Author

William North's *The City of the Jugglers* (1850) is one of the
most original novels of the mid-Victorian period; it is also
the most elusive book by one of the nineteenth century's most
elusive authors. Only three surviving copies are recorded in
WorldCat, with only two listed in libraries in North America.
North was widely published and well known in the 1840s in
London and Paris and in the early 1850s in New York, yet
there is no modern biography, nor is there an entry for him
in such standard works as *The Oxford Companion to English
Literature, The Cambridge Bibliography of English Literature,*
or *The Dictionary of National Biography.*

North (1824 or 1825–1854) was an aristocrat by birth
and a republican by conviction. He came from the cadet
branch of a rich landed and clerical family (relatives included
the earls of Guilford and a bishop of Winchester). In his teens
he broke away from a conventional English classical education (at Temple Grove and probably also at Eton) to study at
a German university. His first book, *Anti-Coningsby; or, The
New Generation Grown Old, by an Embryo M.P.* (1844), a two-
volume political satire on Disraeli and the Young England
movement, published when North was only nineteen, was
rapidly followed by a three-volume political novel, *The
Imposter; or, Born without a Conscience* (1845), and the
shorter *Anti-Punch; or, The Toy-Shop in Fleet Street* (1847).
At the same time as he was writing these books, he was con-
tributing regularly to *Chambers's Edinburgh Journal, Eliza
Cook's Journal,* and similar publications.

North had also translated the French writer Alphonse
Lamartine's *Poetical Meditations* (1848), and on the outbreak
of revolution, he traveled to Paris. He found Lamartine insuf-
ficiently revolutionary, however, and soon returned to London
to publish a new edition of William Beckford's *Vathek* (1849),
with a memoir of Beckford, North's most reprinted work. A
friend of the Rossetti brothers, North was also involved in

1849 in initial plans for the *Germ*, a Pre-Raphaelite magazine. Christina Rossetti distrusted him as a "rabid" Chartist and free-thinker, but North remained on good terms with other members of the family. It was at this point in his career that North published *The City of the Jugglers* and a companion pamphlet, also very rare, *The Infinite Republic: A Spiritual Revolution* (1851). He later told friends that not a single copy of the novel had sold, asserting that if even one purchaser would have told friends about it, success would have been assured.

Certainly none of this literary activity brought North what he thought an adequate income, and after the failure of his short-lived *North's Magazine* in 1852, he decided to immigrate to the United States. There, in New York, North associated with the literary circle at Pfaff's Tavern and seemed to flourish. His Poe-like short stories and poems appeared in *Putnam's Monthly Magazine, Graham's Magazine, Harper's*, the *Whig Review*, the *Knickerbocker*, and the *Saturday Press*. He wrote a farce, *The Automaton Man*, that was successfully produced at Burton's Theatre, and he drew on his experience in France to write *The History of Napoleon III* (1853). But he felt disappointed both in love and in his literary career. He had often discussed, and threatened, suicide, and in November 1854 he killed himself by drinking prussic acid, leaving in manuscript his final and most successful novel, *The Slave of the Lamp* (1854), a satire on New York society and the literary scene, later reprinted as *The Man of the World* (1866, 1877).

This facsimile of North's *The City of the Jugglers* has been scanned from the original 1850 edition now in the Department of Rare Books & Special Collections at the University of South Carolina. The facsimile makes North's book available for the first time since its original publication, both in digital form, through the library's Digital Collections site, and also as a print-on-demand book, in partnership with the University of South Carolina Press.

Patrick G. Scott
Director, Rare Books & Special Collections
Thomas Cooper Library
University of South Carolina

The City of the Jugglers

THE

CITY OF THE JUGGLERS;

OR,

FREE-TRADE IN SOULS.

A Romance of the "Golden" Age

PRO.	CON.
" Every man has his price."	" What shall it profit a man if he gain the whole world and lose his own soul?"

BY W. NORTH,

Author of "Anti-Coningsby," " The Impostor," Lamartine's " Poetic Meditations,"

(translation,) &c., &c.

WITH FOUR HIGHLY FINISHED ETCHINGS,

BY F. H. T. BELLEW.

LONDON:

H. J. GIBBS, 4, TAVISTOCK-STREET, STRAND.

1850.

H. J. GIBBS, PRINTER, 4, TAVISTOCK-STREET, STRAND.

CONTENTS.

BOOK I.

THE OPENING OF THE SOUL EXCHANGE.

BOOK II.

THE GRAND EXHIBITION OF THE SOULS OF ALL NATIONS.

BOOK III.

THE PANIC IN THE SOUL MARKET.

PROLOGUE.

I.

I had a dream! start not, 'tis still
   Allowed to dream—I had a dream!
Methought, obedient to my will,
   An army, like a swollen stream,
Poured from a savage mountain gorge,
   With crimson banners floating,
      In choral song,
      As thunder strong,
   Their foes to death devoting.

II.

I stood upon a jutting crag,
   My long sword glittering and bare,
And sternly counted, flag by flag,
   While swelled their war-cry on the air,
And horsemen, num'rous as the sand
   On ocean's shore uncounted,
      Still swept beneath,
      With song of death,
   On fiery chargers mounted.

III.

At length they paused, 'mid silence vast,
 As if all earth had ceased to breathe ;
And with dread thought my brain, o'ercast,
 Began to throb, and whirl, and seethe,
And from the crowded gorge below,
 And from each crag's wild station,
   Upon me gazed
   Fierce eyes, that blazed
 With fevered expectation.

IV.

And then I knew that all this host
 Was mine to govern, mine to lead,
That earth must now be gained or lost,
 For evermore enslaved or freed;
And with the thought my heart grew full,
 And strength, the child of danger,
   Inspired a power
   O'er that grand hour,
 To earthly doubt a stranger.

V.

I spoke. With eyes the mountain side
 Was shining, as with sombre gems—
" Eternal death to all the pride
 Of coronets and diadems!
Rise! take thy everlasting throne,
 Spirit of truth undying !
   In vengeance rise,
   To paralyse
 The foes, thy rule defying!

VI.

Men are not children of a day,
    As grovellers cant, and canters whine,
They tread an everlasting way,
    Spirits of essence pure, divine.
From state to state, from world to world,
    They rise o'er pain victorious,
        This life a stage,
        The last turned page
    Of progress boundless, glorious.

VII.

Spirits of everlasting time!
    Men, passing citizens of earth!
Dare to fulfil each thought sublime,
    Each passion of celestial birth!
Dare to *be* all that fancy dreams,
    To *do* all conscience teaches!
        Go forth to quell
        The brood of Hell,
    And storm their rampart's breaches!

VIII.

There is a plague—a mad disease—
    That overspreads the shuddering globe,
Infects the ships that sail the seas,
    And wraps the earth with leper's robe—
A burning, savage lust of gold,
    The craving soul's starvation,
        Self's scheme to rise
        To Paradise
    On brother soul's damnation!

IX.

In vain, with words that pierce like swords,
  With love that penetrates like dew,
We offer to these blinded lords
  Of visionary wealth, the true,
The only wealth, the only truth,
  By reason unrejected—
      " The wealth of each,
      Of all," we teach,
  From man to man reflected.

X.

They sleep the sleep of folly's crew;
  No sentinel holds watch.   They sleep—
Thus slept the host the Persian slew—
  They will not hear; we will not weep,
Though we should wade in blood knee-deep!
  They sleep—base, abject, sterile—
      Asleep, they wait
      Their certain fate,
  In torpor's ghastly peril!

XI.

" *March on !*"—Ten thousand trumpets then
  Woke every mountain echo round,
And voices of unnumbered men
  Returned the blast with deafening sound.
" *March on !*"—I madly waved my brand,
  Like heaven's storm-fire gleaming,
      When at my side
      A form I spied,
  A face 'mid gold locks streaming.

XII.

A woman's form, of such bright grace,
    And radiant dignity, methought,
In gazing wildly on her face,
    All passion fled, and, wonder-fraught,
I stood expectant of command.
    She spoke—" To me is given,
        To me alone
        Th' eternal throne,
    The throne of earth and heaven!

XIII.

" *Love* has the power alone to cure
    The mad disease of selfish greed;
The sword of Love is reason pure;
    The wounds of Love can never bleed,
But are themselves best medicine.
    March on !—march on, *for ever !*
        Learn—Truth disclaims
        All bounded aims
    That *now* and *future* sever !

XIV.

" Beware, beware of pride—the curse
    Of spirit chief, as earthly king!
Nor deem *thy* youth's hot flood of verse
    Such song as none but thou can sing!
Armed *cap-à-pié*, my warriors fight,
    O'er earth's broad surface scattered,
        Each son of light
        An errant knight
    Till falsehood's fanes be shattered!

XV.

" And hear my sovereign decree,
　　Which shall in lightning streams go forth,
The Titan, *Thought*, untamed shall be,
　　The strong Prometheus of the North;
And mighty poets shall arise,
　　The clouded heavens clearing,
　　　　With lays to shame
　　　　Dead kings of fame,
Young earth, in rapture, hearing!"

XVI.

And as the peerless accents stayed
　　Above, below, and all around,
In robes of dazzling light arrayed,
　　Stood living echos of the sound;
Great, noble forms of god-like men—
　　Prophets—no more of Edom,
　　　　Or Israel.
　　　　The choral swell
Bursts forth.　Hark!—" Love and Freedom!"

June, 1850.   W. N.

CITY OF THE JUGGLERS;

OR,

FREE-TRADE IN SOULS.

BOOK I.

THE OPENING OF THE SOUL EXCHANGE.

CHAPTER I.

A BOLD SPECULATOR.

It was about four o'clock on a spring afternoon. The City was still in full activity. The gold was rattling on the bank counters, and the clerks were cashing their notes as coolly as if the whole affair had been anything but a gigantic juggle. *Practical* men—too practical to think—were paying in their deposits with a touching and child-like confidence. No suspicion had *they* that they were trusting to a system, which, "like the baseless fabric of a vision," might at any moment dissolve into nothingness. *Practical* men do not understand the currency—they despise theorists who do. They swear by Sir Robert the Devil and—everybody is in debt to everybody in consequence.

B

No matter. It was four P.M. in the City. Attornies were cheating their clients, or assisting them to cheat other people. Merchants were calculating the chances of the markets, like gamblers inventing martingales. Clerks were adding up figures as clocks add up minutes. Cashiers and secretaries were reflecting on the facilities of an impromptu voyage to California. Directors of companies were " cooking" the accounts of their shareholders. Waiters at Joe's, Sam's, Tom's, Betsy's, and other chop-houses, whose proprietors are apparently more proud of their Christian names than usual, ordered countless chops through patent gutta percha telegraphs. Cooks basted themselves with half-and-half whilst roasting before their fires, like Fox's martyrs, bound to the steaks of their tyrants. Crossing-sweepers were industriously clearing streets as dry as carpets and begging of passengers as charitable as cannibals. Usurers were meeting gentlemen who wanted to borrow money at any rate of—nonpayment. Adventurers were keeping appointments with capitalists they hoped to drag into speculations. Capitalists were contriving monopolies by which to crush non-capitalist adventurers. Stockbrokers were playing monkey tricks on the Stock Exchange. Hebrew gold kings were manufacturing intelligence to astonish the stock-brokers. Couriers were dashing off with the commands of London financiers to foreign potentates. Messengers were arriving from the sham, entreating aid from the real sovereigns of Europe. And the plenipotentiaries of the daily press were calmly overlooking the whole ant-hill with sublime indifference to the struggles of its busy insects, generalising for millions the knowledge which, even to those in the midst of the bustle, was too often but semi-obscurity and chromatropic confusion.

This being the state of affairs in the stronghold of the gold-worshippers, the great commercial "diggins" of the eastern world, two individuals—Manichæans of the nineteenth century—descended arm-in-arm the broad flight of steps from the great gate of the Royal Exchange, engaged in low but animated conversation.

Their object was to escape from the crowd, and to avoid being overheard by strangers, as was evident from the cautious glances they threw about them. They paused in the shadow of the Duke of Wellington's statue, which the rays of the western sun grotesquely caricatured upon the pavement. The sun is like all light—a great leveller. As death brings the pretensions, so sunshine brings the shadows of all men to the dust.

"It is an old truism," said the taller of the two Manichæans, "but it never struck me so forcibly before. The world is never thoroughly taken in by an old juggle. Catch a new monster, a child with the legs of an ostrich, or a Bengal tiger that can learn to play at nine-pins, and the mob rushes to pay its half-crowns, and vociferate its admiration; but produce a second pair of Siamese twins, or a latter-day Tom Thumb that may be put into a hat-box, and it is as little appreciated as an old joke of the venerable Miller."

The speaker, whose large black eyes glittered with a peculiar exultation, cast a searching side-glance at his companion.

He was a thin man, in the prime of life, slightly above the middle height, with coal-black hair and whiskers, very large arched eyebrows, and a cadaverous complexion.

His features were aquiline, regular, and even handsome.
But on minute inspection a variety of lines and wrinkles
became perceptible, which united to give his face a
cynical, perhaps malignant, expression. There was
more assurance than dignity in his manner, and though
his frown might have inspired little apprehension, his
smile suggested something dangerous, because undefined.

The personage to whom he had spoken was, on the
other hand, short, stout, and rather rubicund; with
small greenish eyes, that twinkled restlessly beneath
the serpentine fascination of his companion's gaze.

"Yes," continued the thin man sententiously, "new
roads provoke new travellers. There are fools enough,
and knaves enough, and gold enough behind us"—he
pointed significantly towards the Exchange by a slight
motion of his hand—"to build railways from London to
Calcutta, with an extension to Pekin, if wanted. But
railways have found their level. They may still trans-
port railway kings, but cannot trust them in any station
on their lines. Railways are degenerating into facts,
from phantasm Golcondas, as that mad old grumbling
dreamer Carlyle would call them, I suppose. There is
a fellow for you! who, having discovered the Irishman's
axiom that 'Mankind is a great rascal,' gets straightway into a passion, and thinks to turn the river of mind
as a hunter turns a buffalo, by shrieking outlandish
gibberish and compound Anglo-German Billingsgate!
I hate these canting egotistical lecturers, spouters, and
scribblers. If a man has an itch for reforming the world,
let him do something himself, instead of abusing everybody else. Give me practical men, who take the earth
as they find it, and if they can't build their houses on

rocks take the firmest sand that offers. There is but one moral principle, and that is self-interest. There is but one maxim worth attending to in life—'Buy in the cheapest market and sell in the dearest.'"

"True," said the stout man, "but buy as cheap as you will, and sell as dear as you will, unless you have an unlimited market—which, with present competition, is scarcely possible—I can't see the facility of making those rapid fortunes you hinted at."

"Therefore," replied his saturnine comrade, "I come back to my old proposition: the newest speculation is the most profitable. Petty traders gamble, commercial genius descends upon its prey like the eagle. Who do you suppose make the most rapid fortunes?"

"Bill-brokers, perhaps."

"Pshaw! have *you* made a fortune at that tedious game?"

"I have not been so lucky as I might have been. I have had heavy losses lately. But then I was imprudent, I ran great risks—"

"Without which you would have done nothing. Guess again."

"I have it—the Jew slopsellers!"

"Nonsense. The poor rogues scrape together a trifle by grinding the life out of their starved workwomen; and Noses and Son, backed by Rotmuck—I beg his pardon, Baron de Rotmuck—may have done something more with bankrupt stock, devil's-dust cloth, and a perfect Niagara cataract of advertisements. *Any* man may make five hundred per cent. per annum if he only has the capital required to start with."

"Well, I give it up," said the fat man, gasping with curiosity.

" Of course you do. Now answer me an easier question. Does not all commerce amount at bottom to selling other men's labour for your own advantage?"

" Why—yes—that is—I suppose so," said the stout Manichæan, who did not pretend to understand political economy, and felt himself already out of his depth.

He was, it must be owned, a rather shallow Plato, and his instructor a somewhat Mephistophelian Socrates.

" *No,*" rejoined the latter, " I say there is one thing better."

" Indeed ! what is it then?" grunted the stout disciple, completely mystified by this unexpected announcement.

" *Selling the men themselves,*" replied the taller speculator, after a pause, with cutting emphasis.

So sharp, bitter, and to the purpose was every sentence of this man that he might be said, like Hamlet, to "speak daggers." Each of his words was a brass-headed nail, driven into his companion's brain with a miner's hammer.

" Do slave-dealers make quick profits?" enquired the short man, timidly. ·

" Very."

" But are they not occasionally shot by the guns of British cruisers ?"

" Occasionally : the sea-serpent is sometimes seen, Lord John once said a good thing."

" So you think dealing in niggers the best speculation we could embark in ?"

"The best you could *embark* in, certainly."

"But seriously?"

" Why, on the principle of 'Buy in the cheapest market and sell in the dearest,' it stands to reason that a man-catcher who steals his merchandise ready made (begotten, I *should* say), cannot well lose by the bargain, unless he meet by a miracle with a cruiser, and lose the bargain altogether. But I have no notion of transporting black cattle from Guinea to Brazil. I said something *new* was the thing. Well, human bodies, black and white, fair and foul, alive and dead, are regular articles of commerce. *I* propose to enter into a business quite as common, but scarcely recognised on 'Change. In a word—I propose to *deal in human souls!*"

" The devil you do ! What an uncommonly strange idea !—But you are jesting ?"

" I never jest. What I say, I mean."

"Are you the Prince of Darkness, then, or his envoy? Is that a pocket handkerchief or a tail hanging out of your pocket ? Why—excuse my saying it—you must be either mad, or drunk, or making a butt of me ! Pray talk of pounds, shillings, and pence, but don't speak to me of souls. I neither believe in souls nor devil."

"No," said the pale man, with a concentrated sneer, that made the other almost tremble at his own audacity, " nor in any God but Plutus. But you do not understand me. In the first place, never mix up such childish trash as devils, with or without horns, hoofs, or tails, in a rational discussion. Next, be assured that there *is* a devil, minus the D, pervading the very atmosphere we breathe. This spirit of *evil* seems a sort of spice to existence generally, without which it would be confoundedly monotonous and insipid. Thirdly, as to a soul, you have a thinking apparatus in your scull, I presume. You have feelings, especially if kicked down stairs; and you have or have not principles, good, bad, or indifferent, as the case may be. These, or the use of them, men, can and do sell every day of their lives. In common parlance, such queer matters are termed souls. The word is understood, why split straws about an expression?"

"A thousand pardons! I thought you were quizzing me by proposing to deal in souls after death?"

"After death! It is you who are quizzing now! What are you raving about? What do we know of *death?* 'Post mortem nihil est, ipsaque mors nihil,' said Seneca, who continues to describe all beyond as 'Rumores vacui, verbaque inania.' After death! There is nothing to be said after such an absurdity. You were dreaming of Doctor Faustus. O sancta simplicitas! It is in the souls of the living, not the dead, I propose to speculate."

"Well, there is one thing I wish to know," said the stout pupil, overawed to some extent by his companion's air of superiority, caustic fluency, and Latin quotations; "how on earth can you buy a soul without a body to keep it in?"

"What! still in the dark, or rather still among the darkies?" replied the tall philosopher, in a tone which caused the fat neophyte to apprehend an attack in Greek or Hebrew on his obtuse intelligence; "do you think I want to buy men for the sake of putting them in glass cases? Take care of the souls, and the bodies will take care of themselves. Why, one would think I had proposed something really new—to try an experiment which had never been tried before."

"Humph! If your scheme is not new after all, why did you boast of its novelty?"

The dark man looked down upon his comrade, with the good-humoured pity of superior genius.

" All things are old and all things are new according to combination and circumstances," he replied, with less sarcasm in his tone. " I have not told you my scheme yet. I have merely thrown out an idea in order to prepare you to understand it. Look about you—look at Downing-street, look at the Houses of Parliament, look at the Church, the Bar, the Press—aye, look at the leviathan *Timeserver* and its crew; and say whether there are not souls bought and sold, aye, and double-sold in London, wholesale and retail, to an extent beyond all ordinary powers of calculation ? Now observe how clumsily, how indelicately, how imperfectly the thing is managed—and mark how splendidly my scheme will come in to supply all the wants of the age. You shall share the speculation. The capital can be raised in shares. The preliminary expences are not worth mentioning. The very letters of allotment will rise like balloons at Vauxhall—Railways were a joke to it!— The South-Sea Bubble a mere flea-bite! However, talking is dry work; I feel inclined for a cutlet; so we will just turn into the European, and discuss the matter over a bottle of Madeira. By the way, there is a popular prejudice of late against Madeira. It was started for a wager by a fashionable physician. I was dining with him at the time. Where can you show me a stronger proof of the ease with which the world is made a fool of ?"

CHAPTER II.

THE SOUL AGENT'S FIRST CUSTOMER.

A week had elapsed since the conversation of our two
Manichæans, recorded in the preceding chapter.

A man of striking and majestic aspect walked down
Whitehall, in the direction of Westminster Abbey, which,
gilded by the noon-day sun, towered proudly above the
surrounding buildings.

Even so did he himself tower above the crowd amid
which he moved. Taller by a head than the average
race of men, his breadth of chest and martial carriage
alike indicated a fitness for and experience of the camp.
More than one trim guardsman involuntarily turned to
gaze after the passing stranger. Nor was this military
appearance diminished by a long dark brown moustache,
which completely overshadowed his upper lip, and a closely
buttoned surtout of dark green cloth, from the breast of
which a crumpled roll of papers protruded. His features
were noble in the natural and uncorrupted sense of the
word. His eyes, grey in colour, were of a singular beauty.
Their very softness expressed an intensity of self-posses-
sion, courage, and penetration, rarely found in eyes which
shine more brightly with the borrowed light from without. Their brightness was the brightness of the spirit
that flashed through them, as the glances of women
through those useful blinds, transparent from the interior

of a mansion, but impervious to the gaze of the curious in the public thoroughfare. His broad open brow was smooth as a young girl's, yet pregnant with earnest thought. Take him all in all, he conveyed an idea of the grandeur of a Mirabeau without his ugliness, or of a Dante without his sorrows. His profile resembled that of the living poet Lamartine—his full face suggested the features of the dead warrior Napoleon. Strange combination of imperfect comparisons! Such countenances must be seen; they are unique, and are not to be met with amongst common men. Such an attempt at verbal picturing may seem exaggerated—perhaps inconsistent. But this is certain; there are forms of human grace and dignity, that walk the earth in living incarnation, which do not yield to sculptured gods, or poet's dreams of the ideal. Happy the student who has met with such forms, which the great artist, Nature, at times exhibits, lest the vanity of imagination should wax too arrogant of an unsubstantial superiority.

The stranger's rapid progress was arrested by a mob, which had assembled, regardless of the remonstrances of established authority in the shape of blue coats and metal buttons, before a house recently painted and otherwise externally embellished.

Upon the window blinds of the ground-floor, and upon a large brass plate by the side of the portal, were to be read these startling words—

"GENERAL AGENCY"

"FOR THE SALE AND PURCHASE OF HUMAN SOULS."

A porter at the door, in a magnificent livery, distributed to all respectably-dressed people prospectuses printed in ιetters of gold upon superfine satin note paper. To the rabble of more unpretending costume he gave no prospectuses, but occasionally addressed them in the following scornful terms, varying his discourse with references to his more wealthy auditors :—

"Come, move off, my good people, move off; what are you staring at? No admission except on business, sir. Hollo, you in the corduroys, just get away from those railings, will you? nobody will give anything for *your* soul, depend upon it—A prospectus, madam? certainly—Like to walk in and speak to the secretary, sir? (This was spoken to a gentleman who had the air of an M.P. at the least.) Now, then, don't stand in the way, little boys—where are you pushing to?—do you want to be packed off to the station-house, you man with the basket?"

At this moment the gigantic figure of the stranger moving through the crowd, as a man-of-war through the ocean, arrived opposite the speaker. The new comer, laying his hand upon the shoulder of the porter, twirled him round like a top without apparent effort, and passed quietly into the office. A pasteboard clerk, amazingly well got up, with a very stiff white neckcloth, and a very wooden face, received the intruder in a most obsequious manner.

"Can I see the manager?" said the stranger, curtly.

"If you will state your business, sir, certainly," replied the stiff clerk, in measured accents.

"Without that preliminary?" said the stranger, quietly.

"No, sir, I must know—"

"To know nothing is your department, I should imagine," rejoined the obstinate stranger.

" Sir, I really—"

"Nonsense, I mean no offence. If your masters are here, announce me." And the stranger held out a card, on which a duke's coronet was visible, but covered with his thumb the *name*, of which the stiff clerk could only see a small piece of one letter, and even that he could not distinguish.

" The Duke of—?" said the clerk, with a smile like the distortion of a gutta percha mask, " I beg your grace's pardon, but I could not see the—"

" Exactly, that will do; announce me at once."

" As the Duke of—?"

" Just so—I am in a hurry."

The pasteboard clerk did not dare to push his in- quiries farther, and straightway announced the Duke of Nowhere, who was instantly admitted to the sanctum in which the saturnine speculator of our former chapter was seated. Upon the table before him were rows of books and papers tied with red tape. The apartment was luxuriously furnished. He rose politely as the martial visitor entered.

The stranger removed his hat, and thus more fully displayed the grandeur of a brow stamped with intel- lectual indication. He met the sharp glance of the speculator's large black eyes with supreme indifference. There were only one pair of eyes in existence that had power over the stranger; and they were other eyes than speculators'.

On the other hand the enterprising Soul Agent felt a vaguely-uncomfortable sensation at the steady look of his bright-eyed visitor, which seemed to take him in at a glance, to measure and judge him at first sight, and to scan him with a quiet consciousness of superiority against which he secretly rebelled in spirit. He resolved to resist this sensation to the utmost, and recover his natural audacity.

" Excuse me," said the Soul Agent, with easy politeness, " my clerk announced you as the Duke of—I really did not catch the name."

" Nor did he," said the stranger, with perfect suavity.

" Nevertheless, if we are to transact business together, as I presume we may from your honouring us with a call, it is necessary to know your real name and address—in confidence—in strict confidence, your grace."

" As what the *Timeserver* calls a guarantee of my good faith," rejoined the stranger, " while their own is beyond all guaranteeing."

"A great organ the *Timeserver !*" said the Soul Agent.

" A great grinding organ, truly," said the visitor, sarcastically.

" Magnificent leaders, sometimes," hinted the agent.

" Five-guinea yards of balderdash," replied the stranger.

" Vast sources of information."

" For distorting and colouring," completed the visitor.

" Immense power ! "

" Over old gentlemen of weak minds."

" Still it is a wonderful engine, your grace."

" Wonderfully stupid. *I mean to put it down.*"

The Soul Agent stared aghast in amazement. He had shares in the *Timeserver*.

The stranger continued, "Never mind the grace, I may be anything but what I represent myself. I may be an impostor. However, that is of no consequence."

"Of no consequence? But it seems to me—"

"Exactly; I will set your scruples at rest. Look at this bag."

The Soul Agent did look with all the power of his large black optics.

"It contains a thousand pounds in gold. Take it in your hand, look at it, weigh it, feel it. You worship gold—respect me, at any rate to the extent of a thousand pounds. There are others where these came from. Now to business. I wish to buy the soul of a cabinet minister—in fact the F——n Secretary. Can you negotiate the matter for me at any price, and to what extent?"

The dark speculator regarded the cavalier stranger with increasing admiration. He felt that cunning with such a man would be thrown away. But there was much to hope from his liberality.

"On referring to my register," said the Soul Agent, in a cool business-like tone, "I find that the soul of the minister in question is in the market. His exact price will require some calculation, for I find that there is a report of his being mortgaged to Russia, and otherwise diplomatically pledged. I will, however, get our actuary to make a precise estimate, which in a few days I can communicate to your grace."

"Good," said the stranger, "there is no particular hurry as to that matter. Now as to the leader of the opposition?"

"Sold, your grace, sold long ago, by private contract."

"Beyond redemption?"

"I fear so, at present."

"Could an assignment be effected from the present holders?"

"Not unless, perhaps, at a monstrous figure. They value him highly, as highly as a Jew's eye. Indeed, I may remark in confidence that he is very much over-rated by his friends."

"Good. When he is to be had at a discount I may treat with you. The chief proprietor of the *Timeserver*, is he on sale? I will give a liberal price for the rubbish."

"At present he is mortgaged heavily, but will bear additional encumbrance," replied the Soul Agent. "There again the figure is very high, and if I might venture a suggestion, a cheaper bargain might be made with the principal editor."

"Who has no soul to sell at all. Thank you—I have no wish to purchase slaves. My work cannot be done by machines. I can pick up mere instruments, as occasion -offers, at clubs, or coffee-houses, or anywhere."

"I perceive that your grace understands business. It is a pleasure to deal with a nobleman of such evident talent."

"You flatter me."

"Not in the least, your grace. If you could only give me some idea of the line in which you speculate, I could perhaps be of some real service to your grace."

"Thank you," replied the stranger, with distant courtesy, "I have only two more enquiries to make—is there a soul upon your books belonging (if not sold to somebody else) to one Bernard Viridor?"

"To what class does he belong, your grace. I really do not remember the name?"

"He is a young writer, chiefly on abstract questions, and under an assumed name; a poet of the *nascitur non fit* order, and I believe rather a red-hot democrat."

The Soul Agent took up one of the volumes upon the table and turned over its leaves with great rapidity.

"Here is the name," he said, on turning to letter V, "your description is correct—man of genius—young—poor—pretends enthusiasm—mixed up with treasonable movements— associates with suspicious company. May be had reasonable, I should say, if not too nice on minute points of opinion."

"Or broad principles?" said the stranger.

"Principles are very elastic," said the agent, drily, "but this Viridor is ambitious, most likely—may give more trouble than more important people. However, I will undertake the negotiation if fair terms are offered and full powers to treat given, with time to collect information."

"I authorise you to bid as high as ten thousand pounds, with a place worth from five to twelve hundred a year, a seat in Parliament, and an introduction to the first society in England."

"In that case I think we may consider the matter settled," said the Soul Agent, with a grim smile; "a democrat is but an advanced Whig, and every Whig is a Tory on the Treasury bench. This young dreamer is probably in debt, and can be easily reached. Very few souls can stand the test of extreme pecuniary pressure."

"Very few."

"Is he well connected?"

"Yes, his relations are all in independent circumstances and comparatively rich. He is of good family, as they call it."

"All the better! A genius, not to say a democrat, is always cut by his relations. That stings the soul and makes it bitter. It teaches wisdom and destroys childish faith in human nature."

" Whence scepticism, selfishness, and worldliness— that is, venality. You are a shrewd guesser at psychology," said the stranger, regarding the Soul Agent with a sort of interest akin to the geologist's examination of a new fossil.

" A logician, your grace, if you please, not a guesser."

The stranger smiled almost disdainfully.

" You are not so shrewd as I thought, or you would have abandoned logic," resumed the supposed duke. " But I am not here for abstract discussions. You think my affair can be managed ?"

- " Yes, but it may require great delicacy of manœuvre to bring him to treat plainly."

" You can keep the £1000 as a deposit for preliminary expences."

"They will not exceed a couple of hundred," said the dark calculator, placing the heavy bag of gold in a drawer, with feigned indifference.

Nevertheless, the stranger, with that keen intuition of a mind at once imaginative and reflective in the highest degree, detected at a glance by the expression of the Soul Agent's fingers, that there was, as yet, little capital at the back of the new speculation. There is no over-refinement of observation in this statement. For those *who can read*, every square inch of nature is scribbled over with the hieroglyphs of thought.

"We endeavour," continued the Soul Agent, involuntarily infusing a shade more subservience into his tone, " we endeavour to act fairly towards our clients, and to save their money, as far as practicable, in all transactions. In fact, it is our own interest to do so, as rival agencies will open in imitation of our establishment within a few days. However, our immense connections and extended sources of information give advantages to the genuine concern which other firms will vainly attempt to compete with."

"It is a pity that a patent could not be secured for so splendid an idea."

"It is indeed," said the Soul Agent, bowing low to the compliment. "And now, your grace, although I have not the honour of knowing your name, I am prepared, if you desire it, to offer you a few shares in the company at par, notwithstanding that they are already at a high premium in the market."

"Your disinterestedness overwhelms me. I will consider the matter as speedily as possible. Meanwhile, one last proposition. May I take the extreme liberty of inquiring at what price your own valuable soul is to be purchased? I am not a poor man, so you need not fear to name a round sum, or even a great prize of a non-pecuniary nature, for which you are doubtless eligible?"

For the first time during many long years the dark speculator felt the blood rush up to his cheeks, his heart—he had one, anatomically speaking—beat quickly, and his whole nervous system intensely agitated.

Destitute of conscientious scruples, and all ordinary weaknesses of sentiment, he had yet one dominant quality, which from its exaggeration amounted almost to a virtue. He was proud—proud as the type of pride, the fallen but unconquered Lucifer. His dark eyes flashed for an instant with suppressed rage. Lived there a man—was this impassible and incomprehensible stranger *the* man—who ventured to make him the butt of a whimsical pleasantry?   An instant's reflection banished the idea.   The bag of gold in his drawer was proof conclusive of the stranger's seriousness.   Then again, who *was* this mysterious nobleman whose speculations took so bold and extensive a range?   What were his means, and what were his aims? Was he some fabulously wealthy peer, gifted miraculously with the strong intellect of a plebeian student, and grasping in his enlightened ambition the full power which such a position gave him?   It was impossible to guess—it was useless to ask.   Here, probably, was an opportunity for the Soul Agent of securing at one blow a comparatively vast fortune. But then his grand schemes, his brilliant speculations, his independent balance-holding between all parties and factions, his prospectively enormous gains, which became at the best problematical as the tool of another. He threw his pride into the scale, and independence triumphed. He resolved to reject the offer, and whilst he was about it, to do it grandly. But he overshot his mark. He was not a match for the stranger.   Cunning never is for genius.

"I thank your grace," replied the Soul Agent, vainly affecting extraordinary coolness, and vainly hoping to have concealed the inward struggle which the bright-eyed cavalier read, as a mariner reads the signs of a storm in the heavens, " my profession is to buy and sell the souls of other men, but not to barter my own liberty. Besides, I too am rich, and shall be richer, for the profits of such a trade are not easily computed."

"True," said the stranger; "you despise my offer,

not understanding its value. Every man has his price. I believe you assume that postulate. But you imagine that to buy you at your own estimate is not in the power of so humble an individual as myself. It may be so—I am sorry I cannot arrange the matter. You will still undertake my commissions?"

" With pleasure," said the agent; and secretly stung at the irresistible domination of his collocutor's nature, he risked a most adventurous and ill-timed sarcasm.

" Perhaps," he said, with difficulty preventing his voice from quivering, " perhaps your grace might not object to sell your own soul if a sufficiently high price were offered?"

" Willingly," said the stranger, frankly, to the consternation of the Soul Agent, who calculated upon a contemptuous refusal. " Sign me a cheque for a million, and the thing is done!"

" A million!" gasped the speculator; " a million for a soul without a name!"

" It is worth it," said the stranger.

"But without even a name?"

" Produce the money, or prove your immediate power of raising it, and I will tell you my name."

The Soul Agent, who felt his dignity lowered by this strange *badinage*, wished his customer or himself at the devil his master's, rather than where he sat at that moment.

" The price is preposterous!" he exclaimed, peevishly.

" You perceive," said the stranger, coldly, " that it is useless to trifle with me. You are a gentleman of boldness, fertile resources, and experience, but *you* are trying to make a fortune—*I* already possess one. Now to *me*, a million, if there were an object to be gained, would be a mere bagatelle."

A mere bagatelle ! The Soul Agent forgot all personal pride at this prodigious announcement. Bitterly he regretted that he had not accepted the stranger's offer. He saw in the stern though beautiful lineaments of his client the expression absolute of truth and power. He felt that he was indeed in the presence of one of the real kings of men, one too who for a wonder appeared equally rich in spiritual and material wealth. A million ! he forgot the sarcasm in the fact. Could he, the Soul Agent, have made sure at one blow of even a tythe of that sum—and bolted ! Or even supposing this

> "———— Millionaire,
> This creature rich and rare,"

as a certain poet once defined it, *had* had the cunning to guard against all evasion of contract? Still, even as the factotum of such a man ! But it was idle to regret ; he had exposed his weak side—he had allowed himself to be foiled. The stranger would not repeat the offer, at least on terms worth taking into consideration. The chance was lost, but he might yet by zeal recover the opportunity.

Already, without knowing it, the dark Agent had sold himself to his mysterious customer—for a chance.

There is a spiritual as a social scale of infinite gradations. A spirit of the secondary must bend to a spirit of the primary order. Men of genius, the real princes of thought and rulers of the earth, are not so stupid at a bargain as some commonsense bunglers imagine.

"A second customer like your grace," said the Soul Agent, with a courtier-like cringe, "and I should lose all faith in my tact as a man of the world. Luckily, you have *no* second!"

"Perhaps I have the more principal," said the stranger, accepting the agent's homage, and condescending to a jest, but not to a smile, in order to restore his collocutor's equanimity.

The Soul Agent laughed, but it must be owned his laughter was a little ghastly, and smacked of the music in *Robert le Diable.*

"Adieu, for the present," said the stranger, feeling his triumph complete, since philosophy teaches that no man will laugh at a bad pun unless thoroughly subjugated.

"*Good* morning! I trust your grace will soon honour me with a second visit?"

The stranger bowed gracefully, though slightly, took his hat, and departed in silence.

The pasteboard clerk, seeing his master grinning the visitor out, with a politeness very far beyond his usual reserved and dignified demeanour, kow-towed in so painful a manner, that he could be likened only to a wooden doll jerked convulsively by an ingenious application of whip cord.

As he issued from the street door, the stranger gave the porter, who was still at his post haranguing the small boys, a second twirl to get him out of the way, and taking a gold-lettered prospectus from that official's hand, strode rapidly away in the direction of the Horse Guards, where the infallible clock informed him that he had passed full an hour in the society of the Soul Agent.

Within two minutes of his departure, an emissary of the dark speculator was dogging his footsteps.

CHAPTER III.

A CURIOUS FAMILY HISTORY.

TOWARDS sunset on the same day two persons of the greatest importance to this history were assisting the world-movement in a retired chamber of the ducal palace of the St. Georges.

This palace was now the property of Arthur Bolingbroke Darian, ninth Duke of St. George. The extraordinary misfortunes of that famous race, which rival those of the fated House of Pelops in Grecian fable, as also the terribly rapid mortality of the last three dukes and others of their blood, are facts well known, doubtless, to many of my readers. But as some circumstances in connection with these surprising events have been grossly misrepresented, which from my peculiar position I am enabled to correct, I shall not apologise for briefly recounting the facts in their naked simplicity, as they occurred, so far as can be ascertained or reasonably conjectured up to the present time.

Roland Bolingbroke Darian, the fifth duke, married, some twelve years previous to the date of this narrative, the second daughter of the reigning Prince of Falkenheim. He was an only son, and, with the sole exception of the present duke's grandfather, Sir Arthur Darian, and his family, every collateral branch of the race was either extinct or utterly lost to genealogical science.

In the third year of his marriage, the duke Roland, accompanied by his young wife, proceeded to Stamboul, it was supposed upon a secret mission from the Home Government. He there became very intimate with a Russian nobleman of high rank—then Envoy Extraordinary to the Porte.

Some months afterwards the body of the Russian was found, shot through the heart, in the sea, at Pera, and the greatest excitement was caused by the event in the diplomatic circles of Constantinople.

At the same time a most hideous catastrophe divided the public attention. This was no other than the suicide, so much disputed about in the English and French papers, of the young and beautiful Duchess of St. George. By degrees a general murmur of suspicion began to connect the two events, and the darkest hints were thrown out as to the probable guilt of the Duke Roland. No rational doubt, whatever may have been adduced to the contrary, could exist as to the duchess having perished by her own deed, as the bottle of poison was found in her hand, and a written declaration of the fact upon a table in her dressing-room. But with the death of the Russian it was different. He was known to have entertained a violent passion for the deceased princess. The duke had been heard upon more than one occasion to express the strongest hatred of his supposed friend. All else was wrapped in impenetrable obscurity. Fabulous particulars were circulated, but the best proof of their utter falsehood is, that when, at the instance of the Russian court, the grand vizier instituted the most severe investigation, no clue could be discovered as to the mode by which the murdered count had met his fate.

C

The subject had given way to more recent horrors, when, as will be perhaps remembered, a letter appeared in a widely circulated English journal, purporting to be from a gentleman who had long resided at St. Petersburg. This letter, I have ascertained from private sources, was written by a person of extraordinary abilities, formerly employed at the court of the Czar, in the organisation of certain new institutions, which the Emperor was desirous of establishing. On account of his liberal principles, however, and suspected propagandism of republican ideas, he became a political fugitive, and, with great difficulty, escaped across the Polish and German frontiers, arriving, after incredible hardships, in the British capital.

The letter in question most distinctly declared the writer's conviction that the death of the Russian Envoy was solely attributable to the long arm of the Czar himself, who, secretly enraged at the Count's conduct, and suspicious intimacy with a man of such anti-Muscovite opinions as the Duke of St. George, caused him, like many others, to be assassinated by an imperial emissary.

The *Timeserver* most indignantly rejected this theory, and with their "noted ferocity to the fallen," heaped additional opprobrium upon the now shunned and execrated nobleman.

A fine romance was got up on the subject.

The Russian was an old flame of the Duchess. St. George had married her against her consent by flattering the avarice of her family, to whom, though reigning princes, a son-in-law of such standing, with a quarter of a million rental, was an object of no small moment. In an insane fit of jealousy, the duke had subsequently murdered his rival, and the wretched princess, if not more immediately his victim, had hastened to escape the ill-treatment of a monster through the gloomy portal of the tomb!

Such was the insinuated conjecture of the day, and of the *Timeserver*, its misleader and parasite. Those who have perused its French, German, Hungarian, and Italian despatches and articles may surmise that there were substantial, not to say golden, reasons for their persevering policy on the subject.*

Be that as it may, neither the revilings of the press, the coldness of friends, nor indeed any other outward influence, seemed to affect the duke after the death of his wife. He retreated to Syria, and in a lonely Maronite fortress contrived to pass unmolested the few remaining years of his life in a sort of savage royalty, guarded by Eastern mercenaries, and utterly destitute of all European society. If the world were not so mad

---

* A very curious circumstance occurred to the author of this work, in connection with the *real* architype of the *Timeserver* order. An intimate friend, Dr. A——, son of the celebrated German poet and historian, knowing from the fact of their having been fellow-students at the Universities of Bonn and Berlin, that the author was conversant with the German language, came one evening to his house and requested assistance in translating a most important letter addressed to the —— Ambassador, which the latter had placed at the disposition of the great journal in question. The letter contained the most interesting account of the then state of Hungary, which was at the time inaccessible to correspondents of the press. By joint effort the letter was decyphered and translated. It told in favour of the Magyar cause. It was consequently *entirely suppressed,* and no use whatever made of the valuable information it contained. How long will hireling printers and scribblers continue to influence the opinions of a free nation? How long will the more honest portion of the press endure the overbearing insolence of a joint-stock imposition? And people praise the *talent* of its miserable automata! Pshaw! it exhausts the patience of *real* men of letters to behold such childish infatuation!

just now after the sneering school of literature, I would simply say that he had loved and been deceived, and that his heart broke. He was a strong man, strong in mind and body, like all the St. Georges—an old Saxon stock crossed with northern fire. Perhaps the climate killed him. Enough, he died; and after considerable delay, the news reached Sir Arthur Darian of his kinsman's death, and of his own accession to the dukedom.

Sir Arthur set out for Syria to raise a tomb to his predecessor, and to take possession of the vast personal wealth which had accumulated in the late duke's coffers during years of indifference to pomp and lonely exile. Sir Arthur, his eldest son, and two of his daughters— he had a third who was too unwell at the time to accompany him—arrived before Smyrna. The plague was raging. It broke out on board the vessel in impertinent defiance of all quarantine regulations. Of the whole crew, passengers included, only ten persons escaped the virulence of the disease. One of these was a servant of Sir Arthur's. He himself, his son, and daughters, perished amongst the first victims. His son survived him by a few hours, just long enough to secure an empty title for his epitaph. Thus the race of the St. Georges was supposed to be extinct. Sir Arthur had had a second son, it is true, but the desperately wayward disposition of the young Arthur had, on his growing to man's estate, produced such terrible quarrels between father and son, that the latter had eventually broken out into open rebellion, and the former, in a temporary crisis of rage, had allowed his son to depart for the continent without hope of aid or resources for the future. From that time he had been completely lost sight of. No intelligence could be obtained through any of the embassies abroad, and finally even advertisements in the papers had been resorted to without success.

Nevertheless, after returning to England, and hearing the horrible news of the sudden destruction of his late master and family, Thomas Stanley, the young valet of Sir Arthur, resolved to set out upon a desperate pilgrimage in search of the lost heir to the dukedom. Not knowing to whom to apply for means, or where immediately to find the Lady Genevra Darian, who was at a distant Spa with some friends, he set off with his own small savings in his pocket, and commenced wandering over Europe with an extraordinary fixity of purpose that denoted a rare heroism of character. Reduced to actual poverty, he made his way from town to town on foot, picking up a knowledge of the language, and literally begging as he went. He had a turn for reading, and had imbibed the notion, from the generous sentiments met with in books and publications containing fiction or, poetry, that literary men were more liberal in money matters than others. Acting upon this idea, he inquired in every town whether there were any writers living in its precincts, and straightway seeking them out, told his tale with such truthful and honest pathos, that *in no one instance* did he fail in obtaining assistance. Now, we hear much cant about the improvidence of men of letters —scarcely any one makes mention of their equally conspicuous generosity. It is thought a great deal to give two or three poets trifling pensions, and the nobility *patronize* a Literary Fund which doles out paltry alms to distressed talent on conditions of exposure, which render suicide preferable to the average pride of

educated humanity.   Why do not literary men unite
in forming an independent association, conducted
on noble principles, without the degradation of noble
patrons ? There is but one excuse for their not so doing ;
and it is, that strangely disunited as they are in all other
respects, there is no body of men more ready *practically*
to assist one another in pecuniary difficulty than authors.
I know at this present moment at least a dozen men
with whom I scarcely share an opinion, who would if
requisite divide their last guinea with me as a matter
of course, and without even the notion that they were
exercising more than ordinary liberality.   I do not
know one man of any other profession on whom I could
reckon with certainty even in the most extreme case
of emergency.   I loathe the crawling toadyism of
certain scribblers ("before the public, and behind
the age," as my friend Bellew has it), who write
about our sacred and supreme order with a view
to bring even its most insignificant members into contempt for their personal conduct and so-called eccentri-
cities.   Let them beware ! there is, perhaps, a Prose
Dunciad yet to be written, in which some of these
would-be satirists may figure strangely, should they
continue to shoot their nauseous rubbish at our doors.

To return to our wanderer.

More than one poor village poet, whose verses no
printer would print and scarcely a friend listen to,
emptied his purse into the hands of the ragged pilgrim
with a regret at the smallness of the offering.   Many a
provincial editor, besides giving from his scanty private
means, raised considerable subscriptions for the wanderer
by an appeal in his weekly columns.   Nevertheless,

poets and literati generally are neither very numerous nor wealthy, and he fasted not seldom or was indebted to the rude hospitality of a peasant for a night's shelter and a meal.

He made, occasionally, applications to the rich proprietors or traders of the places he passed through. They treated him mostly as an impudent impostor, or got rid of him cheaply by the copper *congé* of a common mendicant.

How are we to account for this marvellous zeal on the part of a mere paid servant? Very simply—he was low in station, but high in soul. *He* knew that the lost duke was the friend of the poor, and that all his disagreements with Sir Arthur had originated in his inveterate assertion of man's equal rights and duties. He recollected the night of young Darian's departure, when in the midst of a drenching storm he quitted his paternal mansion. Stanley opened the door. Darian seized his hand, wrung it convulsively, and said in a firm but deeply affected voice—

" Stanley, you are a good fellow! Serve my father carefully, watch over him. His health is not good. But if my youngest sister, Genevra, marry, follow her and devote yourself to her service. I shall never return, but remember I was your friend."

Darian departed through the tempest. Stanley sobbed like a child. His young master had once saved his life at the hazard of his own, when incautiously crossing a railway on horseback in defiance of an approaching train. But the last pressure of Darian's hand had electrified his heart. Thus, he set out to beg his way over Europe to seek the lost son of a father who had *relented too late.*

How he succeeded in his quest will be seen hereafter.

For my part, I can hardly help shedding tears when I think of that honest, resolute man and his desperate travels, with the fearful and unheard-of recompense of all his toils.

But there *is* a new world for spirits, or earth were a madman's nightmare!

CHAPTER IV.

CERTAIN ILLUMINATI ARE INTRODUCED.

WE now find ourselves, like the gentleman who circumnavigated the globe, precisely where we were at the commencement of the preceding chapter.

The two personages there vaguely mentioned as not holding sinecures in this history were by no means willow-pattern specimens of human clay. Of the dozen or twenty persons of genius living at the present moment on the face of the earth, two are about to be introduced to the reader.

They were both seated at a large table covered with a chaos of letters, books, and papers, of every description. The one was a famous Magyar, the other an English poet.

Basiline Arpath was the most beautiful woman, the most accomplished scholar, and the most impassioned poetess of all Hungary. Like many others, the *élite* of European intellect, she found in England a refuge from the vengeance of the political thieves and murderers who, in central Europe, for the time, feasted on the blood of the patriots, and, by the very stupidity of their crimes, ensured their ultimate downfall. Strange combination, which caused the same land to become the refuge of the hoary miscreant M—t—ch, and the pure and heroic Basiline! of the old and decrepit trickster, and the young and lovely patriot!

But not the eye of the most practised theatrical *habitué* could have detected in the present attire of Basiline the sex to which she belonged. Her dark hair, which was still of considerable length, and once might have served her for a robe, was now parted at the side, and curled upon her shoulders, after the fashion of a German student. Beneath her ivory forehead a large pair of spectacles partly concealed the magnificent blue eyes, with their long lashes, and finely-pencilled brows, whilst interfering with the exquisite lines of her straight, perfect nose, and full, oval visage. Upon her upper lip was a slight semblance of beard, which, without in the least injuring its beauty, diverted the eye of acute spectators from closely criticising a mouth too delicate in shape for even the gentlest of the harder sex.

She had risen from her seat, and now, with the companion of her literary labours, paced up and down the lofty and richly decorated apartment. The Englishman was a man of square and symmetrical build, and certainly rather above than below the highest average stature in this country. Nevertheless, the disguised Magyar was, thanks to rather high-heeled boots, within little more than an inch of her companion's height. She wore a loose paletot of dark blue cloth, which did not betray the graceful and gently undulating proportions of her slender figure; full grey pantaloons, beneath which boots, suspiciously small, were scarcely seen, completed her outward costume.

The poet wore a simple, and, narrowly inspected, somewhat threadbare frock coat and trousers of the student's favorite colour. His arms were crossed upon his chest, which was broad and athletic; his deep-set eyes, of a fine hazel, with their somewhat heavy brows, of a much darker colour than his hair, were the only feature that rivetted attention in a countenance of uniform and delicate paleness, with features regular in form and serenely guileless in expression. An habitual contraction of the brow, the result of intense thought, had given, perhaps, more sternness to their gaze than was desirable ; but they were eyes of strange, magnetic potence, and were yet unlowered to man. His light brown hair was pushed back carelessly from his face. An artist would have called him superb ; a dandy would have set him down as a queer-looking person; no woman would, perhaps, have admired him at first sight; few would have troubled themselves about his looks on closer acquaintance.

They paced the room, conversing in those clear musical tones which are not unfrequently the property of persons whose words express the purity and grandeur of their thoughts. The deep contralto of Basiline alternated harmoniously with the rich barytone of Viridor—that was the poet's name—a name yet known to few, but destined to become one of the most popular in England ere many months had elapsed.

Even while they thus paced the room, the door opened, and the martial stranger entered. His eyes rested upon Basiline with an inexpressible calmness of delight.

"Arthur!" exclaimed the Hungarian, with undisguised pleasure.

"Yes, here I am," said the Duke of St. George, "and rare news I have in my pocket : but how fares it with my friends ?"

The duke took the small white hand of Basiline in his own, and gazed at her for some instants, as if longing to clasp her to his heart. But he suddenly restrained

the impulse, and turned to Viridor, with whom he cordially shook hands.

"We have been busy in your absence," said the
poet, pointing to the table, " your grace will—"

"What! still that detested nickname!" exclaimed
the duke. " Is it quite impossible to beat into your
philosophic scull the belief that I really *am* a republican
without limit or reservation? Call me plain Darian, in
the name of all truths, divine and human; or I shall
think you love to taunt me with the duncehood of my
ancestors!"

" You seriously mean it?" said Viridor, eagerly.

" *You* do not know Arthur Darian, or you would not
question his sincerity," said Basiline, mildly, yet proudly,
with a look of adoring confidence at the duke.

"Well, then, Darian it shall be, now and for ever,"
said the poet, gaily, again squeezing the hand of his
friend with energetic warmth.

And Darian it shall be in this chronicle, says a man
who detests nicknames to the full as heartily as his hero.

The real Dux—duke or leader—is in no want of the
titular prefix. His actions make his simple name the
noblest of titles. The sham Dux, who neither leads
armies nor minds, is not the less a cypher for the absurd
assumption of a dignity to which he has no rational
claim. There were many Cæsars—there are idiot
despots in Austria who still glory in the sarcasm—there
was but one conqueror of Gaul and writer of commentaries, who died in the Capitol at the base of Pompey's
statue.

Where are the modern Bruti?—or is their greatness
proportionate to the pigmy Cæsars', their tyrants?

. "And now for your rare news," said Basiline; "we live in an age of thunderclaps. For my part I have seen things so strange, and so incredible to all but eye-witnesses, that I fancy I am past surprises."

"Indeed, young gentleman," said Darian; then lowering his voice to a whisper inaudible to Viridor, who was standing at the other side of the table at which Darian had seated himself, near Basiline, he added, "would it not surprise you if I told you that I had never loved you?"

"No," said Basiline, aloud, "for I should not believe you."

"Well, *I* own that were you to believe anything so absurd, I should be astonished into thinking you a maniac," said Darian, in his usual voice; "but no more child's play. Viridor, excuse my rudeness in reminding my fellow-soldier of an old camp-adventure. There is no friendship without confidence, and before we part to-day you shall have mine and this young scapegrace's to the full. Now for my news. We live at a curious juncture in moral history. Of course, men were always selfish, rapacious, venal. Nevertheless, for many centuries there flourished a sort of dim substitute for virtue and justice, which has latterly been gradually fading away, doubtless before the advent of a loftier and nobler principle. This principle, soon to be universally diffused by expansion, from the centres of individual greatness, is neither more nor less than the 'Love one another' of the great prophet, at length understood, and after ages of study discovered to be the perfection of wisdom. The fading substitute I alluded to is called *Honour*. Look at modern aristocracies, at modern gentlemen, the class elect of education, of refinement,

D

of moral and religious culture. Listen to their speeches,
their dialogues, their jests. Read their books, their
articles, their reviews, and say whether the chivalric
honour, which alone saved the middle ages from a
relapse into primæval barbarism, is not a dead letter
in the present age. What do you hear on every side?
Sophistry. What do you see? Expediency. 'The end
justifies the means,' is the secret or avowed doctrine of
the day. How false, how illogical, how contemptible
is this cowardly doctrine in the eyes of a philosopher!
It is indeed time that great thinkers should arise, and set
their lion-like paws upon the mediocrities of routine,
who meet an emergency, with a 'dodge,' a crying evil
with a snivelling lamentation, and a refutation or demonstration with a—*working majority !*"

"A working majority !" exclaimed Viridor, almost
savagely, "a playing majority, you mean—a gambling
majority, who risk the happiness of millions for the miserable stake of a little patronage, even for a few
paltry bribes from advertisers in the *Timeserver*, willing
to exchange a douceur of five hundred or a thousand
pounds for a permanent situation !"

"Legally attainable—you forget they always add
that reservation," said Basiline, smiling disdainfully.

"They also state," said Darian, "that the utmost *honour* (! ! !) and *secrecy* may be relied on. Yes ! men dare
to advertise, and the *Timeserver* dares to publish, propositions which the guarantee of *secrecy* alone could render
possible in a city less shameless than this modern Babylon—a Babylon, by the way, as my sister Genevra re-
marked, without the architectural distinction of a tower
worth describing by an Herodotus."

"To show the fallacy of ends justifying means," resumed Darian, " it is only necessary to reflect, that if such a system were fairly carried out, the present always being sacrificed to the future, there would be nothing but permanent violation of the rights of individuals and the principles of justice, with permanent prospects of compensation to a permanent succession of sufferers, sacrificed to temporary pressure. But the gold-worshippers in practice, materialists in theory, and thought-loathing, brute-force blunderers in policy, are now rushing to extremes."

"I would they were *in extremis*," said Basiline, pointedly.

"Extremes meet," said Viridor ; " the popular proverb anticipated what German metaphysicians laboured to prove. I am no despiser of Hegel. I believe that our enemies may go so far as to rush of themselves into the torrent of truth over the precipice of error."

"Profoundly reasoned, my dear Viridor ; you are aware that I have always held that the great struggle of modern revolution, between democracy and aristocracy, sympathetic love for man and superstitiously exclusive selfishness, human *vis inertiæ* and centrifugal force, ignorance and knowledge, conservation and reform, Whiggery and honesty, childish finality and infinite progressive ambition, fear of losing the old and courage in creating the new, genius and duncehood, and by what other synonymes the contest may be described, is at bottom neither more nor less than the grand philosophical question of Materialism *v.* Spiritualism—the system of Death and the system of Life. A crisis is now at hand—read this prospectus !"

Viridor took from the hand of Darian the gold-lettered handbill which the latter had received from the Soul Agent's porter, and with no small amazement read aloud as follows :—

" GENERAL AGENCY

FOR THE SALE AND PURCHASE OF HUMAN SOULS.

CAPITAL　　UNLIMITED.

MANAGING DIRECTORS,

IGNATIUS LOYOLA GREY, ESQ.,

ROBERT RUSSEL BROWN, ESQ.

ACTUARY,

* 　* 　* 　 (Author of the 'Vestiges of the Natural History of the Creation.')

PHRENOLOGIST,

THEOPHRASTUS DONAMANY, ESQ.

PHYSICIAN & MESMERIST,

DR. PARACELSUS WRIGGLEDUM.

EXAMINER EXTRAORDINARY,

LORD BLOWAM & TALKS.

INFORMER GENERAL.

SIR JAMES RATTAM.

" The object of this company is to facilitate those negotiations which, in every civilised community, must constantly occur. It is a long-established axiom that every man has his price. No sensible man, in the present age, even affects that absurd and impossible virtue—disinterestedness. If any man does good to another, he does it because it pleases his own feelings—in other words, from a purely selfish motive. He expects to be paid in gratitude, if not in money. Visionaries and theorists may act from fanciful impulses, but honest men pay their way as they go, and expect to be paid themselves for the trouble of existing. The soul, or galvanic mainspring of the human machine, regulates all its movements. Therefore everything a man does for money, or other payment, is a sale or mortgage of his soul to another person. It is the intention of the Company to undertake every description of Soul Agency, from the purchase of a young wife for an old *roué,* to that of a ministerial or opposition majority. All sorts of *cabinet* work skilfully arranged. Foreign diplomatists bought and sold with the utmost dispatch. Authors of books, and writers for the public press, secured on the most reasonable terms. In all these commissions the commission required by the Company will be extremely moderate.

"Estimates forwarded of the market value of any soul, in any part of the globe. All prepaid communications attended to with the greatest punctuality. The strictest confidence may in all cases be relied on.

"N.B. No letter, unless enclosing a remittance for preliminary expences, will receive attention.

"Office hours from dawn to midnight.

Signed,   { IGNATIUS LOYOLA GREY.
          { ROBERT RUSSEL BROWN."

"A bold, barefaced enterprise, is it not, captain?" said Darian to Basiline, when Viridor had finished reading the prospectus.

"Certainly a wonderfully shameless document!" said

Basiline, herself inspecting the production of the crafty Soul Agent, as if to satisfy herself of its reality.

" Still," said Viridor, " there is in its very daring earthiness a sort of leaning towards the nobler creed."

" They acknowledge, at any rate, the existence of a soul as the prime central mover of all activity—that is something in our favour," rejoined Darian.

" Which is about as great an admission as that the world turns round," said Basiline, playfully.

" It would not turn round if they could help it," said Viridor, laughing bitterly.

" I will tell you where our great obstacle lies," said Darian, gravely, " not in any arguments our enemies oppose to us, but in their utter and marvellous ignorance and obtuseness. The most obvious reasoning, the most noble truths, the most brilliant genius, falls blunted before their ægis of icy stupidity. They neither know nor care, they neither feel nor think. They stand still, they fancy themselves well off, or at any rate are too weak to cherish a strong desire, even of personal improvement, and they say—*Let us alone.* We are compelled, as it were, to kick them before us, since, unlike the celebrated animal seduced by the bundle of hay before his nose, they are insensible to the most obvious prospects of speedy personal advantage. If they only knew their own interest, I would excuse them for not heeding anybody else's!"

" Because, in that case, they would have reached the acme of moral and social policy, which teaches that the bliss of each is the bliss of all, and that individual enjoyment, founded on general suffering, is a pitiful and dreary illusion."

" You do well to retort upon me with quotations from my own system," said Darian, " when you see me rushing into inconsistencies."

The chronicler cannot here refrain from repeating a sentiment expressed by him in the pages of a satirical extravaganza, otherwise much richer in nonsense than wit :—" It is difficult to speak consistently of inconsistent people."

" I propose," said Basiline, "that we now resolve ourselves into a committee on the general state of politics in Europe."

" A council of war," said Darian, " a council of war. We are all soldiers of the great army."

" I would we were as skilful, or at least as resolute, with the pen, as with that meaner weapon, the sword," said Viridor, seriously.

" Alas !" said Basiline, sighing, " it is so easy to fight, so hard to think patiently for a great cause. So simple to die, so troublesome to work, so natural to hate bad men, so difficult to love Good alone, and in it all mankind, friends and foes, for its sake !"

" True, true," said Darian, regarding the beautiful Hungarian's animated countenance, from which she had removed the disfiguring glasses, with ineffable pride and tenderness. " True, it is easier to be dazzling than great. But before we proceed to council, it strikes me that it would be well to let our noble friend more fully into our confidence, in order that no mystery may stand between our free sympathies. Are you not of the same opinion ?"

" I am," said Basiline. " To the friend of your boyhood, and to the man whose aims, hopes, and principles are in such perfect harmony with our own, nothing should be concealed."

" Then, my dear Viridor," said Darian, "prepare yourself for a rather prolix aud romantic narrative. I will be as brief as occasion permits."

" My dear friends," said Viridor, much affected, "for a lonely student like myself, obscure, unloved, and neglected, to have found two such friends, is in itself a greater happiness than I can express. I scarcely dare to believe it, and often half encourage the notion that our chance meeting at the opera, which I had visited for the first time during several years, after so long a separation, our accidental conversation and recognition, with my introduction to Captain Arpath ; and the last week spent in your delightful society, and in such ennobling labours, must be all a dream of pleasure, from which I shall awake—"

" Like Byron, to find yourself famous," said Darian, with vivacity.

" I never flatter," said Basiline, " but I feel well in your presence that a greater than Byron is with us."

" For every age a man," said Darian. " Woe to the age that cannot receive its prophet !"

At this moment, a well-dressed gentleman entered the apartment, after knocking carefully, and stated simply that dinner was on the table, and every one else assembled.

" We will join you instantly, Manton," said Darian. "I did not think of it before, but my walk has given me an appetite ; the story must be deferred. Proceed, my dear Viridor, our friend Manton will lead the way."

Darian turned back for an instant—he was alone with

the Hungarian. A strange smile lit up her features. He pressed her to his heart for an instant, imprinted one kiss upon her beautiful mouth, and rapidly followed on the track of the poet, who was exchanging a few remarks on the news of the day with Manton, a personage whose position will be explained more fully in the ensuing chapter.

CHAPTER V.

A FAMILY DINNER PARTY.

THE dining-hall in Darian's palace was vast in size, and adorned with regal splendour.

Pictures by renowned artists, of modern and ancient times, hung from 'the walls, alternating symmetrically with statuary in the purest style of art. The ceiling of the lofty apartment was painted in fresco by a famous master of the Italian school. The floor was carpeted with the richest product of the eastern loom. The furniture was old and massive. A vast table in the centre of the apartment was covered by an abundant but simple repast. Covers were laid for about twenty persons.

Presently the door at one end of the room opened, and a party, to all appearance of ladies and gentlemen, entered. In reality they were simply the domestic officials—or, as a servile race have made and named them, servants.

The Roman empire is fallen—slavery is said to be extinct in its Christian provinces. But the feeling and the word survive. The Latin *servus*, or slave, has bequeathed his title to the European *servant*. Polite mockery countenances the slavish sentiment, and the proud noble signs himself the obedient *servant* of the plebeian he despises and tramples on. Everybody is the servant of somebody; there are slaves under every roof.

" I remember, some time ago," said Viridor, on a subsequent occasion, to Darian, "a very near connection of mine, an old and hardened aristocrat, expressing, as the extreme of hideous and awful presumption, and, as he thought, by a sublimely impossible hyperbole, the fear that, the next thing, he supposed, his servants would expect, would be to sit down to dinner at the same table as his family! This was *à propos* of a beer-revolution in the kitchen, the surreptitious visit of a Don Juan of the police force, or some similar accident. My reply was, that such would probably be the fashion with his grandchildren, when advancing education and improved domestic machinery had rendered the relative positions of master and attendant simply a question of division of labour, and contract between man and man. He retorted by a bitter sarcasm, implying that I was a *Socialist*. This he regarded as the severest insult within the pale of conventional abuse. Though neither a disciple of Fourier or St. Simon, I confess I bore the imputation with imperturbable tranquillity."

" Yes," said Darian, "even to that shocking pass must we come at last. For my part, I never could hear any vulgar-minded person express contempt for servants without reflecting that they were like all living creatures —immortal spirits soaring upwards towards perfection— and pitying the meanness of the sentiments that have degraded them to their present position. Every feeling, every act, that tends to reduce to a machine a being possessing volition, reason, and affection, is a treason against nature—the Infinite Republic of spirits!"

" And you practice as you preach," said Viridor.

" How else prove my sincerity? Yes, I encourage

my domestics to amuse themselves in their leisure hours with reading and rational conversation. I give them free opportunities of air and exercise. I allow them in the evenings to indulge in dancing or music, if it pleases them. All I require in return is, that they fulfil their duties, as per contract, with fairness and regularity."

" And what is the general result ?"

" As usual, the complete refutation of all old saws on the subject, such as ' Give them an inch, and they will take an ell,' &c. On the contrary, their zeal is positively troublesome. Their cleanliness, their assiduity, their anticipation of my wishes, compel me almost daily to express personal gratitude for services which common menials would never render. They respect me without fearing me—they obey me without cringing. As to familiarity breeding contempt, it is all nonsense ; unless by familiarity be understood a coarseness of manner, which ought never to exist between the most intimate friends. I am, in fact, surrounded, by friends who love me as the Arabs love the chief of their tribe. It is astounding what an alteration a few months have made in their habits, manners, and language—even in the expression of their countenances. They *were* slaves, spies, flunkies, ready to bear contempt, and to compensate themselves by roguery. They *are* free men and women, respecting and respected by one another. Several of them have married."

" And the children ?"

" There is a nursery at their disposal. They can pay for deputies during illness out of their wages. I know my expenses, which, from the simplicity of our living, the enormous saving of a common table, and the utter absence of waste or pilfering, are not one-third of such an establishment under the old system. I know my expenses, and I insist upon their not being increased by one sixpence without my authority. I give freely—I allow no indirect thieving. I have explained to them my views and principles—they understand and sympathise with them. I have told them that I consider property merely as an office of trust. I have shown them that I enjoy no greater bodily comforts than themselves. I have proved to them that I work as hard as any of them, though in a different manner. And what is the consequence? So far from leaguing against me, as most servants do against their masters, I have found by experience that on one of them endeavouring to impose on me, the others have instantly resented the attempt as an offence against their whole body, and at once requested the dismissal of the offender, lest suspicion should attach to the community from the fault of a single member. But as, on reasoning with delinquents in the only two cases that have occurred, I convinced them that honesty was indeed their best policy, I have not found it necessary to give a single domestic his discharge, since no repetition of the fault has occurred in the household."

" This borders on Communism," said Viridor, smiling.

" It realises," said Darian, "what the schemes of Cabet, Louis Blanc, Considérant, and all other followers of Fourier, St. Simon, or Owen, will utterly fail to effect. *They* madly dream of destroying property in all its complicated forms—of annihilating competition—the stimulus and spice of commerce; in a word, of crushing the *freedom* of industry, and reducing society to a machine.

E

We know such chimeras to be antipathetic to human nature, its love of liberty, activity, emulation, and acquisition. *We* take the world as we find it, and develope existing conditions on a logical system. *They* ask for a new chaos, in order to create a new world from its ruins. The hope of progress is in individual genius and individual exertion, the principal fountain of all general improvement. The political revolution we require is material, the social revolution must be moral in its nature. The government must counteract selfishness, the great evil, by taxation and vigour; the press, by reason, and appeals to the intelligence and the hearts of the citizens. When all men cease to be selfish, perfect community of goods may exist without laws to enforce it. Before that period, not all the legislation of all conceivable republics can maintain such an institution for an hour. But, in truth, all perfection, all absolute ideas, are unattainable goals. Existence is an infinite progress, and in the infinite there is no consummation possible."

On the present occasion, the male and female domestics joined with perfect politeness in a conversation on the events of the day. They were dressed simply and plainly; the women rivalling in the neatness, and even elegance of their attire, the costume of respectable milliners or shopwomen; the men, I am compelled to confess, looking very much like clerks, tradesmen, or other more dignified people.

Darian took the head of the table. The beautiful Hungarian—the supposed Captain Arpath—sat on his right, Bernard Viridor on the left of their friend. The *major domo*, Manton, took the foot of the board, and the rest filled up the other places. A remarkably pretty housemaid, who, but for her red hands, looked amazingly like our fair friend Lady Rose D——, actually sat in the next chair to Viridor, and divided her attention between that republican poet and her left-hand neighbour the coachman, who looked rather like Lord Ch——d, only more honest, and told several sporting anecdotes with great modesty and humour, even arguing with Viridor and his master—both accomplished horsemen—on some points connected with the training of the noblest of all domestic animals.

What a thing it is to be a philosopher! Viridor extended his sympathies even to the wrongs of horses, and Darian joined him, maintaining a theory of horse-education which astounded the coachman, and may some day astound the world of grooms and ostlers!

It was remarkable, at this patriarchal meal, that although wine was liberally supplied without distinction of persons, the greatest moderation prevailed. The females, in general, abstained altogether from wine, or contented themselves with a single glass of some light French or Rhenish vintage. The cook only, an artist of some talent, indulged pretty freely, which, considering his recent exertions, was but natural. The repast has been described as simple. It must not, however, be imagined that it was rude, or that it was by any means prepared in the barbarous style of ordinary English dinners. Good cookery is at once the most salutary and the most economical, nor is instruction in this necessary art the least important part of that national education hereafter to be alluded to. The intrinsic cost of a most exquisite dish is often trifling; nothing prevents the poor man and his family from enjoying it but ignorance. Truly a philosopher feels almost ashamed of preaching the, to him, palpable truisms, that Ignorance is the source of all pain—Knowledge of all pleasure.

This truism Prometheus, by the lips of Æschylus, that poet of awful grandeur, more than two thousand years ago declared to mankind. Prometheus, the incarnate wisdom, was, it is true, delivered from the rock of tyranny by Hercules, the incarnate Force. Since then he, and, alas! how many of his Titan brethren—prophets, poets, philosophers—have wandered over the earth, through obscurity, and scorn, and fiery martyrdoms, teaching in vain the great and eternal lesson. They teach it yet. But how few are their converts! Men have comprehended printing, gunpowder, steam, the most complicated machines, the most marvellous calculations, the most hidden secrets of nature—the most simple moral truths they have not comprehended at all.

One would almost imagine that the simplest things were the most difficult to understand.

"Promethus gave fire to man." To what wonderful uses has not man applied the gift! Clocks, locomotives, electric telegraphs, a thousand manufactures, a thousand arts, bear witness to his ingenuity. And not one mortal in a myriad can cook a dish of soup fit to be eaten!

When dinner was over, and the cloth removed, Darian rose, and, accompanied by his friends, retired to the apartment we have already mentioned. But before they took their departure, he handed to the *major domo* the Soul Agent's interesting circular, saying with a smile—

"You have now all a fine opportunity of making money in an easy manner. There will be people enough who will pay liberally for the soul of a spy over my actions. The office would be a sinecure, as I have nothing to conceal, and care not who knows what I do. Only remember, it is 'First come, first served,' in such a matter!"

The domestics laughed heartily at this address.

"Who feels inclined to set up as a Judas Iscariot?" said the senior footman, amid a general fire of jocularity at the bare notion of betraying such a master as Darian.

———

CHAPTER VI.

A SOLDIER'S TALE.

THE evening was chilly, notwithstanding the month was May. A fire was lighted in the grate, which threw strange flickering shadows upon the sculptured supporters of the marble mantlepiece. On a small table before the fire steamed an urn of fragrant coffee. Two long Turkish pipes were in the hands of Viridor and his host—even the Hungarian trifled with a Spanish cigaretto.

"George Sand would have felt quite at home as one of the party," said Darian, with a peculiar tone.

"George Sand!" exclaimed Viridor. "O the wondrous phantoms which the thought of that name calls up! Spiridion, André, Consuelo, and all the living creations of her genius, arise before me at its mention! Do you know, Darian, I once loved that woman, whom I have never seen? I was a mere boy, I read her works—I formed an ideal image of her face—I obtained her portrait—found it realised."

"And why did you not seek her presence?" said the Hungarian, "you who could have so well accorded with her in feeling and in intellect?"

"It was pride," said Viridor; "I was a boy—I had done nothing—I could not bear the idea of a woman's superiority."

"You surely do not imagine that such a woman as George Sand would have measured you by the breath of fame?" said Darian.

" No, but I doubted my own power. Years afterwards, though in reputation a pigmy compared to a giant,
I should not have hesitated, but it was too late."

" What! the ideal had given way to a real passion ?"
said Basiline.

Viridor was silent for a few minutes. A strange pano-
rama of reminiscences of far lands and fair faces passed
through his mind in that brief period. Suddenly he
aroused himself from his reverie.

" I claim your promised narrative," he said, addressing
Darian, with lively interest.

" Re-light your pipe, and help yourself to coffee," said
Darian, " and I begin at once. You," he added, turning
to Basiline, " can correct me if I blunder."

All three drew their arm-chairs a few inches nearer to
the hearth-rug, and Darian commenced as follows :—

" I was born, as you are aware, the younger son of a
baronet of very moderate fortune. When we were at
school together, you, Viridor, had every prospect of becoming incomparably the richer of the two. When I
grew up I was destined for the bar, like yourself. Like
you, also, I felt an insuperable hatred to a profession
which I felt ought to be left open to the talents of every
reasoning man. The conceit, arrogance, and toadying
snobbism of my young legal acquaintances increased my
disgust. I conceived only one clear notion of English
jurisprudence. As the American editor defined England
herself to be a capital country to emigrate from, so I
regarded the English law chaos as a capital nuisance to
get rid of. Visions of a grand simple code, prepared
by a college of lawyers and philosophers, which every
man might carry in his pocket, danced before my

imagination. Meanwhile, I took to studying politics. Soon, beneath all the plausible jargon of economists, parliamentary leaders, party editors, and club oracles, I discovered, or believed that I discovered, gross and fundamental errors. In nine cases out of ten, the fallacy of an argument lies in falsely assumed premises. Like two diverging lines, the farther the reasoning from cause to effect is prolonged, the wider becomes the discrepancy. Ignoble and imperfect principia being once admitted, all sorts of delusion and absurdity follow as a matter of course.

"I resolved to drop my plumb-line into the deep ocean, to adventure amid the vast solitudes of abstract thought, and to build the foundations of my system in the everlasting centres of the universe. I reduced the three great sciences to three simple definitions.

"Philosophy proper (Ontology, Metaphysics, the Logic of Hegel,) I conceived to be the science of the *Infinite Spirit World*, uncreated, eternal, and self-existent, eternally progressing; to seek enjoyment and shun pain infinitely, the only rational or possible principle of any existence.

"Moral or Ethic science I comprised in the two words—Universal Sympathy—or the knowledge that the interest of the one is the interest of all sensitive beings linked by the common law of life, above mentioned.

"Political science I considered to be the application of this truth in the most noble and extended possible sense.

"From these general principles I deduced all details. I knew that Perfection was eternally unattainable, but that it could be approached infinitely. I had no panaceas, warranted to produce milleniums at the first application, but no amount of difficulty could frighten me. I set to work to study the most practical questions of the age. I saw that but one thing was wanted to their solution—MEN—bold men, with clear heads, and capacity for explaining and simplifying to others the ideas they themselves possessed. Unfortunately, I could not resist the temptation of trying to make proselytes. With a terrible faith in the greatness and prevailing power of truth, I preached republicanism even in the bosom of my family. No man is a prophet in his own country. I was virtually turned out of doors one stormy night, leaving my youngest sister fainting on a sofa, and the brave-hearted man who opened the door for me in a state of emotion I have rarely witnessed. My father and elder brother tried to look grand when they gave me my choice between recanting my democratic opinions or banishment from their society. I thought they both looked rather silly, as, without making them any answer, I embraced my sisters and departed. I felt instinctively that I quitted them not to reencounter them on earth, but I little dreamed of the horrible fate that, with one exception, so shortly awaited them.

"A year afterwards, whilst *you*, Viridor, were at Paris, amid the vortex of its Revolution, and at the right hand of that hero of modern days, Lamartine, *I* wandered over awakened Germany, and finally, as an officer in the Hungarian army, went through that terrible campaign which has left behind it seeds of vengeance and glory yet to bloom upon the fertile hotbed of the fallen Austrian empire.

"There is a hideous tale extant of a man, who, being magnetically entranced at the moment of death by a disciple of Mesmer, remained for a space of many months in a state of living death, neither eating, drinking, nor giving otherwise any sign of vitality. It was, in fact, a mesmerised *corpse*, which, on the spell being dissolved, or, to speak technically, on being *de*-mesmerised, instantly fell to pieces in a state of almost liquid putrefaction!*

"A more perfect type of Austria's destiny could not be desired. Preserved and magnetised by the Czar's Satanic agency—we are willing, for once in a way, to couple mesmerism and devilry together—the actually defunct empire is only waiting the first awakening thunder of a new revolution to display its internal rottenness, and crumble into irreparable decomposition.

"Well, all Hungary rose in arms against a government of scoundrels, backed by an army of slaves. To give any detail of my personal adventures, or even of the war itself, would occupy whole days, and require references to maps, without which all description would be unintelligible. Enough that from first to last I was engaged in eleven battles, and nearly fifty skirmishes; that I was present at the taking of seven, and the defence of four, cities and fortresses; that, thanks to my former military tactics, I obtained, by almost unparalleled promotion, the nominal rank of lieutenant-general from the hands of Bem himself; that I was repeatedly in

* By Edgar Poe, the late lamented American poet and novelist, a man of surpassing genius, to whom I shall have more than one occasion to allude. So artistically and naturally was the story alluded to worked up, that it passed everywhere current as an authentic narrative at the time of its publication.

consultation with that man of brilliant and fertile genius, Kossuth, and with the other leaders of the patriots. Perhaps—excuse a soldier's vanity—perhaps, had my advice been taken, Hungary might have been saved. I have studied the *black art*—the art of war—in the pages of history, and in the conversation of veterans. I am convinced, with Napoleon, that it may be reduced to one dogma—rapidity! rapidity! rapidity! We had admirable leaders—Bem, Dembinski, Klapka, and many others, distinguished themselves in a thousand ways. Bem was the hero of the war. But even Bem was no Napoleon. His courage was greater than his resources. By a peculiar stratagem, I would have marched on Vienna at all hazards, fought a pitched battle under its walls, and raised the standard of liberty and rebellion in the heart of the enemy's country. I urged my plan on Kossuth—he approved it. I urged it on the generals, separately and in council.

" 'It is the most dangerous, the most desperate, of all the plans proposed,' said Dembinski.

" ' For that very reason the most likely to succeed !' I explained; 'and if it *should* succeed ?'

" ' We should destroy the empire in less than three months,' said Dembinski.

" The plan he pursued is well known, as also the persevering, but unsuccessful, attempts to penetrate into the hostile territory. Instead of crossing the Theiss as victors, we were ultimately obliged to retreat before superior forces. And then came the strangest and most exciting period of my brief military career. Selected or volunteering for the most dangerous expeditions, I led a life of the most stormy and intense excitement, which I can only compare to a sort of intoxication of activity. I rarely slept, save in my clothes, and never passed a night without being aroused, either by the news of a hostile detachment's approach, or by some pressing necessity of my troops. A strong constitution and frame, combined with a will and spirit of endurance or resistance that nothing could disconcert, enabled me to go through fatigues which none but men inspired with the fierce enthusiasm of national liberty can comprehend."

"Strength," said Viridor, "is in reality a mental, and not a physical quality. Nearly all men of powerful intellect possess great bodily vigour, especially for the bearing of fatigues, watchings, and hardships."

"Every fact of my experience during the war confirmed that theory," continued Darian. " My best officers had been literary men, artists, and members of the learned professions ; like myself, soldiers by inspiration, rather than education. They were quicker at understanding the boldness of my tactics than the regular officers, whose brains were full of petty points of discipline and conventional manœuvres. My aide-de-camp had been editor of a newspaper in Buda—my most efficient artilleryman, mathematical professor of a public school in Prussian Poland. The Poles were the best soldiers in the armies of Hungary. What a nation of brave and noble hearts has been sacrificed in Poland!"

"They will yet rise," said Basiline; " *Resurgam* is written on their tomb in the very unrelaxed oppression which is required to keep them in subjection."

"Let us hope so," said Viridor, sighing. " If we ever could cease to be cosmopolites, our swords should be for Poland and Hungary."

" ' We shall live to fight for both, and not in vain, I firmly believe,' resumed Darian; ' but to my story. I must pass over all subordinate incidents, and come to the, for me, one great event of a war without a parallel in modern history.

" There is a small town between —————— and Pesth ; it contains about eleven thousand inhabitants. In this town I was quartered with a detachment of about six hundred light infantry, and perhaps thirty or forty mounted volunteers, chiefly German students, who had fought, during the siege of Vienna, at the barricades. After the taking of the city, and the cold-blooded murders of Robert Blum and Messenhauser by Windischgratz, fearing themselves to be assassinated with the mockery of a court-martial, they contrived to cross the lines either with forged passports, disguised as peasants and old women, or favoured by the darkness of the night, and enlisted themselves, as a matter of course, under the Magyar standard. They fought like devils. They were splendid young fellows. *Not one of them survived the campaign.*

" There is noble blood enough upon the idiot emperor's soul, and that of his wild-beast councellors, to paint all Hell with crimson! Pshaw! I rave—there are *no words for real passion!* What I *feel* no poet, no art, can describe."

Darian paused for a moment and covered his face with his hands. The thought of his old companions in arms, and of their dreadful fate, choked his utterance for some minutes.

At length he resumed, in a voice terrible from its depth and menacing calmness of passion.

F

" Not one survived. They yielded themselves pri-
soners of war to a detachment of H—y—u's army, and
were shot in cold blood to a man, by the orders of that
vilest of assassins.

" What monstrous treachery," exclaimed Viridor.

" Cowards, who flog women," said Darian, fiercely,
" are not particular to a few murders more or less.   I
must hasten on with my narrative.   It is idle to indulge
in expressions of indignation, disgust, or contempt,
which would end in exciting the brain to madness.   It
is enough that we have sworn the destruction of the
Austrian empire ; that we have sowed, and are sowing,
the seeds of its utter and irremediable destruction.

" Every day we were expecting reinforcements.   A
body of eight thousand Austrians was advancing upon
the town.   Our position was one of imminent peril.   The
town was quite incapable of being defended by so small
a force as I possessed.   I resolved to wait until the
Austrians were almost at our gates, in the hope of the
promised assistance, and then to retreat gradually in the
direction of the expected succours, with which, if sufficiently strong, I proposed to return and recapture the
town.

" It was late in the afternoon ; I was seated in the
study of a certain doctor, at whose house I had established my head-quarters, awaiting a little refreshment,
when my aide-de-camp, the editor, abruptly introduced
a most extraordinary visitor to my notice.

" He wore a ragged peasant's blouse, trousers which
seemed scarcely to hang together, and a sort of som-
brero hat, which was the only tolerably well-preserved
portion of his squalid attire.   His hair hung down, long

and matted, on his shoulders; his moustache and beard mingled in a tangled mass on his chest. His face was pallid and emaciated; his hands and arms were of alarming meagreness; his feet were bare and bleeding from the rough roads. In his eyes was a sort of wild fire which bordered on insanity.

" ' Who are you?' I demanded in the Magyar tongue, which, with my peculiar faculty for languages, I had learned to speak so correctly as not to be distinguished from a native by any but people of the best education.

" No answer. The man seemed to be studying my countenance with intense closeness.

" I tried German. No reply.

" I tried French. The same result.

" Suddenly the man clasped his hands, his face broke out into a smile, and he exclaimed, to my astonishment, in the purest English—

" ' What! Mr. Arthur!—don't you remember me? Stanley—Thomas Stanley—?' He fell back, exhausted, into a chair.

" ' Stanley!' I exclaimed, ' my father's servant! Can it be possible! And what brings you here, and in this beggar's state? What news of my father, of my brother, and my sisters—my sister Genevra, is she well?'

" ' She lives,' said Stanley, faintly.

" ' And the rest?'

" ' I'—Stanley began, but it was evident that he was too exhausted to continue.

" ' Stay,' I cried, 'pardon my selfishness. Ah, doctor! some food, in Heaven's name, and some clean clothes for this man! He is a countryman of mine, I fear he is ill— he is dying!'

" 'No,' said the doctor, ' he is only exhausted by fatigue and want of food ; is it not so ?' he added, in French, addressing Stanley himself.

"Stanley nodded assent, and murmured faintly, 'Since yesterday morning—no food—I heard you were here— I walked,' and he paused from sheer inanition.

"At this moment, one of our officers entered the apartment, and announced the fact that the head of the Austrian column was already visible from the walls, at about two miles' distance.

"Almost simultaneously, a messenger arrived, bearing the news that the Hungarian succours were within four hours' march of the town.

" ' What are your views ?' said I, to my second in command, who was present.

" ' That the town is not tenable for an hour. It offers too many points of attack for our handful of men.'

" ' Right ! there is no use in sacrificing the men. I have made up my mind. Give the order to march at once. You will take the command for the moment. You will march to meet Solaki and his detachment, and return with them to save, if possible, the town from being sacked, and the inhabitants from—'

" ' Austrian mercy,' completed the doctor, with bitter irony.

" ' Just so. I must remain here a few minutes—till this man, who bears, perhaps, vitally important news, recover the power of speech. I can easily overtake you on horseback.' The major departed.

" ' I will stay with you,' said the aide-de-camp.

" ' I order you to accompany the troops.'

" 'I disobey your order, general, at all hazards,' said the editor, coolly.

" ' There is no danger.'

" ' Then I can stay.'

" ' But if I should not escape in time—'

" ' Then there is danger,' said the aide-de-camp. 'I will not desert you living, general.'

" ' Then stay,' said I, ' double rebel as you are, and console yourself by the reflection, that if you are not shot by the Austrians you will be sentenced by a Magyar court-martial.' But as I spoke these words, in a tone of dismal jocosity, I squeezed the brave fellow's hand, which was white and soft as a woman's, in a way that proved my appreciation of his generosity.

" Meanwhile, some bread and meat were brought in, and Stanley, after a few mouthfuls, became sufficiently recruited in strength to inform me of the death of my father, my brother, and my sisters, and my own conse- quently changed position and prospects in the world.

" I cannot say what effect such news might have had upon mé under other circumstances. At the then present juncture, it made but a vague and bewildering impres- sion. I was too much occupied with immediate peril to give much thought to anything extraneous. Stanley's own brief description of his wanderings and devotion to my person affected me much more strongly. I saw *him* before me in his famished and pitiable plight. I could *realise* that idea. All else of his narrative seemed remote and dream-like. Indeed, I *dared* not dwell upon the thought of my family losses at a time when the lives of thousands were possibly dependant upon my activity and decision.

"Already too much time had been spent in words, though not twenty minutes had elapsed since the departure of our soldiers. My horse and the aide-de-camp's were at the door, but a distant sound of clashing arms and trampling footsteps announced the fact that the foremost Austrians were already at hand. At the same time, an old workman of the town rushed into the house with the information that a small party of the enemy had, under cover of a wood, gained a position whence they commanded the road by which our troop had so recently retreated.

"This unexpected misadventure cut off our escape by the plan originally proposed, and left us but one chance of avoiding immediate capture or death. It was a desperate chance, but even a chance is enough to sustain human hopes, and we adopted it without hesitation. Abandoning our horses to their fate, the aide-de-camp and myself hastily put on a couple of peasants' frocks, which were at hand, with suitable continuations, whilst the doctor thrust our uniforms into an empty cask in his cellar. We then, by the application of ashes from the stove, begrimed our faces and hands, and, accompanied by Stanley, whose costume needed no improvement in raggedness and dirt, went out at the back of the house, and, after a considerable circuit, had the audacity to mingle with a crowd of terrified people in the market-place, who cried, 'Long live the Emperor!' and 'God save the General H——u,' on the principle of a man who tries to coax a bull-dog of whose bite he stands in momentary apprehension.

"The Austrians entered the town with fife and drum, and the general, who established himself at the Hotel-de-

Ville, immediately issued a proclamation that a public execution would take place within the space of two hours, being no other than the infliction of fifty lashes upon the famous Basiline, Countess of Arpath, for her high treason and contumacious rebellion and conspiracy against his Majesty the Emperor of Austria and King of Hungary."

Viridor started at the name of Arpath, and looked with evident suspicion towards Basiline.

"My sister," said the fair patriot, in a tone that left the poet still undecided as to her sex, which he had begun to suspect during the last few hours.

"Yes," said Darian, rapidly, as if impatient to conclude his narrative, "the sister of Captain Arpath, the noblest soul and most beautiful form—"

"Arthur!" said Basiline.

"Well, I will not enlarge upon her virtues or her loveliness. Enough, Viridor, that, not contented with stirring up the Magyars to insurrection by her splendid ballads and odes, which ran like electricity from one frontier to the other, this noble girl, scarcely nineteen years of age, actually adopted the Hungarian uniform, mounted horse, and on more than one occasion spurred through the thickest fire, addressed the flagging soldiers, and carried dispatches of the most vital importance to the army for Bem himself. It was in one of these expeditions that she had fallen into the power of the Austrians. H——u resolved to make her an example. He is one of those wretches who almost convincingly confirm the descent of man from the lower animals. Like Greenacre, Manning, and other criminals of their class, he may be said to occupy but a 'mid station between the brute and human being, having all the blind ferocity of the former and all the artificial vices of the latter. He attained his present position by interest alone, having committed, in the early part of his career, several acts of meanness and cowardice, which most unaccountably failed in securing his ignominious dismissal from the service. But to flog women requires no manly qualities.

" I heard the dastardly proclamation. I had never seen Basiline Arpath, but I knew her by her poems—I knew that death would be to her infinitely preferable to such a fiend-like infliction. I resolved to save her at all hazards, even at the expense of her life and of my own."

At this crisis in Darian's narrative, Basiline, who had gradually drawn her chair closer to the young general's, could no longer sustain her assumed character before Viridor. Her head fell upon Darian's shoulder—he drew her towards him with his left arm, whilst their right hands were locked in one another, and their whole attitude and expression denoted the confidence of a love without drawback, the sublime adoration of a woman for her hero, and a lover for his mistress.

Viridor needed not to be further enlightened. For the first time the marvellous beauty of the Hungarian struck him with the force of an explosion. Strange to say, a deep sadness fell upon him at the spectacle. His thoughts wandered away from the narrative he was listening to, and a selfish regret divided his attention with the past danger of his friends. Strange fatality ! This man, whose bold career and high genius the reader has yet to become familiar with, gifted by nature with rare beauty of person, captivating manners, and a heart of the most intense passion and delicate sensibility ; this student of almost universal science ; this accomplished man of the world, without a vestige of worldliness, had attained the age of five-and-twenty, and had yet to utter, yet to hear, the first protestation of love, in the only sense of the word worthy of its sacred ecstasy ! In a great soul, not all the heroic expansion, not all the fiery activity of intellectual ambition, can fill up the terrible void left by the unsatisfied craving of the affections. The most brilliant courtesans are vainly prodigal of their smiles and caresses upon men like Viridor. No study is so absorbing, no wine so potent, no fame so enchanting, as to avert the dire reaction of the thirsting principle of love. Hence the terrible gloom, the lasting melancholy, of many great and noble minds. Difficult to please, they are often unsuccessful in pleasing. Perhaps the respect their lofty character inspires destroys more tender and familiar sentiments. Perhaps a certain profundity in their remarks frightens by its mystery, or wearies by its incomprehensibility, less gifted intelligences. Perhaps even the very strength and sincerity of their emotions cause them to appear easy conquests, and therefore to be underrated by women of ordinary understandings. Perhaps even their very excess of delicacy and chivalrous behaviour towards the sex operates to their disfavour. But this subject is too curious to be treated summarily. We return to Darian's narrative.

"Time passed on," continued the Magyar leader. "Some delay occurred in the preparations for the execution. A feeble hope began to dawn in my mind

that the expected assistance might arrive in time for
the rescue of the prisoner. Nearly three hours had
elapsed since the departure of my troops. Night had
fallen black and threatening. The sky was covered
with dark heavy clouds—occasional flashes of lightning
illumined the market-place, which we overlooked
from the upper window of a house in which we had
taken refuge. The owner of the house was a staunch
patriot, but had so frankly welcomed the Austrian
officers quartered under his roof, that they respected
the sanctity of his wife and daughter's apartments, in
which we were concealed. As there was no light in the
room we occupied, we could stand without risk at the
window, and watch the proceedings of the soldiers in
the square below, as well as the shadows of the Austrian
officers on the blinds of the Hotel-de-Ville, from the
door of which building they were constantly issuing
with fresh directions from the general. It is probable
that considerable anxiety as to the arrival of their
main body prevailed in the Austrian councils. There
were not in the town above seven or eight thousand
soldiers at the time. But a large reinforcement was
expected every instant. I afterwards learned that
H——u had arrived thus in advance of his army by a
mere accident, having calculated on the previous capture
of the town by a large body of Lombard and Bohemian
troops under the Count Xavier von Strahlenberg, who,
meanwhile, had been utterly routed by Dembinski, and
put to flight in the utmost disorder and confusion.

 "At length a funereal roll of the drum announced the
immediate preparation for the commission of the hideous
crime. A square of infantry, drawn up three deep,

surrounded the post to which the victim was to be attached.

"Every other man in the first lines, facing the centre of the square, bore a flaming torch. The smoke of these flambeaux formed black, rolling, wave-like clouds, with lurid edges, above the heads of the assembled executioners and spectators, and imparted a mysterious and spectral character to the scene. At the windows of the houses, and at one end of the square below, were dimly visible the pale, horror-struck faces of old men, women, and children, intermixed with visages of stern and gloomy menace, that seemed like multiplied reflections of the same countenance, adding, as they did, to their national resemblance, one uniform expression of deadly and inextinguishable hatred.

"'Can human or superhuman daring do anything to save Basiline of Arpath?' whispered the ex-editor in my ear, with unnatural calmness.

"'Yes,' I replied, 'if you will yet obey me as your general, an attempt may be made—not altogether desperate.'

"'General I will obey you to the letter. It is useless to economise our lives. Every instant we may be discovered. The first Austrian ruffian that takes it into his head to enter these apartments brings our death-warrant.'

"'Hear, then, my orders. Within an hour our troops may arrive. We must create a diversion that will more than occupy that period. There is but one physical weapon at our disposition, and that is—*Fire*.'

"'I understand you,' said the aide-de-camp, embracing me fervently. 'General, you are indeed a born

leader of men! If we can but leave this house unnoticed, trust me within ten minutes the Hotel-de-
Ville, and the house which faces it, shall be in flames.
I take that upon myself. I can mingle with the
crowd unnoticed, whilst your great height would
render you suspected the moment you attempted to
force your way through the people. I shall not want
assistants.'

"' I depend upon you. Now descend the stairs. If you
are taken, and we in consequence discovered, I shall sell
my life as dearly as I can. I will not trust to Austrian
faith, and courts-martial of hireling cut-throats. If you
escape for the moment, I follow in your track, and in
case you are frustrated in the attempt to fire some building in the market-place, I station myself in the foremost rank of yonder ragged populace, and with one or
other of these English rifle-barrelled pistols which I
have under my blouse, I drive a bullet to the heart of
Basiline Arpath before one blow of the Austrian lash can
descend upon her form.'

" The editor started. ' You are resolved ?' he said.

" What else can I do ? I shall be bayonetted instantly,
unless my first pistol do its work so well as to leave the
other for its master.'

"' Right! right! right! gasped the editor, and with
another rapid embrace, he commenced on tip-toe his
noiseless journey. For an instant he turned back, and
laid his pistols upon a table.

"' In my case, arms would only betray me, if examined,'
he said, coolly; ' each man to his duty. Mine is to play
the fire-king. Friends, *au revoir!* '

" For some minutes after the Magyar's departure, I

listened with a dreadful tension of the sense of hearing. Hearing no disturbance, I gained courage to look cautiously from the open window upon the gateway below. Presently, I saw a man in an Austrian officer's cloak and hat issue boldly from the door; he crossed the square, and disappeared in the crowd without having attracted hostile attention.

"I saw no one else leave the house. It was the Buda editor, who had picked up this disguise from an ante-room on his road. I did not know it, but there was a sentinel at the door. To this hat and cloak we all owed our preservation.

"Almost at the same moment a procession descended the steps of the Hotel-de-Ville. A figure in the midst, covered with a long mantle, and bare-headed, was evidently the illustrious prisoner.

"I now turned to Stanley, who had hitherto clung to my side, his eyes fixed upon my countenance with an air of stupefaction, indicative of either an incipient derangement of intellect, or of intoxication, produced by the wine and food taken after so long a fast. I conjured him to remain quietly where he was, as his ignorance of the language might prove fatal to us both, whilst his state of weakness and exhaustion would render him incapable of any necessary exertion. I explained to him our position and prospects, and perceiving that the victim of H——u's brutal cruelty was already within the fatal square of soldiery, I resolved to dare the descent of the staircase without further delay. Accordingly, I had commenced my retreat, with the same caution as the editor, when I

G

found that Stanley, having concealed the pistols of the former under his tattered frock, was following me with anything but similar stealthiness. However, it was no time for remonstrances. Fortunately the Austrians quartered in the house were all occupied by the coming spectacle of torture. We reached the door in safety, and I found myself face to face with the sentinel. He demanded the password.

" 'Here,' said I, thrusting my purse into his hands, ' or here,' and I shewed the pistol under my blouse, at the same time walking rapidly on, in order to give the man no time for reflection.

" Stanley followed at my heels. The sentinel gave no alarm. He could not have imagined that anything beyond the escape of a couple of fugitive patriots was at stake. Whether merely mercenary or more generous feelings influenced his conduct is impossible to determine. We mixed with the crowd unnoticed, and a sense of freedom of action, however limited, raised my desperate hopes, and fortified me in my perilous resolution.

" Every instant was now of indescribable interest. The noble lady was stripped of her garments, which were of masculine fashion, to her waist. H——u himself stood in the interior of the square of soldiers, and superintended the proceedings. He was engaged in a vivid altercation with one of his officers. It will hardly be believed, but he was desirous of pushing diabolical outrage yet further by the removal—I cannot proceed. Enough, that by the testimony of one of his own soldiers, wounded in the subsequent affray, I learned that the danger of a mutiny amongst the surrounding guards alone prevented him from insisting on his command being fulfilled."

During this portion of Darian's recital Basiline had risen and quitted the apartment. Viridor listened with a brow pale as that of a corpse, on which the cold perspiration stood like frozen dew-drops; whilst the fire of his deep eyes reflected the fierce passion that burned in those of his companion, at the hideous reminiscences he evoked.

" And now," continued the latter, " ensued a scene of horror rarely dreamed of. I pass over *my* feelings on beholding for the first time, under such frightful conditions, the face and form to me without a peer, even in imagination. The glare of the torches plainly shewed me the unabashed glory of a beauty, rendered divine by its heroic resolution. There was a sort of triumph even in its mute agony. I never felt like a wild beast before. But then I must have torn H——u to pieces with my teeth and hands to have appeased the savage thirst for vengeance that shook my whole frame with its strength. I strove to control my agitation, in fear lest my aim should falter, and my plan for saving Basiline prove abortive. I say for saving, because, had she not died under the lash, I think it highly improbable that her life would have been spared by the monsters who then executed the designs of the Austrian cabinet in Hungary. But I must keep to mere facts and bare newspaper description, or I shall never end my history.

" A new cause of delay occurred. There was no executioner.

" Three soldiers were ordered to advance from the
ranks. H——u himself, handed a huge whip of bull's-
hide to the foremost, a mere lad, and directed him to lay
down his musket and commence the torture.

" The soldier obeyed—he looked at the victim—her
eyes encountered his—he staggered backwards, and
fainted at the very feet of his general.

" H——u ordered the eyes of the prisoner to be
bandaged.

" The insensible body of the first soldier was removed.
The second did not hesitate. He said some words in
a bold tone to H——u. The latter replied by a
rapid gesture of command. The soldier did not lay
down his musket—he placed the barrel against his forehead and blew out his brains. A general murmur arose,
but H——u was apparently unmoved. The third
soldier came forward. He prepared himself to execute
the command of his leader. He raised the whip—I
raised my pistol. He struck the first blow. I pulled
the trigger. The pistol missed fire, and the whip struck
only the post above the head of the prisoner. I put on
a fresh cap, but before I could do so, the third soldier
had adopted a new line of policy—he affected drunken-
ness—he reeled and balanced himself, and appeared to
be calculating his aim with imbecile accuracy. The
trick was too gross. H——u struck him sharply with
the flat of his sabre. He still persevered in his assumed
part. The exasperated ruffian then wounded him
severely with the point of his weapon. At this atrocious
action, the feelings of the soldiers could be no longer
restrained; many of them gave vent to such exclama-
tions as—

" ' We are soldiers, not executioners ! We are ready to fight men, not to flog women ! '

" H——u regarded the mutineers in dismay. But their officers contrived to restore discipline by actively arresting several of the delinquents.

"In the midst of the confusion a sudden cry was raised. It was soon re-echoed from mouth to mouth, amid a scene of general confusion and consternation. ' Fire ! Fire ! The Hotel-de-Ville is on fire.'

" My aide-de-camp had been successful. He had seized the moment of the greatest interest in the execution to effect his object with a band of desperate patriots, about twenty in number. They had suddenly entered the rear of the building, and thrown some combustibles into a room filled with papers. The whole building was pannelled with wood, so that to extinguish the flames was almost hopeless. Nearly all the incendiaries were bayonetted on the spot. The aide-de-camp only escaped by falling flat on the ground, and assuming the part of a dead man, until the increasing flames drove the Austrians from that part of the building.

"In the midst of the tumult a rocket was seen to ascend in the distance. I now knew that succour was at hand. I shouted loudly an Hungarian 'Vivat !' It was caught up by the populace. In another minute I was in the centre of a mêlée of Austrian soldiers, and Magyar workmen and citizens, cutting with my knife the ropes by which Basiline was bound.

" H——u and the greater part of the soldiers had retreated to the other end of the market-place. Four pieces of artillery were only awaiting the separation of the soldiery from the townspeople to be turned against the latter with fatal certainty.

" Bearing Basiline in my arms, I endeavoured to gain a side street in possession of the crowd. Meanwhile, retained by the pressure of surrounding bodies, I became the helpless witness of a most unexpected catastrophe.

" Stanley, who, during the preparations for the execution of H——u's inhuman command, had exhibited almost uncontrolable excitement, now quitted my side, and without heeding my repeated calls to turn back, plunged madly forward in the direction of the spot where the Austrian general's plume was visible, surrounded by his panic-struck officers. These, by their extreme eagerness to escape down the street leading to the northern gate of the town, shewed that a more pressing danger than the attack of an incendiary mob threatened their safety. Meanwhile, a gradual separation was taking place in the market-place between the Austrians and the townspeople, so that Stanley found himself crossing a comparatively free space, encumbered only with dead or dying men, who had been trampled down in the confusion. The Hotel-de-Ville, now completely in flames, lit up the square far more brilliantly than the extinguished torches.

" Stanley continued to plunge forward—all eyes were on him. Words occupy time, yet all I am describing happened in an instant. He arrived within two yards of the disordered lines of the Austrians. He shouted in English the words, ' Damn you for a cowardly villain !' and fired both his pistols at H——u, one after the other, killing an old officer at his side, and carrying away the very plume of the general himself. But H——u was yet unhurt, and Stanley, pierced by five bayonets, fell dead in an instant before the first line of the Austrians, without uttering a groan. As he fell, his

eyes turned towards the place where I stood with an ecstatic glare of triumph. I left Basiline, whom I had covered with my blouse, and instinctively dashed forward to Stanley's rescue. In so doing, I stumbled, and fell over something on the ground. It was the heavy whip, with loaded handle, intended for the execution. I picked it up, as being no contemptible weapon, and rose in an instant—just in time to catch the last glance of my devoted friend. He was dead—dead in the odour of sanctity—of exalted heroism. He had lived a menial, he perished a martyr!

"Let men who are apt to treat those of their brethren whom circumstances of education and means compel to minister to the wants and pleasures of more fortunate mortals, reflect that there may be even in their own circle hearts like Stanley's, which demand but the opportunity of action, courage, and self-sacrifice, to acquire the admiration of mankind. All blood is red—every soul is divine. Less is the gulf between the rudest labourer and the most polished gentleman, than between the greatest noble and the least of true poets or philosophers. In the end the strongest must triumph. Aristocracy has crushed the people, and Genius is crushing Aristocracy. Will they never hear us, Viridor, these children of the night, these darkened hosts of spirits? Have poets divined, thinkers reasoned, prophets prophesied, so long, and must, after all, the sword be our Cæsar of appeal? Must we take the scourge of wrath to drive these money-changers and sellers of doves, these place-hunters, match-makers, and tax-grinders, from the great temple of the earth, which they desecrate with their cruelties and defile with their selfish vices?

"Darian, Darian! my dear friend—the only friend whose thoughts ever echoed my own!" exclaimed Viridor, leaning forward with clasped hands, and gazing upon the republican leader, his face radiant with inspiration. "Did not our great Master, the Master we honour by our deeds, whilst ignorance worships his name in worthless formulas, did he not say, 'I came to bring not peace but a sword?' Have nearly two thousand years elapsed, and are we, His heirs in spirit, compelled still to repeat the gloomy creed of discord? Is there no new, no unheard-of chord to strike, which may vibrate in the hearts of nations? True, indeed, is the type of man's exclusion from happiness! The flaming sword yet guards the Eden of love! Proceed, my dear Darian, with your narrative, and pardon my wandering interruption."

"Pardon the eruption of a volcano!" said Darian, with a serene smile. "I have nearly concluded my story. We shall have time for other matters afterwards. Basiline will return, and there is the whole night before us!"

Viridor listened with renewed attention as Darian once more resumed.

"The cause of the Austrian panic became now evident in the shape of several Hungarian dragoons, who, amid the shouts of the people, entered the square from the street opposed to that by which our enemies were re-treating. So sudden was their arrival, that they were present at the first volley of musketry fired by the Austrians, who covered the retreat of their comrades, upon the insurgent populace.

"A struggle and carnage ensued, which baffle all de-scription for horror and confusion. The spread of the fire to the houses behind the Hotel-de-Ville, the ringing of bells, the shrieking of women, the reports, and echoed reports of thousands of muskets, carbines, and pistols, the clash of arms and tramp of horses, all conspired to fill my brain with a sort of vertigo, increased by neglect of food and the extreme excitement of the previous events. I conveyed Basiline, who was insensible, and seized by convulsive shiverings, to the house I had formerly occupied in the market-place, and which was, from the direction of the wind, secure at least from the fire. Then having seized the horse of a fallen dragoon, I mounted and rode in pursuit of the flying Austrians, with the Magyar horsemen, who shouted my name with frenzied delight, as soon as I had communicated it to those nearest to me. When we issued from the gate of the town, a singular spectacle presented itself. The clouds had cleared off without a storm, and the moon, nearly at its full, rendered every object in the plain distinctly visible.

"The Austrians were flying before us without even the pretence of order. Some had left the road and were making for the cover of a neighbouring forest already referred to. Others were trying to cross the swollen river on the right; and immediately in front of us, was a small party of horse, making the most violent efforts to penetrate a mass of infantry before them, so dense and crowded as actually to prevent the cavalry from outstripping them.

" Amongst these I thought I recognised the General H——u. The bare thought inspired me with ferocious exultation. I spurred forward like a madman, followed by some twenty Magyars who were considerably in advance of the rest. We penetrated to the very centre of the Austrian horse, and with a savage delight I could almost feel ashamed of, I seized the terrified H——u by the arm, and inflicted at least a dozen blows with the whip upon his back that literally tore his uniform to ribbons, and drew blood at every stroke. I held him in such a manner that he could make no use of his sabre, even had his terror permitted the attempt, whilst his companions were too eager to continue their flight to turn to his rescue. His yells resembled those of an infuriate bull, and he would have remained my prisoner had not a shot from one of our own party killed my horse under me, and compelled me to relax the gripe upon his arm, which, if I mistake not, will, like the blows of my whip, leave a mark on his body not to be effaced with life. The strength and swiftness of his horse saved him. He escaped with the remnant of his vanguard, as his after-cruelties and butcheries testify. But if you go to Vienna, before the coming revolution, you will know the reason why Field-Marshal the Baron von H——u dispenses with a *valet-de-chambre*.

"I need not add anything further at present to explain to you how Arthur Darian and Basiline Arpath became inseparably united."

CHAPTER .

VIRIDOR'S WALK HOME.

It was long past midnight, as Viridor left Darian and Basiline, in that state of mental exaltation when the brain is, as it were, flooded with electricity, a sort of waking clairvoyance seems to transcend all material obstacles to the spiritual vision, and the soul, half disembodied by its intense sympathy with external life, becomes conscious of a power almost miraculous in its influence.

Some day, when cloudy verbalism has ceased to be mistaken for philosophy, when the dim-souled sneerer at transcendental illumination has been taught that all is not mysticism which is not commonplace and tangible (*plump, haudgreiflich*, as my ex-friend Teufelsdroeck Latterday would express it)—some day, when the grand decree "Let there be light," has been extended to the moral as well as the physical world, this exaltation of spiritual potence, this *faith* "that moves mountains," will be recognised as the supreme moment of intellect, and once more the true Poiêtes, or Creator, the real Vates, or Prophet, will be reverenced by a race who indeed realise the saying of the naturalist that "two-handed walks erect, and regards the heavens."

Viridor walked, or rather, as it were, floated along ; for in his intellectual rapture, he was scarcely conscious of any mechanical function. He did not even hear the objurgations of a cabman, whom his impetus nearly sent spinning down an area; and he shook off the arm of a fair fallen angel, who strove to arrest his progress, without even being aware of the attempt.

He thought of Darian and Basiline—he compared the strange adventures related by the former, with his own perilous exertions during the reign of the Provisional Government at Paris, where, though incapable of ostensible occupation from his foreign birth, he had, as the confidant and agent of his idol Lamartine, played so important and mysterious a part in those days of marvellous excitement and activity. Again he dwelt upon the noble character of the love of Darian and his beautiful Magyar—a love combined with so heroic a devotion to the cause of European liberty. He marvelled at the grandeur of their resolution in deferring all consummation of their passion by marriage, until the achievement of some distinguished triumph for the cause to which they were devoted. He contrasted their delicious anticipations and prospective felicity, with his own mournful isolation. He asked himself wildly, to what signal disadvantage of mind or person he was indebted for such an eternal winter of the passions? He recalled his brief dreams of affection, his bitter disappointments, his dreary satiations, disillusions, and disgusts. Then he rapidly pictured an ideal adventure, a romance of rapid encounter, of mutual recognition, of love at first sight, of sympathy, of delight. And then he fiercely tore away his thoughts from such enervating indulgence, and revolved in poetic phrenzy magnificent sentences, oracles of lucidity, irresistible thunderbolts of truth, and verses of transcendant harmony, which swept him along the pavement as a war-charger its rider, until he also, like his friend in the fore-noon, was checked by a crowd, and abruptly roused from his enthusiast reveries to a sense of the sub-realities of existence.

He found himself in Whitehall, before an illumined mansion. It was that containing the offices of the Soul Agents. Ever since the morning, the dark speculator and his coadjutor had found it absolutely necessary, from the rush of visitors eagerly enquiring into, and offering patronage to the Company, to engage the whole of the house for their business, in place of the modest suite of chambers on the ground floor, which they had originally rented. They bought out the other tenants regardless of expense, and so energetic was their fur-nishing upholsterer (whose soul, by the way, was, al-ready signed, sealed, and delivered, in the strong-box of Ignatius) that the whole mansion was in a few hours fitted up as consultation and waiting-rooms, for the accommodation and privacy of the soul-deal-ing public. The third floor alone was devoted to some dozen soul-appraisers and clerks. These drew up their registers, estimates, and reports, from the notes and informations constantly sent or brought in by a staff of intelligent out-door soul-commissioners and reporters, whose omnipresence in society, and relations, direct or indirect, with every proprietor of a soul worth sixpence in Europe, became subsequently a source of no small wonder and admiration.

But in the private audience-chamber of the original promoter, the dark Ignatius, was the vital mainspring of the establishment. From his clear head and bold

H

invention issued every idea carried out as fact by the association.

As for his fat friend, Robert Russel Brown, he partook equally of the heavy dullness of Sir Robert the Devil and the flippant superficiality of Lord John Twaddle; he was as little capable of understanding finance* as the former, or politics as the latter. But he had a turn for share-jobbery. He was an embryo George Mudson of the soul-market. They called him Lucifer Brown afterwards, just as Mudson was nicknamed the Iron Czar. He became a truly accomplished swindler, and was much courted by the nobility. The subtle Grey, (a *very* distant relation of the Grey-tribe, who swarm Downing-street, &c.—as may be surmised from his talent) the profound Ignatius, was comparatively little spoken of at any time. Brown had the glory, and got the testimonial. Brown also came in for the newspaper battery, and the sarcasms of the comic writers; he grew fatter than a bishop, he grew richer than Aladdin, he bought souls by hundreds, by a scratch of his pen, or a handful of scrip, but his own soul was no more his own than Lord Rattlesnake's. The dark comrade of his way governed him by a look. Brown had found all the original money capital, it is true, but Ignatius had found all the capital in ideas. And everything starts from an idea—a company, a party, a religion, a book, an empire, even a world, must have been conceived

---

* When I say that Sir R. cannot understand finance, I mean that he is incapable of conceiving the higher and more philosophical development of that important science. That he understood how to juggle the public, and fill his own pockets by a law which is virtually a legalised robbery, I do not for an instant dispute.

before it could have been created. Ideas govern matter; nay, they form it, they consolidate it, they realise it. This is one best reason why Materialism is preposterous as a system. The belief in it is itself a chimera. No man can really believe in the impossible, and the material reasoner, by that very super-material act of reason, overthrows the very thesis he would establish.

Viridor gazed up at the new Temple of Corruption. He read the inscription on the illuminated blinds. The broad doorway was thronged with people going in or out of the house. It was all brilliance, bustle, and life.

Suddenly there was a great darkness. The gas was turned off, the windows ceased to be illumined, the crowd dispersed, the gate was closed, and the pale moonbeams fell upon the silent building. Viridor still lingered against a small stone pillar on the edge of the pavement.

" Even so," he muttered, as the change came over the Soul Agent's offices, " even so will your system and your tribe vanish from the earth."

" You remember the shibboleth of Contarini Hening," said a voice at his elbow—" *Time.*"

Viridor turned, and beheld the Soul Agent.

" You quote but a poor authority. I will return the compliment by quoting Bernard Viridor—*Eternity.*"

The Soul Agent laughed. " It is too late now," he said, " to apologise for the liberty of addressing you."

" It is unnecessary. I am a philosopher."

" In that case, I will remark, that had you not mentioned a man whose soul is at a premium in the market, I should have said that your quotation was rather a vague and unsatisfactory reply to my own ! "

"Perhaps it has not yet struck you that man, as a creature of time, would be a monster, and that an eternity is requisite to render his existence a consistent theory."

"And the application?"

"Very simple. You hint that yonder speculation may last long enough to satisfy its promoters. I imply that it will be destroyed soon enough to please me whenever it happens. The swiftness of thought is inappreciable, but time itself is but the succession of thoughts. Somebody said—' Work, man—hast thou not all eternity to rest in?' I say, 'Rest, if it please you, for you have all eternity to work in.'"

"An easy creed," said the Soul Agent, pleasantly, "yet the copy-books tell us that Procrastination is the thief of Time."

"No procrastination can last out eternity," replied Viridor.

"He is a nice sort of mystic moralist," thought the Soul Agent, who recognised Viridor from a lithograph portrait he had procured since Darian's visit.

"An interesting acquaintance, were it only as a study," thought Viridor, who recognised the Soul Agent by Darian's description.

"I should like to discuss these matters more at leisure with you," said Ignatius, in his most agreeable manner.

"Nothing easier—visit me at my chambers next Sunday, if it will suit your engagements, and we will smoke over the subject."

The somewhat mystified Soul Agent, whose brain

was indeed a little obscured by the multiplicity of business he had transacted during the day, exchanged cards with the poet, and they separated with mutual salutations.

As they uncovered their heads in the moonlight, a fanciful spectator might have likened them to one of the fallen spirits of the abyss, exchanging a few friendly words with some old comrade of his former home. So they parted : the Soul Agent to join a mistress, who loved him in spite of himself; Viridor, to seek his lonely chambers in the Temple, where his books and pen were his only companions. The former felicitated himself upon a chance which might facilitate an affair too important to be neglected—the latter revolved a scheme of no ordinary magnitude and originality.

On reaching his dwelling, on the second floor, No. 23, Grace Court, Temple, Viridor's ideas were distracted by a very peculiar fancy.

There was but one key to his chambers, and that was in his possession. From the first day of his occupation he had been under the necessity of giving this key daily to his laundress, for the purpose of arranging the apartments, making the bed, and other necessary proceedings.

Now, since that afternoon, no person could have entered the rooms, and, nevertheless, Viridor took it into his head, that the position of the arm-chair, in which he usually wrote, was changed, and also that his papers were not in precisely the same condition in which he had left them. As, however, the character of the old woman who attended to the matters above-mentioned was above suspicion, he gradually threw off this fancy, engendered, possibly, by over-excitement of the nerves,

and after writing for some hours, betook himself to rest
with the dawn, to dream for a few hours of political revolutions, Soul Agents, and beautiful Magyars, which
latter spectres haunted his imagination with a dangerous
and annoying pertinacity.

CHAPTER VIII.

THE SOUL EXCHANGE IS OPENED.

THE Soul Agency was established. In the columns of the *Timeserver*, the *Morning Ghost*, the *Daily Nous*, the *Cobbler*, the *Humbug*, the *Scrambler*, the *Globule*, the *Evening Gun*, and other daily journals, of all shades of politics, appeared the startling advertisements of the new-born Company.

The world at large, and even the world *not* at large, in Whitecross Street and the Bench, applauded the invention to the skies. The former saw a new field for speculation, and the latter imagined themselves suddenly possessed of property, the existence of which they had hitherto scarcely suspected.

Money-dealers rubbed their hands at the notion of a new relish for their dinners. They had fed on human flesh so long that they rather took to the prospect of a change of diet. They saw the road clear for new juggles and new victims, and they sang *Jubilate*, and rattled the devil's counters in their breeches' pockets.

Ministers, or to speak more correctly, the clique of insignificants who let things take their chance, and confine their notions of government to pocketing salaries, providing for relatives, selling patronage, and keeping down talent—ministers highly approved of the new speculation. They foresaw the possibility of securing a majority so beautifully compact and conve-

niently abject as to save them an immense deal of
anxiety in future divisions. If they could once bring
their political "niggers" to the perfection of training
enjoyed of old by Sir Robert the Devil's Sugar-Question
rescinders, who could say how long they might suck the
blood of sleepy old John Bull ? They might stick in
office till literature had educated the people! They
might dine in Downing Street till virtue had as many
friends as religion ! Till the arrival of the Millenium !
Or in case that event turned out a mistake, until Dooms-
day itself! Oh ! there was a great deal to be done by
ministers on the new system. Lord John Twaddle was
quite in high spirits. Sir George Grub and Sir Charles
Woodenhead were more confident in their mediocre
feebleness than ever.

As for the great Earl Grub, whose plans for getting
rid of our colonies by disgusting them with the mother
country, and goading them to justifiable rebellion, are
so little appreciated by less eccentric politicians, he
thought immediately of a few more constitutions for
Australia, and a few more governorships for his cousins.

But Lord Pumicestone, the only man possessing an
idea in the Cabinet, immediately resolved to bombard
somebody's capital, and formed a vague design, on the
spur of the moment, of invading Italy and Spain, with
a remote view to conquering the world, and governing
it afterwards upon rigidly Pumicestonian principles.

Such were the vague aspirations awakened in official
breasts by the opportunities which the Soul Agent's
speculation abundantly offered.

Precisely similar were the thoughts of those politicians in opposition who had any thoughts at all.

In short, both parties appreciated the advantages of a definite system of warfare, and prepared to measure their purses and talent for driving bargains with the utmost alacrity.

Byron was quite right in calling England a nation of shopkeepers. Life in England is essentially a system of traffic. The power of capital is absolute in the hands of those who know how to use it.

Curiously enough, there is scarcely a man in the country who has the slightest notion of what *can* be done with capital. Nor did I ever yet meet, personally or in print, with a man who even clearly understood the nature of capital itself. As I am not myself a capitalist, and for a secret and peculiar reason do not intend to become one, I can throw out a few hints upon this subject, more dispassionately, perhaps, than persons whose own passion for acquisition blinds them to the rational explanation of this exciting mystery.

I shall take as my text the words of Meyerbeer's celebrated opera—

"Gold is but a chimera."

Now, so far from this thesis being a mere poetical figure, as some may think, or a piece of cant morality, as others may imagine—it is a downright, plain, material truth.

This appears strange and paradoxical. But if any one suspect that I say it for the sake of saying anything smart and startling, he is grossly mistaken. I once *did* write a satirical novel* for pure fun. I did not observe

* "Anti-Coningsby" was written at the age of nineteen years, in six weeks, *currente calamo*. Since then, six years of earnest study and reflection, together with the perusal of some six hundred volumes in various languages, on every class of subject, have left the writer an altered, if not a better man.

that many people found it out, but I myself was perfectly aware that it was a tissue of extravagant nonsense from one end to the other. I have often wished to make this confession, and I do so now, because I wish to establish very different relations with my readers. This book is a true expression of my thoughts and feelings. It is practically and typically founded on the observation and consideration of nature and man, synthetically and analytically regarded. There are certain ideas—advanced spiritual banners. Their shadow is upon us. We so-called writers of fiction, in seemingly throwing the mantle of fancy round the forms of reality, in fact but strip the actor and the stage of life of their paint, trappings, and artificial illusions. We exhibit mind under matter. We are showmen at a great fair—I will not say a "Vanity Fair," lest I should infringe the domain of a rival school. We say, "Walk up, ladies and gentlemen, and see the live lion stuffed with straw—walk up, and see the big names stuffed with impotence!" Such is our vocation, as such is my egotism. I would not put it in a regular preface, for fear everybody should skip it. To return to our text.

"Gold is but a chimera." By gold of course I mean property—capital—in a word, wealth.

Now I think it will be admitted that if a man do not know *what* he possesses, and can moreover have no real certainty that he possesses *anything at all*, the thing which he undoubtedly *does* possess can only be regarded as a chimera—in fact, an idea, and an idea by no means of the clearest.

Before illustrating this position by example, let me,

however, admit, once and for all, that the chimeras are really worth having. There is a satisfaction in chimeras which is indisputable.

Let us, then, suppose that a man possesses a house which produces the sum of £100 a year. Such, at least, is the description which the chimera-cherisher would give of his property.

But suppose that within three months that house is to be burned to the ground, and the tenant with it; what does our friend virtually possess? A house that will bring in £100 a year? No—a piece of land, with a ruin upon it, which nobody cares to buy, perhaps, or build on. In a word, *nothing* in the form of a house, and a rental which is a chimera. Case the first.

Suppose the house insured. This chimera has another element. Either it is a building and a rent, or a sum of ready cash. But if the insurance office fail, or resist payment successfully? Still a chimera. Case the second.

Suppose the house of eternal durability. What can secure tenants, or guard against diminution of rent and value? It is still a chimera. Case the third.

His title may be bad, and he may not know it. An obstinate chimera. Case the fourth.

I could go on to case the thousandth, but I think it would be superfluous.

It is evident that the proprietor of the house neither knows what he possesses, nor whether he possesses anything. At best he has but an utterly uncertain interest in the property, for he may die to-morrow.

Still, he knows he has something.

True—an algebraic X, an unknown quantity, that is, a chimera.

And this rule applies to all property, to all capital, to all earthly possessions.

Death and taxes alone render it impossible to fix the value of anything.

Possession is said to be nine-tenths of the law. Yet, the man is himself possessed who talks of possession as a reality. We possess, in truth, but one thing—a soul and its activity.

Had not M. Proudhon denounced property as an impossibility, in addition to its being a theft, I should have set him down as a blockhead, with all his subtlety of logic. As it is, I by no means rate him as the terrific monster he is pictured. He is like a child in a dark room, groping for the door. Some day he may find the handle, open it, and see the light of day. Till then, I am sorry a thinker of his ingenuity should occupy such disagreeable quarters. There are more dangerous chimeras than his extremely popular just now in the soul-market.

Capital, then, is a chimera—yes, but a very different sort of chimera to different minds.

The thousand pounds which gives the poor old lady thirty pounds a year from the funds is a very different capital from the thousand which produces its annual five hundred to the intelligent tradesman, besides giving employment and subsistence to some twenty or thirty workmen, shopboys, &c.

The Marquis of ——'s half million of rental, which passes not through his hands but through his imagination, as waste water passes through a sewer, is very different from the same sum passing through the factory of the great cotton-lord who supplies half Europe with calico they could not fabricate in small quantities with ten times the outlay in time, labour, and money. And again, how different would be the same capital passing through the multiplying channels which a soul of grand and enlightened enterprise might contrive. That capital might represent the regeneration of a country, the revolution of an empire. In a word, capital is—what the intellect makes it. Stamped with a thought, the piece of representative gold or paper becomes doubled, centupled, infinitely multiplied, or—annihilated, and utterly neutralised.

Sir Robert asks, What is a pound ?

I answer, A chimera, a bit of metal dropped down a drain, or a germ of infinite human activity, pain, and pleasure—the trinket of a fool, or the wand of a magician.

What, then, is currency—what is credit—what is commerce ? It needs something more than a Sir Robert, aye, or a blundering Macgrubbins to boot, to answer these questions.

To be a statesman it is necessary to learn something beyond statistics (particularly Macgrubbin's statistics*). There is a philosophy in politics, which these devil-may-care, happy-go-lucky legislators, know as little of as the sable citizens who, in the words of the humorist,

> " Worship mighty Mumbo Jumbo,
> In the Mountains of the Moon ! "

And this sort of people are talked of as practical,

---

* For some instances of Macgrubbin's accuracy, see " Analogies and Contrasts," a most amusing and instructive work, by the author of " Revelations of Russia," &c. For additional instances of his carelessness and stupidity, apply to the present writer, or to Macgrubbin's own Dictionary of Trade.

I

useful men, lead parties, and govern nations! O my
dear brother literati! do you not think we might do
something more than write articles about our inferiors?
Do you not think that it is high time we should cease
playing the prompters' part to these miserable actors—
cease teaching these overgrown babes of intelligence
to play at government, and take a little of the governing of the world into our own hands, if not as our born
right, like the aristocracy of blood (of blood in more
senses than one), at least as the defenders of the *people*,
which we, and we only, represent, in this age of
transitions?

When the first Soul Agency was established in London, it was high time something should be done to avert
social paralysis. A dismal torpor, not the dreamy
laziness of the luxurious lotus-eater, but the torpor of
a stagnant pool of writhing reptiles, devouring and
leaping over one another, was fast threatening the world
with the realisation of an editor's dream, revealed to the
present writer some months ago in New Bubbleton
Street. This dream was no other than the serene
theory of a *dead level* in intellect, free from those
thickets of philosophy and mountains of genius which
obstruct the path of the unostentatious pilgrim of life.
This dead-level Utopia of "Buntley's" editor was to be
brought about by universal education, which, apparently,
was to stop short at a certain point, and in no case to be
pursued beyond it. Everybody was to be " up to the
mark" (of " Buntley's" editor), and nobody above it.
There was to be a world of able, but no great men;
lots of talent, but no genius. Such was the tendency of
progress (" Buntley's" editor's) prophecied to me by a

very respectable and gentlemanly man in a white neck-cloth. A pleasant theory for a man whose soul was an irregular polygon, full of ups and downs, ins and outs, recesses and projections!

I presume that my article must have been below the ideal dead level of New Bubbleton Street, for it came back one day, looking very dull and heavy, owing, doubtless, to the society of other dead-level MSS. at the New Bubbleton autocrat's. Now, to show how minds differ in this world, I have not been able for years to *read*—even in the last stage of literary poverty, at a club, divan, drawing-room, or coffee-house, where every-thing else was engaged—a single article of the dead-level magazine, without breaking down in the second page of it. And yet this dead-level theory has no lack of partisans. I need not cite examples, and make enemies of half the critics in Europe. So I shall merely observe that I think it a very flat system.

Nevertheless, at bottom it was the old Whiggo-Con-servative notion of Reform; for, after all, every man is a reformer as soon as he fancies he can gain anything by reforming.

And the proof that conservatism is as great a chimera as capital, is, that nobody is ever contented with the present state of affairs. Every class looks to some re-mote Atlantis for their vision of happiness. The only difference between the tory and the radical (I sink the hybrid whigs—as mere chimeras themselves) is, that the former looks back to the past, whilst the latter looks forward to the future for the realisation of his ideal. And the reason the tory is a blockhead, and the radical a rational being is, that while the past is irrecoverably

lost to us, and not to be revisited by any human con-
trivance for locomotion, physical or spiritual, the future
is the constantly attainable land of promise into which
we are ever penetrating yet more deeply, and which
offers inexhaustible domains for conquest, and inexhaustible novelty for our entertainment.

The past eternity is a road that has brought us to an
unsatisfactory present. The future is a railway that
bears us to unlimited anticipation. And to prove that
the future is worth more than the past, if anybody were
insane enough to doubt it, let us take one simple commercial illustration. We can borrow money to an almost
boundless extent by the mortgage of the future, but
no mortal Rothschild would lend one sixpence upon the
security of the past.

The new plan for speculation in Souls, that is, for
dealing in realities instead of chimeras, came just at
the proper crisis. All new inventions do. The world
of men, and even of spirits (*vide* Kepler), is, without
knowing it, a great self-governing Republic. The forms
of their Parliament are somewhat grander than the
standing orders of the House of Commons, and their
speeches and acts somewhat vaster in compass. But
the analogy is perfect. A new religious, moral, metaphysical, or political system, a grand discovery, such as
printing, gunpowder, steam, telegraphs, and magnetism,
a revolution as in France, an emigration as to California, a grand school of poetry or art, all such gigantic,
change-producing facts, are the propositions of the
M.P.'s of intellect, adopted and carried by the universal
suffrage of opinion and feeling.

It was proposed to the age to bring things to a crisis

by straightforward Soul-dealing—and the age adopted the idea.

The whole public rushed into the speculation. The less they understood the nature of the commerce, the greater was the excitement in its pursuit, and the deliciousness of the chimera. Money was to be made out of nothings. They called *human souls* NOTHINGS!— these brain-darkened bipeds of *practical experience!* It took them a long time to find out their blunder. Meanwhile, what victims! what fortunes gained and lost! what hearts broken! what thrones of love, and hope, and happiness, abdicated and overthrown!

The new trade had one good effect, at any rate. Capitalists began to study the nature of a Soul, and to form more correct estimates of public and private characters and abilities, than they had hitherto dreamed of. It was astonishing how stupid people began to find their level, and comparatively honest men to rise in estimation. Vanity and self-conceit were awfully tried by the soul-speculating *régime.*

Some very audacious spirits, however, actually raised their market-prices by downright impudence and brag, not to mention advertisements, which proved a great card in these, as in all other transactions.

There was a comic writer, who had established and ruined seventeen satirical periodicals, besides two tailors, one boot-maker, and a friend (who was obliged to emigrate to the City and turn light porter, after living so luxuriously fast, that not even the weakness of trustful humanity could, in any measure, keep pace with his downward progress). This comic writer, who could make jokes as readily as a child makes faces, published an advertisement in the *Timeserver*, the *Morning Ghost*, and the *Tumbler*, not without a certain "rude sagacity" in its colouring, which is worthy of insertion in Mr. D'Israeli *junior's* "Curiosities of Literature.

I subjoin the document :—

"To the Speculative.—Will be sold, a tremendous bargain, a SOUL of Five-hundred Russell power, warranted not to turn rusty, even if used for very dirty work. Will cut up any amount of books or men per diem, so long as the congenial spirits be supplied for the body, not forgetting the domestic smoking apparatus. Taken altogether (and whoever takes it will find it a taking affair), the Soul in question will be found to answer, combining, as it does, the cunning of the boa constrictor, with the innocence of a pigeon (at a billiard table). The advertiser wishes it to be distinctly understood, that there is nothing methodistical about *him*, and that salary is not so much his object as real stunning employment. Address, pre-paid, to the Crocodile Coffee House, Cuba Street."

The papers teemed with advertisements of similar offers, each possessing its peculiar spiritual advantages. Meanwhile the *Timeserver* proclaimed, in its most inflated bombastic style, that Soul-dealing was a great fact. The *Morning Ghost*, and the *Humbug*, denounced the importation of foreign ideas as an unjustifiable attack upon British intellect, and claimed protection for the Soul merchants of this country against foreign competition. All agreed in giving share-lists of the various Companies, which had now arisen on the model of the Dark Speculator's establishment, and the money articles in all the papers teemed with hints as to the market value of particular Souls. "Ben Sidonia was done for the account at ninety thousand, and a seat in the Privy Council—Jawes was steady—There was a move in favour of Lord Mammysick—O'Slasher was at a discount—A high figure was offered and taken for Musty—Shuffleton was offered on any terms, and refused—A half share in the Earl of Puddleduck was rising as the market closed, but bidders were shy," &c.

Every day increased the rage for this sort of speculation. Even the ladies, who influence human affairs to an extent little appreciated by superficial thinkers, were seized with a passion for slave-holding. The prices they gave were often extraordinary, but, from their natural love of intrigue and mystery, were rather conjectured than known in the Soul-market; just as certain events in romances are, to use a standard Colburno-Bentleian phrase, "more easily imagined than described."

Many of them were less admired even for their personal charms than for their wonderful financial dexterity. Capital in their hands seemed to expand like air. Everything they touched rose to a fabulous extent in the market.

It began even to be whispered, by bankers and students of currency, that smiles and kisses seriously affected the circulation.

Be this as it may, the Royal and Stock Exchanges, Capel Court, and all the other resorts of the Soul-dealers, no longer sufficed for a raging mania of speculation, which acted upon all classes like the animalcule clouds of cholera, which of late settled with such deadly weight upon the metropolis.

A new Soul Exchange was planned, competed for, contracted for, and built, with inconceivable rapidity. Barry was laughed at by all England, when the magnificent structure rose, as by enchantment, in mockery of his yet unfinished Houses of Parliament.

A general report spread through the town, and a great deal further, thanks to the all-pervading press, that the new Soul Exchange would be opened by the Prince of Darkness in person.

The clergy, who had supported the new speculation from the facility which it offered for buying savage converts (which the Soul Agents supplied, wholesale or retail, from India to Otaheite, on the most moderate terms), though bitten by the mania as badly as any other class of the community, were rather shocked, to do them justice, at this marvellous announcement.

However, a Puseyite bishop, who was of a conciliating turn—when it suited his interest, clearly demonstrated that the great precept of forgiveness to our enemies could not be more nobly carried out than on the occasion offered. It was therefore resolved to treat the distinguished personage in question with all the honour and respect due to his rank and sublunary importance.

It turned out, eventually, that the Prince was not in town, and his place was supplied by a committee of noblemen, amongst whom I observed the countenances of the Dukes of N——e, S——d, &c., &c., whilst the procession consisted of one half the people in London, and the lookers-on of the remaining moiety.

In the evening there was a grand illumination, and a dinner in Hyde Park, at which some ten thousand people sat down, for in England nothing can be done, even in connection with the Soul, without the unavoidable ceremony of a public dinner.

END OF BOOK I.

BOOK II.

THE GRAND EXHIBITION

OF THE

SOULS OF ALL NATIONS.

BOOK II.

CHAPTER I.

PARTIES.

BEFORE proceeding to record the extraordinary events to which Free-Trade in Souls gave rise in this famous City of Jugglers, it is necessary to glance briefly at the general state of mundane politics in those days.

Political creeds are simply the outward and practical development of inward moral principles. I have before explained, and so has Balzac of France (a spirit of singular acuteness), that for the philosopher, that is, the observer and reflector, every part of nature is a type, or rather a sort of anagram, of all existence. This analogy arises from a metaphysical cause which I do not remember to have found mentioned in any book. Every fact, every idea, and every relation of facts and ideas, has, like every point of the earth's surface, an antipode or negative. Between the two extremes of un-likeness extend infinite gradations of likeness. Hence the universal and inevitable analogies which we discover at every step in the pilgrimage of science, since without absolute negative there must be resemblance in a precise ratio to the degree of negation contained by the object of analogism.

Let those who read the above paragraph, and consider the necessary connection of all things past, present, and to come, reflect a little upon its import before they consign to contempt even such sciences as astrology, chiromancy, phrenology. Nature writes her revelations in a thousand forms. Yet under all forms there is but one Truth, which fills eternal space and time with the vastness of its elaboration.

The political institutions and opinions of a nation are plain evidences of the standard of morality it has attained. In reality, therefore, the great parties in a state are the professors of various moral systems. Leaving certain critics and supposed wits who occupy much print and paper in these days to ask amazedly, "What the—— does the author mean by such sentences as the above?" and then proceed to shew that as *they* do not understand his meaning, *he* must necessarily be a blockhead, I shall at once give as plain an account as possible of the chief parties, varying of course in relative proportion, but little in character in different countries, which at that time existed upon the face of our remarkably imperfect planet.

All mankind, then, were, always have been, and still are, divided into three great classes :—

    I. The Idol-worshippers, or Aristocrats.

    II. The Gold-worshippers, or Plutocrats.

    III. The Fire-worshippers, or Democrats.

and a supplementary class of bipeds, who, being in fact no-bodies, can scarcely be regarded as men at all, who, never-theless, are, statistically reckoned, as numerous as all the other classes put together, which I shall therefore charac-terise as the Bosh-worshippers, or Somnocrats, in the allu-sions it may be necessary to make, in the course of my story, to their nonentity.

In accordance with the saying that the first shall be last and the last shall be first, I shall commence my description of these classes by the most useful, the most enlightened, and the most misrepresented of them all.

The Fire-worshippers, or Democrats, derive the main articles of their faith, political, moral, and religious, from the great Persian prophet Zoroastes, whose pure and lofty system may be conceived from the following brief quotation:—

" Teach the nations," said Ormuzd, the supreme prin-ciple of Good, "that my light is hidden under all that shines. Whenever you turn your face towards the light and follow my command, Ariman (the spirit of evil will be seen to fly. In this world there is nothing superior to light."

Such are the words of the twenty-second chapter of the *Zerdusht-nameh*, and such is the sublime belief of the worshippers of fire, that is, of light, truth, genius, and virtue. All existence is a perpetual progress, an endless conquest of Evil by Good, of darkness by light of falsehood by truth, of mental and bodily serfdom by human dignity and liberty.

The true Democrat fights under the banner of Oro-masdes, against the fiend Arimanes. His aim is to enlist all mankind, aye, and in a sense yet too grand for mortal comprehension, all Spirits of the Infinite, in the army of light—that is, of boundless liberty, and infinitely progressive happiness. The true Democrat* well knows the insanity of a selfish grasp at enjoyment based on the misery of his immortal brethren. He well knows the irresistible power of the God he serves, and the futile opposition of his opponents, who dream of pleasure in the shadow of sympathetic pain.

He sees that there is no standing still, no conservation, no whiggo-finality, in nature. All celestial science forces upon him the conviction, that in the infinite star-world there is a perpetual spiral motion within motion, revolution within revolution, never for two minutes allowing any heavenly body to occupy the same point in space, or ever return to the same point which at any previous period it had occupied.

In the spiritual, moral, and material world he finds the same eternal principle of progress. It is useless to talk to him of *waiting*. He cannot wait, any more than a comet can pause in its eliptic career. In his belief the best moment for Reform is the instant anything existing is known to be capable of improvement; the best right to power is the intelligence to exercise it; the best course to follow is to speak the dictates of his conscience in defiance of all temporary interests, and to die for the smallest truth, rather than to lie for the most luxurious living !

* I have prepared a work remarkable, at least, for one quality—brevity, in which I have endeavoured to state plainly the result of the most advanced eclecticism, in the form of an ontological, moral, and political system, which will be published at a price accessible to the humblest student, the instant the reception of the present volume shall have indicated the advisability of such a proceeding.

He is a Republican, because he himself would deem it a crime to accept a crown from any source but the free election of a nation. He is tolerant, because he abhors the falsehood of belief regarded as an act of volition, or of religious teaching as a trade and profession. He is humane, because he knows that all the wealth of the earth cannot buy one instant of happiness comparable to the supreme delights of individual and expanded affection.

And he is a Christian, because Christianity is the religion of democracy, of faith, hope, and charity; exalts the humble, makes a servant of the would-be master, ordains more than justice between man and man, and points even beyond the tomb to a progressive felicity, determined by present moral advancement—a heaven in which there are many mansions, and because its Divine Founder baptised, not with water, but with fire—not with form, but with spirit.

The Gold-worshippers, or Plutocrats, are creatures of a very different stamp. They are Materialists in their way of thinking, and what is called matter of fact in policy. They do not believe in any principle at bottom but expediency. They lose sight of the main chance in trying to look to it too greedily. For the main chance is happiness, and they waste so much time in grasping at the means, that they have no leisure left for the end. In fact, more than two-thirds of them downright mistake the chimera money, for the reality enjoyment. I have known Plutocrats, who were so occupied with gold-digging—there are mines of that metal everywhere—that they never, to their dying day, knew what it was to thoroughly enjoy a good dinner, and take their time over it. Not only their higher mental faculties, but even their animal senses, were miserably uncultivated. Fresh air, trees, grass, and the glorious blue sky, had no existence for them. They grubbed away their lives in dusky holes, which a Fire-worshipper, with the fiftieth part of their means, would never have lived a day in. They snatched a chop or steak daily, in a great coat and hat, on a narrow bench with a straight back, in an uncomfortable attitude, and having bolted their food, which they washed down hastily, with curious liquids, of devilish invention, bitter taste, and bilious results, they returned to their dusty holes— counting-houses in the city, or elsewhere—got satiated with figures, dreamed of chimeras in the shape of profits, which profited nobody, and returned home to their families, weary, dull, and glad to go to bed, too tired to dream, and very dismal beings altogether, *I* fancy.

No class of men abuse visionaries and theorists like Gold-worshippers. On the same principle, the greatest rascals always rail at dishonesty ten times as loudly as other people. The fact is, a downright Plutocrat is the most utter visionary extant. He has an *idea* that he is rich, and that is all. He himself is a slave and a slave-driver at the same moment. His task is to squeeze the largest profit out of the labour of poorer men than himself. But with all his squeezing he is a mere money-collecting machine. Perhaps his wife and daughters lead a pleasant life on the strength of it ; perhaps, eventually, some spendthrift son or nephew has the satisfaction of scattering the thousands in a way about as meritorious as that of its accumulation. It is a piece of disgusting imbecility to praise any man for the industry shewn in raking together a fortune. In nine cases out of ten it is a vile instinct, on a par with the propensities of certain animals who have a passion for burying all sorts of things in the ground. There are more misers than is imagined. As for making provisions for their families, it is mere egotism. If a man's son, nephew, cousin, or other relative, be well provided for, what merit is there in giving such an one a superfluous amount of wealth—that is, of concentrated power over the labour of his fellow-creatures? If the said kinsman be in want of the necessaries and comforts of life, why not share with him during life, and enjoy the spectacle of his happiness? Happy will be the hour for society which, denying to men all power of testamentary disposition, shall compel them to exercise during their lifetime the generosity and humanity for the want of which no post-mortem liberality can compensate. But of this hereafter—To revert to the characteristics of the Plutocrats.

There is a bad perseverance in their dispositions. Neither priest nor reasoner can turn them from their desolate purpose. They have no conception of a higher intellectual life. Whether prime-ministers or traders, old clothesmen or attornies, they are equally incredulous of all motives but self-interest—that is, self-interest in the strictest sense of personal gain. They know the strength of this motive, and they appeal to mankind by its agency alone, for they set down all people as fools or impostors, who profess to hold such principles in disregard.

They are all Jews in heart, if not by circumcision. The Mosaic law is their favourite book of reference.

An eye for an eye, and a tooth for a tooth, is their grand dogma. These are the men who support capital punishment. They have the worst opinion of mankind. They know how capable they themselves are of every crime dictated by cupidity, if not defended by the danger of penal retribution, and they attribute like feelings to all the human family.

They are so distrustful and cautious where any feeling is concerned, that they constantly throw away even the most palpable pecuniary advantage; and so stupidly reckless where mere lucre is at stake, that they daily figure in the *Gazette* as victims of over-selfishness and miscalculation. Their Christianity is mere Judaism in disguise. They are false, dishonest, hypocritical, and mean. They cringe to your face, and rob you when your back is turned. They are so cowardly in the dread of selfish loss that they can be frightened into anything —even into generosity. And they cordially hate the poor. They believe that poverty is sufficient motive for any degree of vice or crime. But they have no pity for the victim, though they hear every Sunday a divine prayer for relief from temptation. They have made poverty itself a crime, and they would have crucified the Saviour over again, had he lived in their times, not for publicly urging rich men to share all their possessions with the poor, but because he was a man without property himself, and "had not even where to lay his head." They would have imprisoned him for libelling such respectable men as the Scribes and Pharisees, and they would have locked up the Apostles as incorrigible mendicants. Only the other day they gave the modern Barabbas of railways a testimonial, and they allowed

Waghorn, the enthusiastic originator of the Overland Route to India, to die of a broken heart, in poverty and ' disappointment. They support the *Timeserver* newspaper, and even the *Timeserver* is unequal to their representation.

The Idol-worshippers, or Aristocrats, are, strange as it may sound to unphilosophic ears, the least important, though the most showy, of the great factions of the age. They are the disciples of an exploded system, which they cling to with love, yet have not the ability to maintain by arms. Slowly and surely they are committing suicide as a class, alternately yielding one point after another to the opposing principles of the democratic and plutocratic parties.

Had they the greatness or courage to throw themselves into the arms of the Fire-worshippers, to destroy, as it were, their exclusive life by a glorious act of self-sacrifice, they would rise from their ashes to-morrow, like the wondrous bird of fable, and by their new character of enlightened benefactors of mankind and leaders of progress, become even greater in their regeneration than in their old wornout character.*

* It was my intention to have proposed a plan of this nature to the late Lord George Bentinck, which would have brought him into power almost immediately. My republican freedom, however, was too far in advance of the " stable mind" to be appreciated. Since then I have seen the folly of any attempt at coalition between men of thought and their most troublesome scholars. They know no medium between tyranny and flunkeydom, though to the full as apt for the latter as the former vocation. Well, my noble boobies, if you will not be our friends, you shall be our instruments. We will drive you before us with the sword of reason and the whip of satire. We are the stronger. Even whilst I write, the hour is striking, and the balance turns in our favour. The press is no longer the fourth estate, but the first! Hear this, and sneer, if you will, my lords and gentlemen. I do not sneer—I strike!

But they have neither the devotion nor the intelligence, as a class, required for such heroism. On the contrary, deluded by the hollow cat-like caresses of their deadly foes, the Plutocrats, they have by a thousand concessions endeavoured to conciliate that implacable and heartless race. Fools! when by making one tithe of those concessions to the honest, working, suffering people, they might have defied for ages the brood of deadly vermin who, slowly and surely, are devouring every vestige of their ancient glories, whilst the wise sons of light look on with stern indifference, prepared to crush the Plutocrat, so soon as the destruction of the helpless Aristocrat shall have been satisfactorily accomplished by his agency.

These Aristocrats, or Idol-worshippers, found their practical creed upon the Greeko-Egyptian Mythology. Their education is Greek, or primarily Egyptian, at the fountain-head. They fill their minds with traditions, legends, and fabulous pedigrees. Like the Greeks and Romans, they believe themselves the descendants of the Gods. They fancy that something of the ancestral hero or demi-god still mingles in their blood. Though they admit that the first man was made in the image of his Creator, they have a secret suspicion that the family likeness is better preserved in their own case than in others. They flatter themselves that they are china and the populace wedgewood; that they have some mysterious superiority, quite apart from education and other natural influences. They despise everybody but themselves, and they despise one another also.

Any man may profess Democracy or Plutocracy, and be recognized as a real Fire or Gold-worshipper by the

followers of Moses and Zoroaster. But to be received
by the Idolaters it is necessary to be something more
than an Idol-worshipper. You must prove your descent
from the Idols themselves (*Eidola,* or chimeras), not
that there is much reality in these pedigrees—on the
contrary, they are notoriously easy of fabrication.
Men live by contriving them. It is the Aristocratic
chimera which is found to answer, whether sham or real,
with equal virtue—

> " For well we know that serving men and grooms
> Oft give the lie to half an hundred tombs."

I have now briefly described the three leading forms
of opinion in the civilised world. They will be rarely
found in their pure and unadulterated strength. Few
Fire-worshippers are free from a dash of idolatry—or,
at least, of Hero-worship—a noble weakness, but still a
weakness in the eyes of a philosophic Gueber, whose
Gods are the eternal abstractions, the never-to-be-at-
tained, but for ever approached, ideals of beauty, happiness, and wisdom.

Let who will stay to worship Cromwell. The true
Fire-worshipper has left Cromwell behind him, nay,
perchance, he may be Cromwell himself—a new incarnation, revived and strengthened for a grander and more
terrible contest.

In like manner the Aristocrat and Plutocrat, with
feeble dashes of Democracy, are mingled in infinite
variety of proportion, till, in the end, results the Bosh-
worshipper, or Somnocrat, who does not know his own
opinion on any subject but his immediate wants, who is
swayed by every latest speaker, ignorant of every principle of policy, and, whatever his station may be, from

the peer down to the ploughboy, in terrible want of a rational and initiative education. He is a mental sleep-walker. He is one of the mob. He is the human ether in which the real Aristoi of intellect float like the vessels on the seas. He does not read this book, and if he did he would not understand it.

Thus the reader, being far from a Bosh-worshipper, will understand what I mean, in the course of the hundred volumes I may have occasion to publish before Fire-worship becomes the established system, by the terms—Idol-worshipper, Greek or Aristocrat; Gold-worshipper, Jew or Plutocrat; and Fire-worshipper, Gueber or Democrat.

As, however, life is uncertain, and I may possibly die before completing this work, much less the other ninety-nine threatened volumes, I entreat the young thinkers of the age to treasure up in their memory the above association of ideas (mnemonically arranged for the purpose), in order that they may escape the infernal confusion of all real moral distinctions which the brilliant but contradictory journalism of the day is so apt to induce.   *   *   *   *   *   *   *

The sun is setting. I hear the murmur of the human ocean, the mighty hum of the vast and potent city—I feel as an orator addressing a mighty army. Young England! it is your cause I am pleading! Your would-be leader has been thrown down long since, with his antiquated follies—but it is no leadership that I would wish to usurp! A curse on the hateful ambition which tempts the sacrifice of principle for power. Better to be loved by one spirit in Nature than to be bowed down to by all the hosts of heaven. Youth of England!

give me a little corner in your hearts; believe in my sincerity, even should you deride my pretensions.

There is but one real pay for the soldier of thought— the affection of his fellow-citizens.

L

CHAPTER II.

AN ANGEL VISIT.

IN this world one thing is as important as another. Twice two make four. Every atom of the universe vibrates in accordance with every other atom. Above all, the lightest breath of passion reacts with intense potence upon all passionate entities. Hence the loves or love-dreams of such a man as Bernard Viridor are by no means unimportant to an episode in modern history like the present. Just as every body in space must be *somewhere*, must occupy some portion of the infinite extension (*vide* Baruch Spinoza), so a strong and reckless Fire-worshipper must be doing some very considerable amount of good or evil, by commission or omission, during every active moment of his being.

Therefore, my dear brother Fire-worshippers, let me entreat you to beware of falling in love just at present. For my part, I wish I could ensure my heart against fire (of that description) until the Republic (metaphorically speaking) were fairly established in the five great empires of Europe, and sundry smaller nationalities.

For the last few weeks Viridor had been much troubled in his mind. Almost daily for several hours in consultation with Darian and Basiline, he had gradually allowed his interest in the beautiful Magyar to deepen into an intensely painful sentiment. It is superfluous to say, that never for one instant did the idea cross

Viridor's imagination that she could be more to him than the wife of his dearest friend. In these grand natures justice and honour are instincts too powerful for question or sophistication. Basiline was Darian's. Viridor knew it. Darian was his friend. The poet-philosopher would have despised himself had he allowed one covetous thought or impure desire to rise in his breast with regard to Basiline. Yet he felt as one

> " From Paradise an outcast,
> Who weeping sits at the forbidden gates."*

Why had not Basiline a sister, the counterpart of herself, to make his happiness as she made Darian's ?

Viridor strove to resist the fever of vague desire that consumed him. He was not one of those who can quench the flame of the spirit in the degrading satisfactions of the flesh. To use the phrase of our ducal Republican, Viridor was a volcano in eruption. For years past, from the dawn of manhood, and the first storm of youthful passion, the sails of whose vessel were swelled by fancy and boyish sensuality, he had exercised

---

* Lamartine's " Poetic Meditations." I could wish for the sake of the marvellously beautiful ideas and images contained in these early poems of Lamartine, that they should become popular in England. My translation was a true labour of love, for I gained neither money nor fame by the work. The Press almost universally ignored the book on account of the cheap form in which it was published. A single thousand copies only have been sold, although Lamartine said, in a letter of exquisite delicacy, written to me on the occasion, " Henceforward my work is as much yours as my own." It would seem that my poems were destined to as just a fate as his policy in *its* translation, according to the *Timeserver*. I would fain see this neglect remedied, not from personal interest, but because I should like to share with others the enjoyment of such writing as France's greatest bard's, with whom but one living poet, Alfred Tennyson, can be even compared by a student superior to all bias of national or stylistic prejudice. The translation has, at least, one chance of publicity. Though the reviewers scorned it, the publisher stereotyped it.

a stern control over his feelings. I do not mean that he had been a Puritan. Such folly were incompatible with the nature of one imbued with the profoundest knowledge of man's mental and physical requirements. But he had remained cold, calculating, and indifferent with regard to the fairer sex. He had cherished his ideal—he had no longer dreamed of seeking it. Once or twice he had caught vague glimpses of seraphic forms, eyes lighted with the true fire, but they came like shadows, and departed. They eluded his grasp, or dissolved into commonplace phantoms, in his eager embraces. They borrowed their enchantment from distance. He lost the impression before it had placed its stamp upon his heart. He was still Viridor the lonely, the sombre inhabitant of the unmeasured Vast, the dweller amid Titan thoughts—dim, nameless, abstract rulers of the Infinite world of spirits.

He had concentrated the rays of his spirit on two points in existence,—Humanity, that is, the liberty and happiness of mankind; and Friendship, that is, the immediate interchange of sympathetic ideas with men of noble feelings and lofty intelligence like his own.

But the noblest and most expanded philanthropy, however it may elevate the mind, partakes often of the sad dignity of Prometheus on his rock—the vulture grief yet lacerates the breast, and Jove (the worldly tyranny of inferior spirits) yet taunts his victim from the established throne of power.

And friendship, how rare is its perfection? In boyhood it shines most brightly—it is indeed a passion, as D'Israeli boldly describes it.

I recollect in a critique on " Coningsby," the reviewer

denouncing that passage, one of the best and truest in the work, as an example of preposterous exaggeration.

There is little chance of sympathy in opinion between the author of "Coningsby" and his satirist. Yet I am glad to take this opportunity of reparation for an attack, however well deserved, far too extravagant and personal to admit of literary justification. In my opinion the Protectionist leader is a man of brilliant imagination, keen perception, profound analysis, and at bottom noble and generous sentiments. Selfish ambition has blasted him like a lightning-stricken oak. His intellectual life, his splendid invention, are paralysed by the falsity of his position. At heart he is a Fire-worshipper. His aristocratic fury is a mania, a melancholy disease. An aristocrat of nature's making, what hideous madness drives him to sell his soul for the homage of an aristocracy of acres, whose nobility, indeed, perpetually springs from the dunghill which they throw in the teeth of the parvenu?

But it is not even yet too late. He stands high enough for heroism. Let him shake off his own chains, let him liberate the *noble* slaves on whose subjection he weakly prides himself, let him renounce the insane project of mounting to heaven on a Babel tower of material grossness, let him be himself once more in defiance of party and in contempt of office, let him stand forward as the impartial champion of the truth of the people and his own nobler nature, and I will not hesitate to entreat his pardon for all the ridicule I have heaped upon him. For, by the light of heaven! this man's genius is deserving of a grander cause than the mere advocacy of high rents *versus* Manchester cotton-spinners!

To return to Viridor and friendship. It is only in boyhood that friendship can satisfy the heart. It has no guarantee of duration. How many devoted friends does a man, in the course of his life, lose sight of for ever! How many disappear gradually by unaccountable coldness! How many are lost by a chance word, an accidental slight, a difference of opinion, or a coincidence of admiration! We soon grow accustomed to these losses. We respect and esteem our acquaintance whose characters command our appreciation, but we no longer build our happiness on individual attachment. We know the evanescence of friendship, we enjoy it calmly, free from the lover-like jealousy, doubts, quarrels, and reconciliations of boyhood. Youthful friendships are too often indiscriminating impulses, the friendships of manhood are founded upon judgment and reason. All this the young poet felt, and was lonely even with his friends.

Viridor could not banish from his thoughts the vision of the Hungarian's beauty. In the middle of his political and philosophical analyses he paused, laid down the pen, and mused on Basiline. The tones of her voice, her exquisite gentleness, combined with such heroic daring, her graceful attitudes and motions, all combined to perplex and unsettle his mind. He could not be said to love Basiline, for the utter absence of hope prevented him from contemplating such a possibility. He thought of her as of a beautiful type, of something he longed for, yet despaired of finding.

But desire, like faith, is a potent magician, and often does much to bring about its own fulfilment.

It was evening, and Viridor sat alone in his chambers.

His sitting-room was a large dreary-looking apartment. The walls were of panel, in colour of a dingy brown, which once had approximated to white, but was now dirtying fast in the direction of mahogany. The high mantlepiece was of carved oak. There was but little furniture in the room. The most important item was a large square table in the centre, at which Viridor, seated in an old arm-chair, was then writing, or rather trying to write; for he drew caricatures on the margin of his M.S. in an absent manner, and especially made several attempts to delineate a profile of exquisite purity and delicacy, which resembled in part the ideas originally formed of the virgin mother, in part the ideal type of Faust's Margaret, with a certain indescribable *espieglerie* which belonged neither to the saint nor to the sinner in question.

He was interrupted in the creation of these re- markably slight works of art, by a gentle knocking at the door. For full an hour he had been listening with the keenest attention for the footsteps of his expected guest upon the stairs; nevertheless, he was taken by surprise after all, in a moment of abstraction. He rose hastily, almost sprang to the door, opened it, and admitted a female figure of slight, graceful outline. The lamp upon the table had a non-transparent shade, consequently the only parts of the room it lighted to any extent were a large circle on the table and a small circle on the ceiling. The latter, by the way, was very deceptive in the notion it conveyed of the colour of the plaster, which the smoke of more than one tenant had darkened without the interposition of renovating whitewash.

"How glad I am to see you!" exclaimed Viridor, taking the hand of his visitor, and raising it to his lips; "I hardly ventured to hope you would really come."

"I promised, so I kept my word," said a voice of silvery softness.

"Pray be seated," said Viridor, and he looked round for a chair. There were several in the room. But on one was a pile of papers, on another books, on a third a drawing-box, and he was ultimately obliged to offer the seat which he had just risen from, and to seat himself provisionally on the chair covered by the smallest pile of papers. Indeed, not only did books and papers encumber the chairs, tables, and mantleshelf, besides various more orthodox receptacles, but they were even scattered over the floor, and in one corner of the room, underneath an easel, formed a chaotic pyramid of books, MSS., drawing-boards, and old gloves, which filled the members of the party of order who came there with downright despair.

From week to week Viridor had contemplated a clearing up and arrangement of this literary chaos. But his incessant occupation, and repugnance to all mechanical exertion, had caused him to postpone the mighty effort, until the confusion had reached a pitch which would have daunted the boldest of reformers. As for allowing any profane hand to touch his sacred medley of Sybiline leaves, it need scarcely be mentioned that the bare idea filled him with horror.

"Never touch a scrap of paper in my rooms," was Viridor's injunction to his laundress, delivered in so solemn a tone that the old woman would have committed sacrilege off-hand in the nearest cathedral rather than have transgressed this injunction of the poet's.

It may be imagined that the papers became a rather dusty chaos in time. Viridor's chambers were a good place to read Goethe's Faust in.

The lord of this sombre domicile removed the shade from the lamp, and thus revealed all the disorder of the scene, which his fair visitor regarded with no small amazement.

For his part, Viridor drank in the beauty of a face which it will require all the art of description I possess, not to mention what I may steal or borrow, to pourtray but feebly to the eye of the indulgent reader.

Reversing the usual formula of novelists, I may say that it was a face more easily described than imagined. That is, every word of my description may be correct, and yet may fail to convey to another the impression which I desire to reproduce.

The age of the stranger might be about seventeen years. The innocence of the child seemed to mingle with the conscious dignity of the woman in her fair oval countenance. Her broad longlashed eyelids drooped with a charming modesty. Her half-opened mouth, faultless in its classical formation, revealed teeth white as the cliffs of England seen from a distant vessel, regular as the pearls of a lady's necklace. She was pale by the natural complexion of her fair clear skin; and her silky hair, which was banded on either side of her forehead, was of a rich yet far from deep brown, a sort of intermediate tint between blond and auburn, which, like her finely marked brows, looked dark in contrast with the forehead it encircled.

When she spoke she fixed her soft calm eyes upon Viridor's features with an inexpressible gentleness.

The rudest libertine would have hesitated to insult such incarnate purity. The most abject worshippers of gold or rank could not have ventured on an impertinence, though she wore but a little black shawl of the humblest manufacture, and a plain cotton dress faded in colour by repeated washing. A close straw bonnet, lined with blue silk, completed her external attire, and formed an artistic setting for the gem of beauty it contained.

It is wonderful how much beauty gains by a wise selection in the hues of its adornments. I should like to see some ladies I meet occasionally, introduced into a picture with their rainbow glories. And I should like to see some artists I know take lessons in prismatic harmony from certain other scientific enchantresses of my acquaintance! It would be a mutual profit, I assure them.

" Well," said Viridor, " I hope you have not been chased by any more mad cows, since I had the pleasure of seeing you?"

" O no sir," replied the stranger, in a voice which made even the most trivial words pleasant to the ear, " I have not dared to walk in the park since. I'm so frightened."

" They should remove the cows," said Viridor, "it is too bad to risk their frightening or tossing every little girl who likes to take a stroll in the sunshine."

" Poor things!" said the stranger, simply, "they do enjoy the grass so! I should not like to turn them out. O no! I can walk somewhere else, in the streets, or anywhere. Though I don't like walking in the streets, people are so rude."

" Have you often been insulted, then, in the street?"

said Viridor, with a slight flush, and a tone of lively interest.

"Not exactly insulted. But gentlemen speak to me, very politely sometimes, but still it is hard that because one is all alone, one should be treated like—like —"

"Ah!" said Viridor, coming to the rescue of his fair visitor, who seemed embarrassed for a phrase, "and what do you say to these impertinent people?"

"Oh, I never say anything, I look at them very severely—so—" and the stranger frowned in a way that made Viridor smile.

"You laugh at me?" she said, returning his smile with unconscious fascination.

"Yes, I don't think such a severe frown as that would have much effect upon these rude men we were speaking of."

"But you only see the comedy, you know I can't look as I do when I am really offended. Nobody can act feeling, can they?"

"Well, I think not, myself. At least I do not think any one could deceive me by the expression of his features. Yet they say that hypocrites succeed to a great extent in the world."

"Very likely. But they must be very stupid. It must be so much trouble. I don't care what people think. I do what I like, and I always like to have my own way."

"Always? but that is rather selfish, is it not?"

"Perhaps it is, but I *do* like it; so it is no use pretending I don't. Oh! what a pretty picture, what a dear face—the lady's!"

And the stranger rose and went to the easel on which

an unfinished sketch was standing, for Viridor was in
the habit of relaxing his mind from severer studies by
the cultivation of the arts.

"I am glad you like it," said the poet, "for I
painted it, but it is not yet finished; indeed it is scarcely
begun, it is a mere daub, pray do not criticise it too
closely."

All this was no affectation of the painter's, but strictly
true. Nevertheless his visitor continued to regard the
sketch with evident delight. And here I will venture
on a word to my artist friends. Next to the poet and
philosopher, I rank the artist. I love beauty as another
form of truth, I find art to be subject to the same grand
philosophy as ethics or politics, and as much in want
of radical reform as either.

As in policy the imperfect carrying out of high and
noble principles is infinitely preferable to the best
working system of base and inequitable expediency,
so in art the attempt to pourtray the beautiful and
the sublime, however feeble, is still incomparably greater
than the most successful triumph of mere mechanical
imitation.

There is an absurd mania pervading the artist youth
of the day, in favour of very accurate copyism of individual nature. In one sense they may be called a
model-school, for we recognise our friends the models
with painful facility. Like babies crying for the moon,
they seem to have grown jealous of the sun, and to
have conceived the idea of competing with the daguerro-
type on its own ground. This is a chimerical project,
both from physical and spiritual causes. Their details
may be correct, but their general effects are discordant

and unnatural. Instead of making nature the basis, and breathing into it the breath of life by art, they destroy the freedom of their original designs by reducing them to conformity with nature, that is, model nature— stiff, constrained, artificial, and lifeless. Hence the wooden character of many elaborate paintings, which painfully remind one of the late Madame Tussaud's wax-works. No insult is intended to the wax-works, by the way, which sometimes nod and wink their eyes so cunningly as to deceive the unpractised spectator. But the wooden style of painters deceives nobody—but themselves. They fancy they are artists, whilst the philosopher knows them to be mechanics.

There is more genius, more real art, in many a wood-cut of Leech or Gavarni, or etching of Hablot Brown, not to allude to the outlines of Rotsch or the grotesques of Doyle and Grenville, than in dozens of paintings of vast pretentions, which it would be invidious to particularise. In one thing the most cultivated and least cultivated tastes agree. And that is in preferring the roughest sketch, with meaning in it clearly conveyed, to the most finished piece of light-shade and colour-work without it.

For my part, I like to watch the effect of paintings or drawings upon the feelings of persons of delicate minds, but ignorant of art and artists. *They* are not caught by mere copyism. *They* know which represents nature best, the mind or the model. *They* feel the difference between a work of intellect and one of mere machinery.

The stranger admired Viridor's daub—there was *nature* in it, *real* nature, spiritual nature. She subsequently

M

regarded with indifference Parodummy's picture, which sold for a thousand pounds, and represented a curious collection of exquisitely constructed lay figures in great variety of attitudes or contortion.

This is how Viridor became acquainted with the fair stranger.

He was walking across the Regent's Park, near the railings of the Zoological Gardens, which there offer a gratuitous, but very remote view of the lions, when he saw a young girl running, in the greatest alarm, before a cow, which, with tail erect, was sadly belying the gentleness of her sex. Viridor drove off the cow with his stick, and returning to the fair fugitive, found her in a state of alarm, palpitation, and breathlessness, which did not admit of his acting otherwise than he did, in offering his arm and endeavouring to reassure her by every means in his power.

When they gained the long walk, and the frightened girl began to recover from her terror, and to feel herself in perfect safety, she was profuse in her gratitude for Viridor's interference, exaggerating very naturally the danger he had run in her defence.

Viridor, struck by her beauty, and sensibly affected by the repeated pressure of her small hands, which, though gloveless, were white and delicate as a princess's, could not bear the thought of parting from her without cultivating a further intimacy. As she stood by his side in the golden sunset, which they regarded in silent sympathy of admiration, he felt a long chained hope and desire become wakeful in his breast.

Who should say that chance, or rather the happy combination of harmonious spirits, whose will, conscious or unconscious, is the synthesis of Destiny, had not thrown in his way thus unexpectedly the long-sought jewel of his desire? What, if in the love of this fair child of poverty and obscurity, he should discover the noble heart and sweet consolation he had begun to muse on as a dream?

His whole being was moved even to its foundation. The ice melted, the stern spirit of endurance gave way, and passion entered where stoicism had crouched in desolation. The fire of manhood was lighted up, and his heart demanded its satisfaction with a voice which no cold reasoning could silence.

Viridor had no scruples, he had no prejudices. He cared no more for disgracing his proud relatives by a *mésalliance* than for enraging them by his ultra-republican opinions. He worshipped the sacred fire of conscience, the light of truth in thought, in feeling, and in action. He was not one to sacrifice real happiness to chimerical ambitions. The ordinary ideas which such occasions suggest scarcely presented themselves to his mind. He had but two apprehensions—

Had this lovely daughter of the people yet learned that she possessed a heart? If not, was he the man to teach her that knowledge?

Viridor was not vain. He was proud, even to occasional arrogance, towards the petty intellects he had to cope with in his war against folly and baseness; but he was free from personal vanity. He had either been unsuccessful with the sex, or unconscious of his successes. He had associated altogether too much with men, and too little with their gentler comrades. He was somewhat

stern and unbending, little skilled in small talk, utterly
hostile to coquetry, flirtation, and dandyism. He fancied
himself destitute of personal attractions. He had no
confidence in his powers of pleasing women. He attributed any slight triumph he had gained, rather to
pity or politeness, than to any honest appreciation of
his efforts. In a word, he had a dismal presentiment
that he was about the last man in the world a beautiful
girl of seventeen could fall in love with.

He was wrong. His fair companion had fallen in
love with him already, and with a love far more powerful and lasting than his own dawning passion. She did
not know it, she did not reason upon it. But for the
first time in her life she clung to the arm of a man in
confidence and joy. She looked up into Viridor's face,
and his dark eyes seemed to shed rays of soothing happiness upon her soul.

Before they separated, Viridor had, unknown to his
companion, read the inmost secrets of her thoughts. He
found in her feelings of exquisite refinement, and a
pure, loving, and just instinct of thought, combined with
an affectionate, impressive, and rather obstinate character. What chiefly pleased him was the constant
reference she made to her " dear father," for whom she
seemed to entertain a species of admiration. Above all,
Viridor gained the conviction that love was to her a
mystery yet to be revealed.

When he asked her to visit him, she assented without
hesitation. If not ignorant of the so-called impropriety
of such a proceeding, she was indifferent to worldly
opinions. She came punctual to her engagement.

Viridor made tea. He had bought a cake and some other delicacies, which she partook of, with artless satisfaction. She laughed heartily at the student's clumsy contrivances, and the deficiencies of his *ménage*. She begged him to smoke, if he wished it, as her father always had his pipe of an evening. He was now out of town, and she was staying with her sister, who was married to a newsman. They had a small shop over the water. They would not mind her being out for a few hours, and if they did, she did not care, for she had a will of her own—not that she would annoy her sister for the world. Her sister was the dearest girl, and not at all like her. Quite the reverse—her sister was dark, and very pretty, with large black eyes, and her husband James—that was Mr. Mullens—was so fond of her. They would think she had gone to see Laura. Laura was her friend—the only friend she had in London—such a nice girl—only one year older than herself—But really she must be going, it was getting late, it had struck nine long ago. And she rose to take her departure.

Viridor rose also. He took again her little hand in his own.

" Grace," he said (he had found out that her name was Grace Morton at their first interview), " dear Grace, I am many years older than you are, but—"

" But what ? " said Grace, smiling, and helping her host, in his turn, out of an embarrassment; " but you never saw anybody half so pretty as I am? Now do say so, you may as well pay me a good compliment whilst you are about it !—not that I believe anything men say, they are such deceivers, as the young lady said in the play the other night."

Viridor stopped the mouth of his pretty banterer with a kiss, as anybody would, I am sure, have done under similar circumstances. As she retreated from his embrace, her form, supple as a reed, rested for an instant almost supported by his arm.

" When shall I see you again?" said Viridor, eagerly.

" Never," said Grace, severely, " if you presume so quickly on my pleasantry."

" Grace, dear Grace ! " said Viridor, " forgive me for my freedom ! " and for the first time in his life the proud Viridor bent his knee to a mortal. The noble object of his early passion could not boast of such homage as he yielded to the dignity of the lowly and neglected child.

When he rose, the head of Grace rested upon his shoulder without any effort on his part. They stood thus for a few moments in the enjoyment of feelings it is unnecessary to descant upon, when a sudden sharp knocking at the door aroused them from their dawning love-dream.

Viridor recollected an engagement which he had hitherto forgotten.

" Farewell, dearest," he said hastily, with another kiss, which this time escaped objection—"To-morrow?"

" Yes, to-morrow," whispered Grace, drawing her little shawl about her.

" The same hour ? "

" Yes," whispered Grace, in a tone almost inaudible from emotion.

Viridor opened the door. The Soul-Agent entered. His great dark eyes at once took in the shrinking form of the young girl, who hastened to slip away, whilst Viridor thought of Faust, Margaret, and Mephistopheles, and wished Ignatius at the devil his prototype's.

CHAPTER III.

VIRIDOR AND THE SOUL AGENT.

MOTIONING the dark speculator to a chair, Viridor followed Grace Morton from the room, and once more took leave of her upon the staircase. He returned with the pressure of her small hand yet tingling upon his own, but with an aspect and manner completely changed in expression.

A minute ago he had been all tenderness, childlike playfulness, and pure emotion. In a word, he had been the Viridor of Grace.

He reappeared the severe and critical thinker, the man of intuitive penetration and indomitable firmness of resolve. The Soul Agent beheld again the mysterious being he had encountered on his former visits, with the same pale tranquil countenance, and mild inscrutable eyes, before whose gaze his own was ever lowered. There was no trace of confusion of consciousness on Viridor's features. A the waves close over a pebble which disturbs their glittering surface, so did the thoughts of the poet close over the departed maiden.

Few men possessed greater self-command when necessary than Bernard Viridor. He had studied in the school of suffering. For seven years past, from the date of his nineteenth birthday, and return to England from a foreign university, his life had been passed in battles—battles more terrible than Darian's, with foes more implacable than the Croats of Jellachich, or the Cossacks of the Czar.

His father, a man of independent fortune, had destined him for the bar, but a subtle pettifogger of the worst class of attornies—worst, because covering their rascalities with every external appearance of respectability—adroitly lured on the older Viridor into throwing away five hundred guineas, and his son into the bargain, upon certain articles of indenture, by which Bernard became for five years the articled clerk of the said adroit pettifogger.

The young student, fresh from German club-rooms, salons, and lectures on psychology, history, demonology, and other dusky sciences, signed the deed with a dismal presentiment of impending evils, and the obscurest notions concerning the nature of the profession he was entering into.

He soon became enlightened.

Having nothing to do in the office, which he was supposed to attend daily between the hours of ten and six, and the working clerks being frequently interrupted in their conversation, gymnastics, operatic *sotto voce* reminiscences, and other unbusiness-like and illegal amusements, by their necessary labours, he was unable to get through a very considerable amount of that valuable work, Sir William Blackstone's "Commentaries on the Laws of England."

One of the first things he lighted on in that Arabia Petræa of the law-student was an utter denunciation of the practice of preparing for the bar by the routine of an attorney's office.

Viridor bitterly regretted the false step taken in the

dark by his father and himself. Meanwhile, he was occupied in solving an insoluble problem. This was no other than the union of the noble and joyous career he had marked out for himself, and the dry and detested vocation which had been chosen for him.

Had been chosen for him? No, that is incorrect. He had had the choice between Law and Church—between Mr. Lumber's office and an English university. An English university! after three years spent in all the freedom of German student life ! It was like going back to school. Viridor was full of ambition. The germs of grand designs already slept on his soul. He would enter the world at all hazards, he would do something for himself. He would become independent.

Already he had learned that dependence, even upon a father, is servitude. True generosity is the rarest of all virtues. What is ordinarily called by the name is a mere sham. Nine fathers out of ten expect, for every hnndred pounds of allowance given, their hundred pounds' worth of free-will sacrificed as return. Viridor soon felt this ; and it preyed upon his mind, like a cancer on the breast. He over-rated the value of the obligation, instead of looking upon it as a mere act of duty, like most young men of his age. Instead of taking casual reproaches as to neglect of business or extravagance at their real value, as expressions of anxiety for his welfare on the one hand, or petulance of temper on the other, he allowed them to lacerate and excite his feelings, naturally susceptible, to a painful degree of intensity. Hence, perpetual jars and disagreements, attacks and recriminations. Hence the devotion of Blackstone and Coke upon Littleton to the infernal

gods, and the irremediable loss of Mr. Viridor senior's
five hundred guineas in the abyss of Lumber the pettifogger's pocket!

The elder Viridor was a gentleman of the old school,
though little more than twice the age of his son. A
man may have amazingly old ideas at forty even,
especially if he inherits them with his plate from his
grandfather or great-grandfather before him.   Old
Viridor, then, was a Tory, and, I believe, admired George
the Third, and held Pitt in reverence.   He took in the
John Bull and " Blackwood's Magazine," reading the
Morning Herald with rigid punctuality.   In his library
was much calf and morocco, and a complete edition
of the classics, both Greek and Latin authors.   But
had you looked for a poem or romance later than the
time of Sir Walter Scott, you would probably have
been disappointed in your search.   In conclusion,
Mr. Viridor was a tall, handsome, imposing-looking man,
courteous and affable in his manners, universally liked
by his acquaintance (except those he had cut or been
cut by owing to a certain fiery temper of his), and
particularly pleasing to ladies, for whom he had a most
chivalrous and honourable respect.   Add to this, that he
had a taste for reading, and considerable knowledge
of art, evinced in a fine collection of pictures and
engravings, that he possessed all gentlemanly accom-
plishments, and something under a thousand a year
from landed property, and the picture may be considered
tolerably accurately sketched.

He had been left a widower during the childhood of
his son, and had married a young lady of great personal

but no pecuniary attractions, which I consider a point in his favour.

In truth, Mr. Viridor was far from mercenary. His vice was not so much gold as idol-worship. He worshipped power, position, worldly and recognised respectability. And he had a spice of the tyrant in his composition. He liked to guide, to govern, and to plan. He liked blind obedience to his commands. He liked the very branches of his trees to grow the way he ordained. He was the architect of his own house, which was built as never house was built before or since. He had his coats made according to his special system. He was born to command, but could scarcely obey even the clearest dictates of reason opposed to his own stern volition.

He tried to mould his son after his own thought, instead of allowing free development to the youthful faculties. He was not content with a legitimate influence, he would have governed Bernard absolutely, and for this purpose resorted to means of undue severity.

But it was too late. Years of foreign travel and study had emancipated young Viridor's mind. He already lived for himself as an individual incarnation of an individual spirit, with aims, ideas, and ambitions peculiarly its own. He was totally unfit for passive obedience to a father, or the constraint of a lawyer's office. He rebelled against both, at first secretly, then openly. Viridor the elder never for an instant imagined that he was at all in fault. He allowed his son a hundred and fifty pounds a year; there was an excellent career open before him, with ample and certain expectations in the distance—what more did he want?

A little happiness, a little peace and quiet affection, a relief from eternal lectures, or, still worse, silent but severe looks of reproach for trivial and involuntary faults, and last, not least, a little less acrimony on the subject of occasional small pecuniary advances, rendered necessary by Bernard's utter ignorance of the value of money.

Viridor, indeed, was rarely extravagant, but he had a horror of appearing mean. This is the real secret of many a comparatively innocent spendthrift's wastefulness. Hence he was always in debt, and always anxious and careworn about things, the importance of which he over-reckoned, but which he had neither the self-denial nor resolution to avoid.

In addition to the above requirements Viridor desired more than all to escape from the profession of the law in every shape, for which he had gradually conceived an implacable detestation. Not one particle of his soul ever entered into his legal studies. Like Darian, he saw nothing in English law, common and civil, but a monstrous mass of evil forms mingled with good principles, crying loudly for reform. He would be a legislator—but never a lawyer.

A crisis arrived—a few hot words from the father were taken literally by the son, whose passion for absolute free agency could no longer be restrained. The office of Lumber was deserted for ever, the allowance withdrawn, and Bernard Viridor thrown upon his own resources.

Had Viridor the younger possessed any worldly prudence, he might easily have conciliated and managed his father. Had Viridor the elder relied upon paterna

N

affection, and not paternal authority, he would have certainly succeeded to some extent in swaying his son. But the latter did not consider his interest, and the former was too obstinate and proud to take any trouble to study the mysterious though candid disposition of the embryo poet.

Thus, with mutual misunderstandings, they parted. They did not meet again for years.

The ruling passion of Viridor was for literature. With considerable versatility he had already produced a variety of tales, poems, and translations. They had been printed, and what was more, paid for by the proprietors of sundry not very distinguished periodicals, now mostly gone to that "ulterior bourne" which Mr. Carlyle occasionally hints at, as the probable destination of all earthly entities.

At the moment of his quarrel with his father, he had fortunately made a most brilliant hit by a political satire he had ventured on in a style and tone quite novel and extravagant. It was reviewed in almost every paper in the kingdom, praised and abused with equal exaggeration, immensely read, and sold like wildfire.

(By the way, I wish I knew a wildfire shop, that I might make an investment in that article. Will any dealer in that *comparatively* useful description of fire do me the favour of enclosing his card?)

Accordingly, on the strength of his satire, and a limited power of drawing upon his publisher in advance of his next work, Viridor quitted the Arabia Petræa of law to pitch his tent in the Arabia Felix of the *belles lettres*.

The change was mightily agreeable. It was the air of liberty and life, from frowns, inuendos, and lectures. Oh, if parents, rulers, and legislators, all who have authority over an individual, a province, or a nation, would but learn the downright inefficiency of severe measures, in operating real reform, either in a child or in a multitude! If they would but throw all brute-force dogmatists and latter-day prophets over the bridge—in spiritual signification—and strive to govern by the only two principles that have real power absolute over thinking spirits—REASON and LOVE! For I tell these semi-thinkers, these incomplete entities (*êtres imparfaits*, as George Sand terms them), these weak deriders of that transcendant optimism which is neither more nor less than sublimated Christianity, and more especially I tell this same latter-day fury,* much read in German illuminism, with small understanding of its revelations, that both they and he are objects of great and serious commiseration to the earnest seekers of light, and hopeful leaders of crusades without end,

---

* This man pretends to pity Lamartine! That poet and statesman has his faults, like all men of genius. But when I remember the days of February, 1848; the hero-orator at the Hotel-de-Ville; when I compare the works of Lamartine and of Carlyle, the subtle refinements and lofty elevation of the former's ideas, with the crude indigestions of Kaut, Fichte, Goethe, Jean Paul, &c., of the latter; when I ask myself what Carlyle would have been in the place of Lamartine; when I consider the respective places they will occupy in history; when I see in the one the poet, hero, and historian of all times, and in the other the paradox-monger, imitator, and word-gushing pamphleteer of a passing day—I do not pity—I laugh. And this Carlyle speaks contemptuously of George Sand. Silly Scot!

"Du gleichst dem Geist, deu Du begreifst,
 Nicht mir—"

Would be no inapt reply from that glorious spirit, whose very *blunders* are worth all the " slush element" of Carlyleism I ever waded through.

against Pain, Ignorance, and Falsehood, that trinity of everlasting hatred.

(Pen ! pen! cease thy digressive mania, or this history will remain a fragment to the end of time !)

The next two years of Viridor's life were years of marvellous fortune.   In the most unexpected way, by literary successes of various kinds, including one anonymous drama's triumph, he obtained and spent more than a thousand pounds sterling. But he had to make great mental efforts for his years, and what was worse, to endure an amount of care and excitement disproportionate to the untaught fibres of his sensitive organisation. His health gave way. On coming of age, he found himself in miserable health, pressed by debts, incapable of energetic exertion, and deprived, by a sudden turn in a law-suit, of property the sale whereof was to have produced his future means of independent income. It was a period of general reaction and pecuniary scarcity, produced by the mad speculations of the preceding year. Literature was, as it were, suddenly becalmed. Viridor's new book was a comparative failure. He risked his last hundred pounds in a publishing speculation, which failed, owing to his illness, inexperience, and the neglect of his subordinate agents. As if by magic, he found himself without resources, with exhausted credit, neglected by his relations, forgotten by his friends (at least, so he imagined), and, by way of a climax, arrested for debt and thrown into prison.

Strange to say, his mind, relieved from its tension by this extreme plunge into misfortune, no longer preyed upon the frame it had well nigh exhausted. He recovered partially in health, and when he managed to arrange with his creditors, emerged, as one out of a dream, from the dismal scene of his incarceration, to find himself reconciled with his father, broken in spirit, and obscure in position—a mere shadow of the once brilliant Viridor—vegetating upon a miserable pittance, and so utterly changed in character, that for some time a lunatic asylum appeared his probable, if not certain destination.

For nearly a year he lived in utter solitude, doing literally *nothing* but walk about in a state of hopeless melancholy, and gaze with childish interest at the shops or passing carriages of the metropolis, or the fields and trees of the suburban landscapes. Twice he attempted suicide, and twice by a singular chance escaped alive from the ordeal. Some inferior percussion caps in the one case, and the unaccountable non-effect of a large dose of opium in the other, were the causes of this escape.

Then came a violent reaction. He arose suddenly from his lethargy, applied himself to study and literary labour with restless assiduity, and found, to his own surprise, that his genius had developed itself in its torpor, that he had learned not only to understand but to sympathise with his fellows, that the boy had ripened into the man, the neophyte into the high-priest, that the dreams of his young vanity, which he had so bitterly condemned, might after all become developed into realities. He saw the nullity of his factitious reputation and fleeting success. But the broad road was before him. He no longer trusted to blind inspiration, but he began to see his way to the real fountain of truth

and grandeur. He resolved before all things to edu-
cate his mind. He undertook the severe toil of *thought.*
By day and night he meditated on the great fundamental principles of the sciences, the arts, and their
practical application to life. He recognised, at length,
that in all things the most sublime and noble system is
the truest and the best. He kept that grand idea
before his eyes, even in his lightest contributions to the
floating literature of the hour. He was respected, if
not applaudĕd. And thus, during years of poverty
bordering on actual want, and petty sufferings without
limit, he arrived at the triumph of fully developing and
comprehending that living philosophy of the age which
even Darian was yet incapable of pursuing and elabo-
rating in all its details. And this wondrous systematic
intellect and lofty intuition it was that made him, at
the period of our narrative, a personage of such secret
but vast importance in the great movement of the
European world, at an age when many men are still
struggling through the noviciate of a profession, or
blushing at their youth amid the circles of the Idolators
and the Gold-Thugs.

This was the soul, rudely and imperfectly described,
hich the subtle Ignatius had undertaken to bargain for.

It may be imagined that the philosopher who reckoned
his disciples amongst the natives of every civilised
country of the globe, was in small danger of being
won over by the propositions of his adversary.

Nor would the dark speculator, in all probability,
have attempted the negotiation, had he at all comprehended Viridor's then position. But in the eyes of the

agent, Viridor was simply the needy man of letters, the gentleman of broken fortunes, and the young man of five-and-twenty, who had his way to make in the world.

He did not know that Viridor had but to ask for thousands to receive them without a question or a condition, that myriads were prepared to rise in arms at his word, that the destiny of millions of men were as surely dependent on the impulse given by his spirit, as the descent of the scale is dependent on the ' additional pound thrown into the balance by the meter.

The spies of the Soul-Agent could penetrate the cabinets of ministers, but not the changing council-chambers of the supreme Illuminati. They could betray the secrets of freemasons' lodges, but not the formless mysteries of spiritual brotherhood; they could enter the club of the conspirators who desired physical-force revolutions, but not the united souls of philosophers who, with the invisible lever of thought, moved all humanity from its inmost centres of action.

It was the third interview of Ignatius the Plutocrat, with Viridor the Democrat. He had made no progress as yet towards subduing the scruples of the Fire-Worshipper, nor could he be said to have lost ground himself, since every inch backwards in his system was a foot in advance towards the purer creed.

It was, after all, an unequal contest—the false glitter of gold against the true light which it reflects, the metal that can be consumed against the fire that consumes it. Granted, that the latter operation requires some chemical science not possessed by every dabbler in experiments at the Polytechnic Institution.

"Pray do not stand on any ceremony," said the

Soul-Agent, "if I am in the way, say the word, and I will leave you while it is yet time to recall a more agreeable visitor."

"Thank you," said Viridor, "I had no wish to prolong the interview. Well, what news from the Soul-market?"

"Nothing particular to-day, except a rise in the value of out-door agitators and demagogues. One very violent fellow was bought for five hundred pounds by the Duke of Rackrent."

"What do they want with him—is he to be silenced, or proclaim his apostacy through a speaking trumpet?"

"Neither—he is to go on more rabidly than ever."

"What, to excite a riot, and give excuse for strong repressive measures?"

"Precisely. It is a dangerous plan, and a doubtful. I told the duke so, but what can one do with these blockheads? However, I am but a plain Soul-Agent. I neither care for nor interpose in politics."

"Have you no opinions, then, on the subject?"

"Yes; but no passions."

"Do you mean that you are indifferent to the well-being of the people?"

"Not at all, I wish them all happiness. But I believe that the man who does something practically useful is the greatest benefactor of society. Now, I have founded the Soul Exchange, and put men in the way of saving more time, that is, money, than they can possibly do by any other recent improvement in machinery. If they would only do away with speeches in Parliament, and vote point blank on every bill proposed, the effects of the system would be wonderful."

" Wonderful," exclaimed Viridor, " considering that two bills out of three are blunders! We should be inundated with laws which would eat one another up in the execution!"

" You are quite right about the blunders. But let me ask you one thing—is there any blunder possible that could do more harm than procrastination?"

" Perhaps not. Because, after all," said Viridor, meditatively, " a positive evil is more easily grappled with than one arising from mere inactivity and uncertainty. A bad law could be repealed, and would serve as a test for the remedy required."

" Exactly so, it is easy to discover improvement when there is something to improve. Look at the number of amendment acts. The great vice of government is laziness. Oh! if we had but a man like yourself at the head of affairs we should soon see a new life breathed into the old machinery!"

"Say, rather, that you would soon see the old machinery replaced by new. You are aware that I care little for traditions, glorious old constitutions, and other worn-out lumber, inherited from our ancestors."

" I am aware that you care only for your country," said Ignatius, trying to look sincere, which was a great effort on his part.

"Quite a mistake," said Viridor, " I do not care for my country at all."

" No?" said the crafty agent, brightening up, and hoping that, after all, the literary politician was not so ridiculously virtuous as he pretended. "You do *not* care for your country? Why should you?"

"Why indeed?" said Viridor, "I was born here, it is true; but I have travelled. I speak English; but I can also speak French, German, and Italian. Why should I confine my desire to benefit mankind to a single country of the many by which the earth is covered?"

"If you were but Foreign Secretary, such sentiments would do you honour," said the Soul-Agent. "Now I have no doubt but that you have formed a plan of European policy already, in case of accidents," continued Ignatius, with an almost inperceptible tinge of irony, provoked by the absurd idea of Viridor entertaining such projects in his present obscure position.

"I am ready to take office to-morrow," replied the philosopher coolly.

"Have you devised a settlement of the Eastern question?"

"Yes," replied Viridor.

"Should you become First Lord or Home Secretary, I presume you are ready to propose a remedy for Irish pauperism?"

"Most certainly."

"And to pacify the discontented farmers?"

"That also."

"And the landlords?"

"I am prepared to redress even their grievances."

"And to preserve the colonies?"

"Unquestionably."

"And to reduce the expenditure?"

"Of course."

"And yet keep up the national credit?"

"Most decidedly."

" And satisfy the clamorous for an increased franchise ? "

" Fully."

" In short, you are armed at all points ? " said the Soul-Agent, with a mixture of respect for the confident audacity of the young author, and suspicion of his sincerity in all he professed.

" I have studied and reflected upon most of the important topics of the age, and as I believe rather in the application of *à priori* principles than of partial experience, I should not hesitate to undertake any responsibility, so long as I could satisfy my conscience by devoting my whole energies to the carrying out of the ideas I have faith in."

" What! you reject experience—the source of all wisdom, knowledge, and even principles ? "

" I do not reject it, I profit by it to the utmost. And the first thing experience teaches me is, to beware of trusting to experience. A grain of judgment is worth a pound of precedent. It has been said, that there is nothing new under the sun. The fact is, there is nothing old. Beyond the sphere of mathematical truths there is no repetition in nature or life. No two generals or statesmen were ever in precisely the same position. Besides, even the fact that one course of action succeeded on a previously similar occasion is no proof that even *then* another course might not have succeeded *better*. I am for obtaining all possible knowledge of the circumstances in which I am placed, but I reserve to myself perfect liberty of acting upon the information obtained."

"What a pity it is that you are attached to no party," said the Soul-Agent, "that talents of the high order you possess should lie as it were idle, when they might be turned to such profit for your fellow-creatures."

"You think so?" said Viridor, who wished to encourage the agent to speak out.

"Undoubtedly. I have before hinted to you that there is more than one opportunity for you to enter the political arena with every prospect of attaining the highest position."

"In plain terms," said Viridor, "you have a bid for my soul?"

"In still plainer terms," said Ignatius, encouraged by the easy tone of the poet's remark, "I have three *bonâ fide* offers for you, of the most brilliant nature."

"Can you mention to me the terms?"

"A seat in Parliament in every instance."

"That is little. I can exert more influence by a scratch of my pen than I could by a dozen speeches to men who had made up their minds not to be convinced beforehand. What more?"

"In one instance, a place worth eight hundred a year?"

"Very little—I could make as much by scribbling nonsense, if I wished to sell my soul to public caprice."

"In the second case, an estate for qualification, bought out and out, clear of encumbrance, by subscription."

"A pleasant prospect truly. I should encounter my subscribers at every turn. They would point me out

to their friends, and say, ' Look there, that is our speaking machine ; we got it up in fifty shares of so much per
man !' We may dismiss that."

" Ten thousand pounds in hard cash, is the third
proposition, with a place into the bargain, if you desire
it, and social advantages not to be surpassed."

" Who pays the ten thousand pounds ? "

" A single individual. The transaction may be made
strictly confidential. Between you and me, it comes
from a man of very high station, and, I suspect, ultra-
liberal opinions."

" I know the man," said Viridor, who was well aware
of Darian's *ruse*, the object of which was solely to
increase his (Viridor's) importance and influence amongst
the soul-dealers.

" You know him ? " said the Soul-Agent, who, though
he had easily ascertained the name and rank of his
first customer, was, owing to the incorruptibility of
Darian's attendants, unable to gain particulars of the
latter's personal associates.

" Well," said Viridor, " it is the Duke of St. George."

" And what do you say to his offer ?"

" That it is a joke."

" A joke ? " said the agent, reddening, " a joke?"

" Nothing more. Arthur Darian holds the opinion
that a soul which can be bought is not worth having."

" And so you are content to be this young duke's
aide-de-camp, free, gratis, and for nothing ? " said the
Soul Agent, whose eyes were gradually opening.

" Not so ; I serve no man, party, or nation—I seek
for truth."

" And you are content to renounce even the means of

o

carrying out your principles. You reject the only road to power. You resolve to continue in comparative poverty, obscurity, and helplessness, when by accepting either of the real offers I have to make you—"

"I might become a slave to creatures I despise."

"You are, then, resolved?"

"There needs no resolution. I am true to my faith."

"Confound his faith!" thought Ignatius, "I shall lose my best customers. I have engaged to find them a soul to animate their unwieldy bodies of voting clods and talking sticks, and I find nothing but an obstinate fanatic. Let me see you to-morrow, and learn your final decision," said the dark speculator aloud, rising to go, "I entreat you not to throw away such opportunities for mere fanciful illusions. The man who belongs to no party is a cypher ignored by all."

"The man who devotes himself to any party, in the sense you understand it, is something still worse."

"How so?" said the agent, dismally.

"He is a cypher to himself, as well as to everybody else."

"I cannot see the force of what you say. Man is a gregarious animal. You yourself are always speaking of harmony as the grand principle of happiness and progress."

"True," said Viridor, "but remember that there is no harmony without difference in music, and that no two notes, unless divided by a full tone, can possibly harmonise, whilst every nearer approach, short of absolute unisonance, produces the most appalling discord. For my part, I am my own leader of the opposition, my own pope, and my own master of transcendental eclecticism. I wish other people would think as freely. Freedom of opinion, combined with toleration, is the noblest mental condition I can imagine. The difference between such independent spirits, and the servile supporters of Jack This or Bob That's measures, is as great as that between the straw in a bundle on the pavement of a stable and the single valuable tube through which a thirsty Yankee sucks his sherry cobbler in the dogdays!"

"Ha, ha!" laughed Ignatius, with a forced hilarity, "I see you are not in a vein for serious discussion," and he took a hasty leave, anxious to escape without further displaying his chagrin at the failure of one of his most important negociations.

"Wait till I buy your soul and publish your memoirs, my poor Mephistophiles of the nineteenth century!" muttered the poet with a smile, as he also took his hat, and in a few minutes followed the Soul Agent down the dusky staircase from his chambers.

Very opposite were their destinations.

CHAPTER IV.

THE TIMESERVER.

IGNATIUS LOYOLA GREY quitted Viridor's chambers in a far more pleasant frame of mind.

Since he had become a Soul Agent by profession he had gained some curious experiences. The great fact —by the bye, Ignatius was the originator of that much-abused formula—the great fact of his experience was the astounding ignorance which prevailed in the world as to the relative value of the most valuable of all commodities.

He was constantly buying and selling, for his clients, souls, not worth their weight in electricity, at the most ridiculous prices, and, on the other hand, disposing of real diamonds of intellect for a few pieces of dross which would not have purchased the favors of the most facile Aspasia.

That very morning he had bought three Irish M.P.'s, an Italian *chargé d'affaires*, and a Cabinet Minister's mistress, for a total of six thousand guineas, after considerable chaffering; whilst a man of science in difficulties had been easily bargained for at a solitary hundred.

As for Viridor, the longer he resisted all the Soul Agent's temptations, the stronger grew that worthy's passion to effect the purchase; indeed, he only awaited the first sign of relenting on the part of his temptee to make, himself, an offer which should throw all the others into the shade, and make Viridor's soul his prey before anybody else had time to outbid him. Ignatius well knew that he could then make his own terms with his clients. Curiously enough, all three parties were anxious to make Viridor's soul their property.

The Aristocrats wanted him because they required men of talent to support their falling cause, and could produce none themselves.

The Plutocrats wanted him, because they fancied that his writings were of a dangerous character to their gods, and threatened the pillage of their plunder-caverns.

And Darian, as we have seen, bid for him on the. Fire-Worshippers' behalf, by way of mystifying the Soul Agent.

Meditating on these things from his special point of view, Ignatius emerged from the temple without feeing the porter who opened the useless wicket. He dismissed the splendid carriage which awaited him, with an impatient gesture, and the words " *Timeserver* Office—two," and continued his way on foot, towards the city. At Blackfriars-bridge he paused, and leaning over the parapet, contemplated the water in profound meditation.

" This country," murmured Ignatius, " is on the verge of a great moral and physical convulsion. The men in power are too feeble to bear up against the storm which is coming. Before long there will be only two political parties in the country, Republicans and Limitarians. I must make friends with the stronger party. But which is the stronger ? The king of to-day is the vagabond of to-morrow. The convict of yesterday may be the hero of its anniversary. What folly to be always calculating the future! It is speculating on female frailty in the arms of beauty—foreseeing indigestion in the freshness of appetite. At the worst, one can but die!"

The Soul Agent turned round gloomily, and for a few minutes regarded the diorama of varied human countenances which in spectral gloom flitted across the bridge, coming, one by one, within the rays of the nearest gas-lamp, and the vision of Ignatius.

They were a rare collection of wild caricatures, those faces! What havoc had Nature made of her ideal types of human beauty and dignity! What fatal accidents, corroding and destroying influences, had worked upon those masks since their first infant outline! To gaze upon them was enough to rouse the soul from apathy, to drive it to reform, or rebel against a state of things whose history was written in such fearful characters.

There was a thin mechanic, with his pinched and sallow features, careworn brow, mouth painfully contracted, and sharp anxious eyes vainly peering forward into a future of unresting toil and privation. He caught the Soul Agent's glance, and an expression of defiant hatred darkened all his countenance. Chartist and Socialist as he was, the well-dressed lounger, the idle gentleman, was an abomination in his eyes. Hunger breeds hatred, and the poor man soon imbibes the belief that his poverty is the rich man's crime.

Then came a young girl whose countenance would have been beautiful, but for a reckless and insolent boldness that sat upon it, like a reptile on a marble goddess. There was an unnatural flush upon her cheeks, the flush of wine—she was too young for paint—there was a smile of forced voluptuousness about her full lips, a vicious humidity about her large dark eyes. Her shawl seemed to have slipped from her shoulders, and fell, not ungracefully, in half studied, half careless folds, displaying the round and swelling proportions of a figure which many a queen might have envied. She paused, and stared familiarly at the Soul Agent. There was a time when that sharp, sarcastic visage would have repelled and frozen her heart in an instant. But what cared she now? she saw only the man, the black coat, white linen, and kid gloves—in a word, the possible customer.

"Pray, sir," said she, "are you the ghost of Hamlet's father?"

"Not that I am aware of," replied the Soul Agent, a little disconcerted by this sudden address.

"You look quite a 'grave man,'" continued the girl, still quoting Shakespeare, that poet of the people, "I hope you have not dropped your heart into the river."

"I never had a heart, my dear," said the Soul Agent, in his most biting tone, "and I suspect you would have been better without one yourself."

The girl passed on with a disdainful toss of her head, and a twitch of her obstinate shawl, whilst two city clerks presented themselves to the criticism of Ignatius.

How very pale, thin, threadbare. and cypher-like they looked! Fourteen hours a day they made entries, and added up columns of accounts in a dusky warehouse. Their lives passed away like revolving water-wheels. Some day they will die, and be replaced by other machines like themselves.

They were walking Number Ones, and added together, they made—Two. If ever they caught a snatch of pleasure, they were too tired to enjoy, or too bewildered with the change to appreciate it.

Next followed a fat cheesemonger, with a round, unmeaning face. He had passed so much of his life amongst cheese and bacon, that he felt almost a cheese or a pig himself.

Then passed a sweep, and an Irish bricklayer, with a brick-dust complexion and a short black pipe, and an old woman who resembled Sycorax, and three more girls of easy virtue, who stopped to sing the Soul Agent a verse of a strange song; and many other quaint masks, with souls behind them, catching a feeble glimpse of existence through the dim and distorted medium of their perverse senses.

All these the Soul Agent carelessly scanned, till, hearing a clock strike the half hour, he strolled leisurely towards the office of the *Timeserver* newspaper.

In a dismal court, not far from the Thames, stands the vast factory from which issues a stream of words singularly resembling in character the river in its neighbourhood.

If beneath the turbid waters of the Thames there be cats and dogs in a state of advanced decomposition, beneath the flowing paragraphs of the *Timeserver* there are ideas and suggestions no less foul and insalubrious. If the Thames water, unfiltered, be poison to the stomach, the tone of thought in the *Timeserver* is, to minds that cannot sift it of its hackneyed fallacies, to the full as dangerous. If the Thames, with all its hidden filth, be still useful to the world, so is the *Time-*

server, with all its lies in masquerade. Both have their uses and their abuses. Neither of them have a pure drop in their veins. Both are daily recruited from sewers of corruption. As there is more merchandize embarked and disembarked in the Thames than in any other river, so there is more news conveyed and misrepresented by the *Timeserver* than by any other journal. Of the two, it were difficult to say which we swallow with the greatest repugnance, Thames water, or *Timeserver* articles.

The Soul-Agent arrived at the door of this literary Pandemonium. He was a great man there; though few, even of those employed in the establishment, were aware of the fact. Scarcely noticing the few persons he encountered, and who saluted him with suspicious awe, he made his way along a passage, and up two flights of stairs, to a mysterious-looking door of red cloth. On ringing a bell at the side, this door flew open, as did also a second door covered with iron plates, which faced him as he entered. Having passed the second portal, Ignatius found himself in a small snug chamber, with a large office table in the centre, and a fire burning in the grate, which, in fact, consisted of several letters undergoing annihilation at the hands of a gentleman whose back only was visible.

There was but one other person in the room.

He was an elderly man, with a very bloated face, a slightly humped back, and disproportionately short legs. His nose was large and red, his eyes small, and half buried in his fat cheeks. Eyebrows or lashes he did not, to appearance, possess. His dress was clerical in cut, with the exception of a heavy gold chain round his neck.

At the noise of the Soul-Agent's entry, the person occupied in burning the papers looked round, and nodded in a familiar, though uneasy manner. He was a large-featured, coarse-looking man, something like the barristers one sees in courts of law, bullying witnesses. His head was nearly bald. His dress was that of a cockney sportsman. There was profound cunning in his sharp greenish eyes, and a sinister expression about his large jaw, which could not fail to strike even a superficial observer.

" Good evening, Grey," said the sportsman, " you are just in time to give your opinion. The Austrian re-mittance falls short this week."

" It is the third time since the close of the war," said the humpback, in a mild croaking tone.

" What do you propose to do ?" said Ignatius.

" Do ? Confound the rascals, give it them in a thun-dering leader, teach them to pay their debts of honour, d—n them !" replied the green-eyed gentleman.

" Yes, spare the rod and spoil the child," said the hunchback, " but the times are changed."

" So shall the *Timeserver* be, by jingo !" growled the sportsman sullenly.

" I mean," insinuated the small gentleman, " that we have not so strong a hold on them as we had. They can do without us."

" Yes, for the moment," said Ignatius, " but if there should be a new outbreak ?"

" Pshaw, the rascals do not see an inch before their noses," rejoined the sportsman, " they trust to their infernal bayonets too much, like everybody else just now."

" I will see the ambassador this very night," said the Soul-Agent sternly, suddenly assuming a tone of leadership, which his companions rarely resisted; " we must remember that though, as a *quorum*, we represent the committee of shareholders, we have to account for our acts. Besides, Twiggins, you are really too hasty altogether; you made us give ourselves the lie last week point blank, about the Roman business. Even the *Timeserver* is not unassailable, and the cursed *Daily Nous* watches us like a cat after a bird. They are a little timid in Bobbery Street, but they will take their opportunity, depend upon it, if we indulge in any glaring inconsistency just now."

" I thought we had thrown consistency overboard long ago," croaked the dwarf, with a mock humility which Ignatius fully understood.

" Yes," replied the latter, " as a principle, but not as a blind. It is all very well for a French *mouchard* to deny himself the luxury of a shirt, but he cannot dispense with a dickey."

" Comparisons are odious," said the cockney sportsman. " However, let Grey see their poor devil of an Ambassador, and we will hang fire till we get his answer, eh?" And the speaker, having delivered this sentiment with great assumption of importance, looked towards the dwarf for his approval.

" Just so," said the humpback, whose eyes were riveted upon a piece of paper, on which Ignatius was scribbling a few words.

" Will that do, Mr. Somers?" said the Soul Agent, passing the slip of paper carelessly to the dwarf.

Its contents ran thus—

" Tread on dangerous ground, but very gently, in the Austrian article."

The dwarf, whom we have heard called Mr. Somers, appeared to read these few words with acute attention several times.   Once or twice he raised his pen, as if to alter, but refrained on detecting the eye of Ignatius fixed upon him with a peculiarly indifferent expression, that he had learned to interpret differently.   He therefore contented himself with underlining the word *very*, and handed the paper to Twiggins.

" All right," said the sportsman, thrusting the piece of paper into an envelope, and dropping it through a letter-slip in the floor.   " I hope, for the editor's sake, he has not written his article beforehand."

" Not he," said Ignatius, " that sort of men have but one spur—necessity.   Not even wine can stimulate the brain of an old hack scribbler of all work.   By the bye, has the Pope written to explain the deficiency?"

" O yes, there was a letter from the Cardinal Raggolini yesterday," replied the dwarf; " the Rotmucks are holding back with their loan, like Jews as they are."

" Not a bit of it," interrupted Twiggins, " I have obtained a piece of information which explains the whole business.   Baron de Rotmuck shewed a great deal of pluck in the matter.   He asked the Pope to remove all objectionable laws respecting his countrymen.   The Pope and the Cardinals refused.   Rotmuck obtained a private interview with Pio.   'I'll tell you what,' said the baron, 'your Holiness may be Pope of Rome to-day, but I am master of Europe to-day, to-morrow, and the day after. I am the greater man of the two.   But I have my fancies. I know you and your long-robed knaves to be capable of cheating a Jew, or even a Greek, and that is saying a great deal. No matter; have the extreme condescension to kiss my great toe, and the loan shall be taken up at all hazards to-morrow!' To this the Pope replied, that he would pray him out of purgatory (and into a worse place) first. 'Then,' said Rotmuck, coolly, 'if your Holiness require money, I shall raise my demands, that is all; so you may guess my terms, you who are fond of having your toe kissed by the people.'"

"Who told you that story?" said Ignatius, laughing at the off-hand style of Twiggins's anecdote.

"Why, if you *will* know, I had it at dinner yesterday, from Ben Sidonia himself."

"His romances are good," said the Soul Agent, "and so would be his speeches, if any man could make head against facts as plain as the sun at noonday. But Hebrew heroism is a scarce commodity, I fancy."

"We shall be no losers by supporting the Pope," said the hunchback.

"No," said Ignatius, "the standing orders will do for *him*. To turn to a more important matter—the ministry is shaky."

"Very," said the dwarf.

"The odds are two to one against its escape on the A.B.C. question," said the sportsman.

"These poor Whigs," said Ignatius thoughtfully, "they are so fond of office, they want the salaries so much. They are so liberal with every thing but money."

"They have no bottom," said the sportsman; "though they have an uncommon talent for finding the gap in a fence if there is one."

P

"And if they go out, how long can the landlord party keep their ground? Can they take office at all?"

"*Pro tem.*," quoth the hunchback, significantly.

"Till a grand battue comes off," said Twiggins, "with Free-trade reformers as sportsmen!"

"After that, the deluge," said Ignatius.

"What deluge?" said the short committee-man, querulously.

"The deluge that will drown us with them, if we do not get an ark of safety built in time," replied the Soul Agent, with marked emphasis.

"What the deuce do you mean?" said Twiggins, in alarm.

"I mean mischief—and from the democrats."

"The democrats? pshaw! we settled them on Kennington Common."

"You frightened a mob."

"The Charter is a humbug."

"I trust it may prove so. Do you know what its first point means?"

"What, Universal Suffrage? why, a vote for every man in the country above twenty-one years of age."

"And that means—REPUBLIC."

"O, hang the Chartists! I am not afraid of them or their oracles," said Twiggins, laughing; "besides, we have made the middle classes believe that they are robbers and pickpockets."

"You will find the real leaders of the movement party something different from the Chartists you talk of," said Ignatius; "I tell you they are *Republicans*— men of the Cromwell, Mirabeau, Mazzini, Lamartine,

Kossuth order. They have both policy and courage ; I know something of their method."

"Ha, ha!" laughed the dwarf; "a few ragamuffins to break windows at half-a-crown a head, and we can command special constables enough to beat the grand army of Xerxes, in numbers."

"And in courage?" sneered Ignatius. "But you are mistaken; the middle classes are suffering too bitterly from restricted currency, over-taxation, and colonial bungling. They are beginning to see their own interest, and it pulls with the people. So must we, if we mean to live out the tempest. As for the ministry— make hay while the sun shines. And now a word on France."

"On chaos you mean," croaked the dwarf.

"Regular wild-duck shooting!" muttered the sporting shareholder.

"The Mountain will triumph."

"When?" squeaked the dwarf.

"Ay, when, indeed?" exclaimed the sportsman.

"To-day, to-morrow, the day after. I cannot tell. It gains ground daily, as it has gained ground since '83. We must moderate our tone. If my advice were followed, we should abandon the poor ape of the Elysée at once. Louis Napoleon is an impotent phantom, a mere *nominis umbra*. In a word, I consider that every commercial interest of the *Timeserver* depends upon our taking a bold course. Our subsidies are failing us from those we have supported, our name stinks in the nostrils of the public, we are burned in effigy daily. In my opinion, we must either take the lead in liberalism, or perish."

"Humph!" said the dwarf, with that air of stolid scepticism which seems to defy conviction, "I think we had better look before we leap. As far as an extra lift to the Manchester school goes, I should not object."

"No," said Ignatius, "especially when they come forward to annihilate our property, by throwing open the news market to every publishing adventurer. What are we to expect, if penny morning papers become the order of the day ? When an advertisement we charge a crown for is to be had for a shilling ? when, with no stamp, no advertisement, no paper duty, we are compelled to exert all the resources of our capital, machinery, and organisation, to compete with rivals that undersell us, even on the certainty of loss ? What are we to do, I say, when it becomes necessary to reduce our price three-fifths, and quadruple our sale, if we do not manage to enlist friends amongst the masses of the people ? when the sudden rise of new journals, advocating new principles, and conducted on new systems, threaten to eclipse even the *prestige* of our name ? when our enormous dividends not only are threatened with diminution, but with utter extinction ? What are we to do then ?"

"Shut up shop, I suppose," replied the sportsman, with a grim laugh. "But you are giving way to strange fancies, you have taken an extra glass of claret—you surely do not mean seriously half you say ?"

"I mean all, and more than I have thus vaguely hinted at. I mean that we live in an age, when days count for years of more torpid history."

"*I* see nothing of the fiery element you seem to dread so much," said the hunchback, "everything seems quiet. The people are put down, abroad and at home. The continental press is gagged, the bayonet is king everywhere—even in France."

"Trust me," said Ignatius, solemnly, "we are smoking cigars on barrels of gunpowder (once more to quote my friend Contarini). Up to the moment of explosion, we are safe enough; after that—advertise for our arms and legs in any papers you please."

"Well, what do you propose ?" said the dwarf, in the querulous tone of incapacity, combined with repugnance to the acknowledgment of superior resources.

"Aye, what ?" said Twiggins, carelessly, as if he would have disguised the involuntary respect he felt for all the propositions of Ignatius.

"To strike in to-morrow on some great topic, with twice the boldness, twice the liberality, and twice the brilliancy of a leader in the *National* or *La Presse.*"

"Well, as you like," said the sportsman, "*vive la bagatelle.* Life is a toss up—the best shot misses his bird sometimes."

"I wash my hands of the responsibility," said the dwarf, shrugging his shoulders — a very necessary operation, by the way, in his case.

"*A la* Pontius Pilate," muttered the sportsman in his beard.

"I undertake all the responsibility," said Ignatius, coldly, restraining the curl of contempt which played about his mouth corners.

"Perhaps, then, you will write the instructions for the editor," said Somers.

"No," said Ignatius, "we must have new blood in the affair. We must have a little of the real stuff about it, or the articles will look too much like mountebanks in mufti. You may dress any man in Bond Street, even a crossing-sweeper, but you can't teach him to walk and look like a gentleman. The old style wo'nt do; and the new ideas will bother our old stage thunderers. I have my eye upon a man who will serve our turn, if we can enlist him for the moment."

"Is his soul in the market?" yawned Twiggins, who was growing sleepy.

"Not yet. Perhaps we may borrow it for a week or two."

"At what rate of interest?" said the dwarf.

"At none at all—but a few words in the proper tone, and a lie which nobody can tell but myself."

"Ha! ha! ha!" laughed the two committee-men, "and who is this gullible Phœnix of democrats?"

"Bernard Viridor."

"Bernard Viridor! *He* write in the *Timeserver!*"

"Yes," said the Soul Agent, "and now, gentlemen, good evening. I must defer seeing the Austrian ambassador until to-morrow, unless I meet him at Lord Rattlesnake's *soirée.*"

It must be confessed that the Soul Agent had profited by the lessons of Viridor. Strange infatuation! Ignatius yet dreamed of bending to his will the spirit which already began to regulate the pulsations of his own strange destiny.

As the three Parcæ of the *Timeserver* were about to quit the apartment, there came a sudden ringing at the bell, which betokened urgency or importance on the part of the ringer.

Ignatius pulled a string, and the doors flew open, one after the other.

A courier rushed into the room, flung down a packet upon the table, and leaned exhausted against the door.

Ignatius tore open the packet, and glanced rapidly at its contents.

"It is the Austrian remittance," he whispered, and scribbled on a fresh slip of paper, almost at one stroke of his pen, the words—"*Butter for Austria, orders revoked.*"

The two committee-men nodded assent, and the decree was committed to the letter-box, like the accusations, of old, to the mouths of the Venetian lions.

"They will take care of you below," said the sportsman to the courier, who bowed low, and staggered from the apartment.

"Dead beat," said Twiggins.

"Dead drunk," corrected Ignatius.

"We can divide the notes to-morrow," said the dwarf, with a hideous leer, turning his key in the lock of the outer door.

There were two other locks on the door. Ignatius and the sportsman each followed in turn the example of their companion, and left the chamber of mystery, like the gold of the robbers,* accessible "not to one, nor to two, but to three."

Such are the precautions which rogues are obliged to take one against the other, in the great City of Jugglers.

There is no honesty amongst thieves—it is quite an exploded fallacy.

The three jugglers descended to the street, Ignatius last of all.

The dark speculator leaped into his carriage.

* The story alluded to will be found in Rogers's "Italy."

" Can you drop me at my club?" said the sportsman.

" Certainly. You will not come with us, Somers?"

" No," said the dwarf, hobbling away, " I have an appointment to keep."

" With his mistress, I suppose," said Twiggins, sarcastically.

" I should like to see the Juliet to such a Romeo," said Ignatius. " But I know all about it; it is the agent of Lord John Twaddle he has to meet."

" The devil it is! He takes bribes, then, on his own account? that is against our compact," said the sportsman, moving his huge frame uneasily in his place.

" His soul is Twaddle's though; what can we do?" resumed Twiggins.

" Buy Twaddle himself, if you like—I will go halves in the speculation."

" We must buy him d——d cheap then," said the sportsman, "for his whole party may be at a discount to-morrow."

" So may we ourselves," said Ignatius, " if we let either Somers or Twaddle cast their shadows over our columns. I have a great mind to sell my shares in the *Timeserver*, and start a rival."

" It has been tried too often," rejoined Twiggins, incredulously.

" A man in battle may escape a great many bullets, and yet be shot at last," muttered the Soul Agent.

With which pithy sentence, we will conclude this lengthy chapter.

CHAPTER V.

MODERN ILLUMINATI.

Day is the season for action; night is the season for thought.

In the day-time, the glare of sunshine and the turmoil of business distract the mind, and force attention to immediate objects. In the hours of night, forms become vague, details melt into obscurity, and the spirit is enabled to concentrate its power upon the essences of things—upon the supreme abstractions which embrace all minor distinctions.

Viridor gazed upon the stars, the calm and beautiful companions of his long vigils. He strove to collect, as in a focus of light, the rays which had by turns illuminated his studies. That night he desired to be all he had ever felt himself in his most exalted moments. A sudden dread came over him. A black phantom stalked at his side. Cold sweat burst from his pores, the pulsations of his heart seemed to cease, and the giant Despair for an instant threatened to paralyse his whole spiritual being.

He had dreamed a dream which that night was to realise or destroy. He had claimed an empire which that night was to see acknowledged or denied for ever. He had preached a religion—that night was to hail him prophet, or brand him as fanatic.

A new and extraneous influence had disturbed the

balance of his soul. The fire of human had dimmed the
flame of spiritual love. His ambition had lost its unity;
selfish desire had mingled with the passion of the universe. He remembered the moral of the weird romance.
Glyndon and Zanoni danced before his thoughts till they
vanished, or merged in the pale spectre of their creator,
who, like the phantoms of his art, had also fallen—fallen
from the Empyrean of the Gods, into the chaos of the
earth-lusts, and the shadows of the threshold.

"O, Bulwer, Bulwer! what fatal timidity could check
thy bold career? what nameless doubt could cause thy
faith to waver? What secret chain debarred thy soul
from liberty? So much—and yet no more. So near
—and yet to pause. The ears of the world—and yet
silent. Speak, speak!—or for ever slumber. And I—
I feel the salvation of a world streaming through my
veins, and Doubt freezes the torrent. My spirit sees;
but clouds obscure my vision. My conscience dictates,
but my brain abjures obedience. My science teaches,
but my tongue refuses utterance."

Thus musing in feverish depression Viridor strode
along. He prayed inwardly to all the spirits of the
Infinite for strength in the great crisis of his destiny.
He strove to exalt his intelligence by contemplating the
present condition and possible future of his human
brethren. The Asmodeus, Imagination, removed for him,
not only the roofs, but the very walls and doors of every
house he passed,—or rather rendered them transparent
as those palaces of crystal described in necromantic
legends. He saw the juggler-citizens, each in the narrow circle of his own petty lights, intrenching and forti-
fying himself against the dishonesty of his fellows, whose

delusion he contrived. He saw the thousand evils of a system of society founded upon man's pettiest instincts. He saw the endless chain of common cares and miseries that bound men to one another, without uniting them in spirit ; that made, of every one, an old man of the sea to some neighbour-Sinbad. He saw the greatness of existing ignorance, and the smallness of existing rulers. He saw the people crying for labour, for education, for food, bodily and mental ; and the arbiters of their destinies playing comedies at Westminster, sacrificing truth to party interest, conviction to personal vanity, and the people to everything. All this he saw— and more than this ; he saw himself, and others like him, men of thought and action, of power to conceive and realise the desires that burned within the age, excluded by a brute-force tyranny, an idle subterfuge, a legalised conspiracy of orthodox social banditti, from all part and share in the direction of the community to which he belonged ; that is to say, he found himself a shareholder in a company, without a voice as to the distribution of his own property—an existing fact, whose existence could not be denied, and yet was not admitted.

The blood of Viridor boiled in its veins. He felt a rebel in his heart against the dogged crew of dunces and conspirators who stood between him and his heritage. His own wrongs alone justified, the wrongs of millions necessitated, his resolve. It was no common oath that Viridor registered, as from the depths of his soul he murmured these ominous words—

" Justice for the people—at all hazards, at every cost. Better were the anarchy of light, than the sombre despotism of darkness. Away with all temporising, with

all half measures. If there be a Truth, let us declare it.
If there be a Right, let us combat for it. If our cause
be just, why should we hesitate to set fame, fortune,
and life on the cast? Hundreds, perhaps thousands,
have done so. They sleep in death, or starve in exile,
beneath the envenomed calumnies of their enemies. The
slaves of privilege and of money, the haters of enlightenment and liberty, the advocates of bayonets and
bloodshed, of police-spies and passports, have thrown
down the gauntlet, and defied us. They have said, 'We
are strong, and might is right.' Let us prove to them
that we are the stronger—and that justice is mercy."

Thus did Viridor revolve in his breast a war terrible
and decisive against the whole oligarchy of Europe. Ever
faithful to his grand philosophical dogma that ideas are
the origin of all things, he forged the weapons of his
party in the Etna of his soul. The Vulcan of the terres-
trial gods, he prepared the thunderbolts of truth by
which whole armies of giants are stricken down and consumed to ashes. He said, "There is no treason but
falsehood, and every honest man is its avenger!"

In this frame of mind, he entered an hotel near
Charing Cross, and straightway directed his steps to a
large room on the first floor of the building, in which
some twenty of his brethren were assembled.

All paused in their conversation at the entrance of
Viridor. Those who had already seen the poet, crowded
around him, eagerly grasping his hand. Those to
whom he was personally a stranger, did not require to
be told his name. His portrait was in all their
hearts.

As soon as the first greetings were over, Viridor, as

Grand Master of the Supreme Illuminati, was requested to preside.

He accordingly seated himself at the head of a table, amply provided with writing materials, and covered with a crimson cloth, in the centre of which, a figure of liberty, with various emblematical devices, was worked in golden embroidery. The other Illuminati took their seats round the table. Their physiognomies would have deeply interested a Lavater. Never since the birth of history had been assembled twenty such faces as were there present. Differing from one another in the most marked manner, in age, in nationality, in individual character, there was, in all, a varied expression of intelligence, earnestness, and enthusiasm, unknown to the vulgar herd. There was not, amongst them, a single example of the coarse, animal, malignant countenances to be met with in every public assembly, even in the Houses of Lords and Commons, where any one who will take the trouble to observe, may see creatures on two legs, which it seems almost farcical to set down as men.

About one half of the assembled council were Englishmen. Amongst the remaining portion were representatives of the German, Polish, French, Hungarian, and Italian nations. Every minute increased the numbers of the assembly.

At length Viridor rose to open the proceedings. Before beginning to speak, he cast one more anxious glance towards the door. At that instant it opened, and the majestic figure of Darian appeared on the threshold.

"Gentlemen," said Viridor, a sudden radiance overspreading his countenance, "I have the most sincere de-

Q

light in presenting to you a new member of our sacred
and eternal order, in the person of Arthur Bolingbroke
Darian, commonly known as the Duke of St. George,
a true democrat and citizen of the light; late general
of the patriots in the Hungarian Republic."

All eyes were fixed upon Darian, as his friend uttered
these words in that clear, ringing tone so eminently
adapted to command the attention of an assembly.

The impression produced by the new comer was decidedly favourable. Few eyes could regard without
admiration, the face and figure of the republican chief.
There was something irresistibly prepossessing in the
look of his eye, which was not always the case with
Viridor, who at times unconsciously adopted a sternness
of demeanour, which the ignorant might have mistaken
for *hauteur*.

Darian seated himself on the first vacant chair he
could find, between a dark and bearded Roman and a
white-haired German philosopher. The silence, which had
been momentarily interrupted, was restored, and Viridor
again prepared to speak. He looked, perhaps, somewhat
paler than usual, and a slight dampness caused his long
silky hair to cling to his temples. Not a single line, not
even the almost habitual contraction of his brows,
disturbed the marble serenity of his broad smooth forehead. His deep, inscrutable eyes flashed with a singular
brilliance. Tears glittered on their long dark lashes—
tears forced from the heart by intensity of sympathetic
exaltation. He stood, poised firmly, like a statue of
Destiny, drawn up to his full height, his arms folded on
his chest, his head slightly bent, in order to behold the
faces of his auditors. With a rapid glance, he scanned the

visages of all who were present. In every case, he read courage and resolution, confidence and hope. With a voice that startled his hearers by its concentrated feeling and thrilling distinctness, he began his address :—

" Lovers of light, and brothers in the war of liberty! We have met to-day, for no idle purposes of oratorical display—for no contemptible gratification of vanity in verbal contentions. We are all animated by one great desire —to fulfill to the utmost our destinies as men; to limit our ambition, not by our necessities, but by our powers; to act upon earth in accordance with our glorious nature as eternally progressive beings. The same sympathetic love for all living spirits animates our hearts. The same unquenchable antipathy to all voluntary infliction of pain—that is, tyranny—in whatever shape, fires our intelligence. Whatever our individual creeds or systems, we agree at least in the one great moral necessity of union to happiness. We see no hope for men without union of thought, union of sentiment, and union of action. My friends, do I speak your thoughts ?"

" Well spoken !" exclaimed all the Illuminati, as if with the voice of one man.

Viridor resumed, in accents yet more deep and penetrating—

" To effect great objects, great means are required. We behold gigantic evils, and history teaches us their wondrous ancientness. We are told by the cowardly, and the weak, and the selfish, that they are incurable— that they are necessary. The apathetic tell us not to hurry, to await the natural course of events, to trust to time and patience.

" But what *is* the natural course of events ? Every

step taken by man towards a better and a nobler life!
What cognate law fixes a limit to the extent or the
rapidity of progress? None. Let us, then, dare to
measure our possibility of success; not by the dull cant
of those rushlight spirits, who boast themselves pre-
eminently practical, because the circle illumined by their
rays is but a few feet in diameter; but by the broad in-
ductions of our own reason from history, science, and
reflection.

"To make men united and happy—I speak only of
approximate union and happiness, for all ideal states of
perfection are unattainable as absolutes—to make men
united and happy, two things are mainly requisite:
Love—mutual sympathy, benevolence, and abnegation
of selfishness in its worst sense; and Knowledge—that is,
the power of rendering nature subservient to our wants.

"Love, Christian love (there are no Christians *yet*),
destroys poverty by its practice of regarding sins of
omission and commission with equal severity. Thus, if
the Marquis of X.Y.Z. allow certain of his fellow-men to
starve to death, he having ample means to relieve them,
he, as a pretender to Christianity, or even humanity,
must conscientiously regard himself as a *murderer*. He
is indeed a far baser murderer than the highwayman,
who violently robs upon the road; for the latter may
have the pretext of desperation and want; but the former
commits *his* murder in cold blood, without risk, and from
a far meaner motive. This appears a little harsh at first
sight; but on minute inspection, it will be found that the
conclusion is irresistible. Begin by supposing the case
of a drowning man, whom you could save by extending
your hand, but do not; and pursuing the illustration of

the idea by examples gradually more remote, you will find that though distance lend enchantment to the view of crime, it cannot diminish its responsibility. The coward, who rolls a stone from the summit of a mountain to crush his foe in the ravine, is certainly no less criminal than the ruffian who boldly drives a stiletto to the heart of his enemy.

"The conscience of the present age must be awakened, its morality enlarged, its philanthropic efforts aggrandised and stimulated. Sects must be annihilated, but Christianity must be revivified. Bishops must become extinct; Church pluralists, deans and chapters, cannibal vicars, and starved curates, be spoken of as melancholy traditions; but the little children and the poor, *which Jesus loved*, must be cared for, and fed, and clothed; even though tithes be abolished, Church property confiscated, and the white surplices of the trained professors of a religion which is too grand, too noble, and too beautiful for the mechanical exhibitions of priestcraft, be converted into shirts for the labourer, and robes for the fair daughters of the people, no longer driven to sell their souls and bodies, for bread, to the lust of the debauchee, or the avarice of the speculator !"

A burst of sombre approbation followed this uncompromising analysis, and the Grand Master continued his address, in a calm but not less earnest strain—

"By the doctrine of love, the hearts of men must be revolutionised. By the teachings of science, their intellects must be liberated, and exalted.

"Knowledge is the primary source of all wealth and all material comfort. The most expanded charity, without expanded education, is utterly unable to defend the cause of the people against their deadly and only real enemy—*Poverty*.

"There is a poverty of the mind, as of the purse, a poverty which it is as essential, nay, more essential, to remedy.

"This direr form of poverty pervades all classes. Its evil effects are most terrible in the highest positions. To combat the ignorance, therefore, of the so-called educated classes, is the most important of the duties of a true democrat and worshipper of light.

"Their greatest ignorance is their greatest crime. They refuse to recognise that the real interests of the people and of themselves are inseparable. They reluctantly admit that justice and policy are two forms of the same idea. All their power, all their fountains of enjoyment, spring from the labour of the many, directed by the science of the few. Yet they dream of an indolent luxury, a voluptuous routine, without mental effort or research. They do not feel that property exists but by sufferance; that to work for the community, is the condition of every temporary possession of wealth; that the duties of an office neglected, entail loss of place and salary; that the resources of a country must either be developed in proportion to its population, or devoured by its inhabitants, who eventually devour one another, for lack of other nutriment. And this is no poetic exaggeration, but a fearful truth, and every man who perishes from more or less immediate want, suffering, and care in a community, is a ghastly illustration of the principle I have exemplified.

"All progress originates in individual genius. The world will be governed, reformed, and regenerated for ever, despite all obstacles of time. If the governing powers of a country prove themselves wanting in the ability to govern, they will assuredly fall, and other more potent spirits arise in their room. There is no *or* in the case, no danger of the world perishing by the folly of a single incarnate soul, or of a single generation. The sons of light rise above the howling objurgations and monstrous apprehensions of all 'latter day' explosions. They mount the ladder of eternity with fearless step; neither dismayed by the chaotic darkness below, from which they have emerged, nor by the dazzling clouds of flame above, towards which they are ascending. The soul is an eternal pilgrim, student, and reformer. Good and Evil, are spiritual light and shadow. We have helped to make the past—we are making the present, we are planning the future.

"Such, Oh my friends, is a feeble outline of the principles I would fain hope all here subscribe to!"

"All, all!" responded the Illuminati, in tempestuous approval, whilst their inspired leader thus concluded his harangue :—

"If I have been prolix, forgive me. I believed that to express fundamental ideas, in which we could unhesitatingly unite, was, above all, the primary duty of the glorious position in which you have placed me—a position which it were mockery to add, I should but insult by comparison with the thrones of worldly rulers. By your free choice you have elected me your President. I confess that before entering this hall, my soul trembled beneath the weight of so sublime a burden. But it trembles no more. I read in the noble countenances around me, the purity of a triumph over all petty and

hateful ambitions. It has been our unanimous desire
that all fruitless discussions should be avoided. Nevertheless, as I see before me many men older, wiser, and,
I would fain believe, even more zealous in the cause of
liberty than myself, I entreat you, my brothers in hope,
to correct me if I have erred, to question me if I have
been obscure, and to supply my deficiencies where I have
failed in expression.

"It now only remains for me to point out briefly the
chief positive objects, to the attainment of which, according to my judgment, all our efforts should be
directed in this country.

"And, firstly, without universal suffrage, without a
parliament elected by the people, it seems to me that
all progress is impossible, unless out-door agitation be
adopted as a permanent system, and intimidation be
substituted for reason, as an element of government.
What have we seen of late years? *A reign of terror!*
Pale Fear, enthroned as king—an obtuse and selfish pack
of legislators, frightened, literally *frightened*, into one
measure after another, by the determined menaces of
external politicians.

"Witness the Reform Bill, and the pitiful Whigs,
ready even to join in a rebellion projected by [the
stronger spirits who inspired them. Witness the triumph
of the Anti-Corn-Law League!

"It is useless to reason with the corrupt and loqua-
cious band, who, under the banners of Whiggery or Protection, waste the life and resources of the country in
their paltry struggles for place, patronage, and power.
The suffrage we must conquer from their fears, not sue
for from their intelligence. The serfs of Robert the

Devil, or Lord John Twaddle, must be swept away, to
'make way for honester men.' The great doctrine of
equal political rights must be philosophically and
morally inculcated by every means in our power, more
especially amid the educated classes, who have been so
accustomed to hear the truth vilified and travestied in
Timeservers, Slaughterly Reviews, and other repositories
of hireling calumny, that they have quite lost sight of
the real bearings of the question.

"I leave it to you, my friends, to point out, in turn,
the arguments most effectual in support of this supreme
and vital object to all legislative reform.

"It is the only road to the realisation of the great
ideas which every philosophic lover of his race must
cherish and contend for.

"*National Education,* universal, gratuitous, and
liberal, absolutely free from all sectarian influence.

"*National Life Assurance,* by which the government
guarantees to every honest man, willing to labour, the
opportunity of working, or support without degradation,
with provision for the orphan and the aged, to the
amplest extent of human necessities and comforts.

"*National Justice,* free of all charge, and therefore
accessible to the poor, as easily as the rich.

"*A National Currency* adequate to the wants of ex-
panding commerce, and destructive of all monopoly of
the circulating medium.

"*A National System of Taxation,* levied solely on
property and income according to just estimates of value,
and not on the present plan of indiscriminate plunder.

"*A National Army* consisting of every adult in the
commonwealth, open as a profession to all classes, on the

Prussian or French system—by examinations for promotion, and entirely without purchase of commissions. The standing army to be employed in public works.

" *A National Navy*, destined as much for colonisation as for defence, and

" *A National Emigration System*, offering every reasonable encouragement to colonists in the shape of passages, free, or on credit, grants of land, with every practicable information and assistance.

" My friends, there is nothing visionary or Utopian in these great and inevitable demands of the age. It is a fine thing for, men who never yet could devise a plan, worthy if even capable of execution, to denounce the poet or philosopher who assumes the statesman, as a dreamer and an impostor. I see before me the authors of books and editors of journals, in which the noblest principles and most subtle difficulties of policy, legislative and administrative, have been handled with consummate talent. It makes me smile to hear such minds compared—yes, compared disadvantageously as candidates for the exercise of national trust and power, with country gentlemen of sporting renown—dandies of May Fair, and denizens of 'tape and sealing-wax' offices. Literary men, unless at the same time landholders or millionaires (which removes all objections at once), are sneered at by the toadies of the Aristocrats or Plutocrats. But what could ordinary statesmen, with their barren inventions, ignorant confidence in their limited experience, and cautious timidities, have done during the late revolutions in Paris, in Rome, in Hungary? We know what they did—they ran away like their masters. Intrigue, brute.force, and gold, have restored them for the moment to power. Yet even in these triumphs they are forced to cringe to the giant they have chained. Without the venal slaves and reckless renegades of the press, they would vainly seek for Mamelukes to carry out their designs. Let us not be daunted by the hollow semblance of strength which they present. Within, all is rottenness. Sooner or later human reason must reject such miserable abortions as Thiers and Lord John Twaddle, whose dwarfish, insignificant forms, marvellously typify the pettiness of their undeveloped intellects.

" My friends, we are the miners of thought—true ideas are the diamonds we seek to discover. Let us display such jewels as we may find, to the eyes of our fellow-men, that they may recognise their beauty, and have faith in their reality. Let us speak our convictions boldly, in the simplest and most intelligible form. Let us proclaim our designs in the most fearless tones. Let us show the people that our hearts, our intellects, and our lives, are devoted to their liberation; and if the tyrants rejoice over our graves, let us leave our memories and our words to a posterity that must avenge us by its admiration, whilst our immortal spirits yet bravely continue to scale the ladder of everlasting perfectibility !"

The speech of the Grand Master was followed by enthusiastic acclamations. One after the other, all the Illuminati present rose to give in their adherence to the principles and measures which Viridor had advocated. With regard to the practical suggestions of his address, the most valuable developments and the most lucid arrangements were proposed, and demonstrated to be capable of easy execution. The stale cobweb objections.

of apathy and ignorance were swept away, till not a vestige remained to harass the mind of the assembly.

The most philosophical mode of primary education, and the best system for national universities, open to all classes and sects; the annihilation of pauperism by a universal benefit association supplying the place of a degrading poor-law; the extinction of mendicancy and professional thievery, by labour guarantees and emigration; the communion of employers and employed, by national and corresponding labour-registries in every town, for gratuitous advertisements and information; a new plan for model-dwellings; the reduction of the national debt, by rejection of the gold standard as the base of currency-laws, and its gradual conversion into circulating medium; the vast economy in cost, and increase in utility, of the military organisation; the taxation of the dead as the most rational of all impositions: the facilities of buying and selling land without expense; the suppression of adulteration and overcharges by shop-keepers; the utter abolition of arrest for debt, except as fraud; the facilities of credit, and impossibility of money scarcity, with an adequate currency; the advantages accruing to literature, education, and commerce, by the abolishing of all taxes on knowledge; the economy in collecting the revenue, by the consolidation of assessed taxation, and dispensing with custom-houses; the effects of sanitary reform nobly carried out; public libraries and amusements for the people; and many other vitally-interesting topics were touched upon and discussed with clearness, brevity, and enthusiasm. Then followed some profoundly important statements as to the condition of the various states of Europe, and the prospects of true democracy; analyses of the various social and communist theories prevalent in France and Germany, and resolutions as to their hostility to all real liberty.

Much I regret that neither space nor time permits me to record speeches, of which single paragraphs were often more suggestive than whole sheets of Hansard. But at present I must content myself with relating the extraordinary proposition which terminated the proceedings of the night.

All had spoken but Darian.   He rose, at length, and said, with impressive gravity,—

" You are aware, my friends, to what mad lengths barefaced venality and selfishness have gone in this city, and thence in every capital in Europe. The human soul is now bought and sold in the market-place, like cattle or vegetables. To say your soul is your own, is no longer regarded as a sign of courage, but of wealth. Soul-dealing has become a raging speculation.   Everybody dabbles in it who takes any active part in the world.   But we are no participators in the commerce; the souls we gain for our cause, are not to be gained by purchase. Yet these priceless spirits are made to suffer exquisite torments, by the corrupt mob which surrounds them.   The soul-dealers are carried away by chimerical estimates.   They are induced to persevere in their abominable traffic, by the gross ignorance of the speculative public.

" Brothers of the light, I have devised a scheme which may succeed in awakening the deluded multitude from their hallucinations.

" I propose to establish, with the least possible delay, a *Grand Exposition of the Souls of All Nations!*"

"It is a grand idea!" exclaimed Viridor, and all the Illuminati, in admiring wonder.

But how is such an exposition possible? you will perhaps exclaim, O reader, as, indeed, the Illuminati themselves did not fail to demand.

All things are possible to genius like Darian's. Read on, and learn. There is something to be learned in the next chapter for those whose spirits are awakened.

CHAPTER VI.

THE GRAND EXPOSITION.

It was not long before Darian, backed by Viridor and the secret council of the Illuminati, made public the adventurous proposition with which our last chapter concluded.

Darian, availing himself of the opportunities which his rank and vast wealth afforded, soon found a committee of distinguished names with which to appeal to the " flunkeyism" of the public. The committee was ultimately constituted, in about equal proportions, of all the three great ethico-political parties.

Nevertheless Darian, as President, with Viridor and other Illuminati as allies, possessed a decided preponderance in the committee. This was partly owing to their perfect union of will, partly to a leaning, more or less decided, towards liberalism, not to say Fire-worship, on the part of their aristocratic and Mosaic coadjutors.

The dark Ignatius, who had still a lingering notion of forming an advantageous political alliance with Darian, and of availing himself of the literary genius of Viridor, was a most influential supporter of all their propositions.

By his supreme command (which, as his wealth and importance increased daily, owing to the prodigious amount of business transacted at the Soul-Agency offices), a series of articles and reports appeared in the *Timeserver*, extolling to the skies the Duke of St. George's mysterious and original enterprise.

This caused the *Daily Nous* to " smell a rat"—which, indeed, was but natural, as Sir James Rattam, of letter-violating repute, was one of the committee. So the *Daily Nous* shook its head, and suspended its judgment. A young and lively contributor begged very hard to get a slashing satirical leader inserted. But the Editor told him, confidentially, to go and be hanged. So the *Daily Nous* suspended its wit, as well as its judgment.

The lively contributor *did* hang himself—from a gymnastic pole—and went through a course of fencing, pistol-shooting, and billiard playing, to dissipate by perspiration the gall of his disappointment.

The *Morning Ghost*, however, took up the proposed "Exposition" very kindly, and gave divers accounts of the dinners of the committee, which were worthy of the Arabiannights and the poetry of fashion.

I rather like the *Ghost* for one thing. It is not so ill-natured as many of its contemporaries. I attacked the *Ghost* once with unnecessary ferocity. What was the result ? A review, upon the whole, favourable, in many respects far more so than I deserved, unjust, it is true, in estimating the moral of my book,* but more than just as to its artistic merits.

* The " Impostor, or, Born Without a Conscience" (phrenologically illustrated by the Author). This is another of the labours I shall always remember with a certain regret. In picturing the character of a subtle and consummate villain, I now see the danger of rendering vice attractive whilst exposing its mysteries. The work was, after all, but a wild, reckless sketch, which it were waste of time for any reasonable being to peruse, unless reduced to desperation by ennui, and on the verge of a "fashionable novel," from which mournful affliction, Heaven defend all friends ! Curiously enough, at the mo-

The *Assinæum*—edited, if my memory of Paul Clifford be not deceptive, by the celebrated and versatile Mac Grawler—was extremely verbose in its recommendations as to the conduct of the proposed exposition. Whether any hope of "surreptitiously accumulating bustle" influenced their conduct, I cannot tell, any more than what was paid by Mr.——, to exclude the advertisements of my work from their columns.

The *Morning Cobbler*, the *Humbug*, and the *Globule*, were also favorable to the Grand Exposition of Souls.

But the *Evening Gun* took the opportunity of attacking, with great spirit, the whole system of soul-dealing. The *Exponent* and *Sectator* were also beginning to rise boldly in defence of a more daring liberalism than had been yet popular with established journals. Neither was the sharp thunder of the *Diapason* silent. The gibes of the *Hunchback* were full of dubious bitterness, but the leviathan *Timeserver* belched defiance of all opposition. The greater number of the weekly press seemed prepared to stem the torrent of demoralisation which threatened the age; and several of the provincial papers especially, made noble, though for the time ineffectual, exertions.

Meanwhile, Darian and Viridor bore the wondering distrust of their friends with secret confidence in their approaching triumph. Subscriptions were collected, prize

ment, I, a mere novice, was dashing off the history of Mesmer de Biron's unparalleled crimes and follies, a master in the art, to wit, Sir Edward Bulwer Lytton, was devising the horrors of his "Lucretia, or, The Children of the Night." "Children of the Night," indeed, both books! Books founded upon the same idea, as evidenced by a hundred curious coincidences in their pages. To have written "The Impostor" at twenty, was a blunder; to have published "Lucretia" at forty, something worse than an error. He who would paint Hell, should paint also Heaven. Poison for tens and antidotes for units, are no good elements for works of popular circulation.

masks modelled and cast, and a vast building prepared for the coming display of the earth's spiritual resources.

At length the day for opening the exhibition was announced, and the following prospectus issued to the astonished public :—

"GRAND EXPOSITION
" OF THE
"SOULS OF ALL NATIONS.

"It being a recognised fact in the present age, that 'the use of language is to disguise thought'—that hypocrisy is the rule, and sincerity the exception—that the expressions of human countenances are as artificial as pasteboard masks—and that no man in his senses believes open candour, in word, look, or deed, to be either rational or politic, we (the committee) have come to the conclusion that to exhibit any amount of human souls in their true character, it is absolutely necessary that the said souls should be deprived of that reasoning faculty which, when they possessed it, was mainly employed for the purpose of abusing the credulity, and misleading the ideas, of their fellow-citizens and acquaintance.

"Before resorting to this extreme measure (of human veracity), the committee were recommended to consider the ancient saying, '*in vino veritas*—in wine, truth '—but though convinced to a great extent of the truth of the saying itself (which probably was originated by Bacchus in the act of rolling under the Olympian mahogany), the committee were dismayed by the prospect of the difficulty and expense of maintaining so large a number of persons as their catalogue contains, exhibited in a permanent state of veracious intoxication. They also dreaded, in thus throwing open the portals of the souls, lest the bodies which they inhabited should suffer by the draught, and the Exposition ultimately become dead drunk—in a sense far more shocking than that ordinarily implied by the phrase.

"The Exposition, therefore, will consist of a choice collection of souls of every class, order, and species, which, unable to vibrate steadily between reason and imagination, have had the misfortune to lose their balance in favour of the latter function. These spirits out of their equilibrium, commonly known as lunatics, from a certain tendency to abandon this miserable earth for its snug little satellite, the moon (supposed to contain less water to damp the spirits than its primary); these eccentric individualities, whose natal stars are comets and other celestial monsters, will offer to intelligent soul-dealers the most admirable opportunities for investigating the value of the invisible merchandise.

"Prizes will be given for the most extraordinary political, social, and scientific madman, in the shape of brazen masks, expressly designed and fabricated for the occasion.

"(Signed) &c. &c. &c."

*　　　*　　　*　　　*　　　*　　　*

The eve of the exhibition arrived; and Darian, with Basiline upon his arm, accompanied by Viridor, Ignatius, all the committee, and an immense number of their personal friends, commenced a tour of inspection, preparatory to the admission of the general public on the following day.

A temporary building of vast extent had been erected, in front of the Duke of Supperland's palace, in St. James's Park. The building was, in form, a huge rotunda, surrounded by wooden columns, which, together with the walls, were so adroitly painted as to represent, even to deception, stone long exposed to the action of the elements. From the simple capitals of these pillars arose a vast dome, surmounted by a colossal bust of Ignatius Loyola Grey, which Darian and Viridor had insisted upon, despite the modest objections of that worthy gentleman, who too soon, in the jealous hatred of his aristocratic and plutocratic allies, reaped the reward of his weakness.

In the interior, there were, circle within circle, rows of square cages, some twenty feet in length by twelve in breadth. Each of these was divided into two compartments—a bedroom, lighted only from above, and a sitting-room open on one side—which was protected by ornamental ironwork, as a wild-beast den by its bars. Each of these cages in the rotunda contained one or more lunatics, of the most varied descriptions. Above each cage was affixed a brief account of its inmate or inmates, and the cages were so arranged, side by side and back to front, that none of their occupants could see or communicate with one another—nor, indeed, had they any suspicion that they formed part of a Grand Exposition ; having been brought blindfold to their present abodes, and being quite unconscious of one another's proximity. The walls facing the cages, which were, in fact, the backs of other similar dwellings, were splendidly tapestried, and the passages between covered by magnificent carpets. The dwellings of the lunatics were

variously furnished, from the height of extravagant
luxury to the depth of most abject simplicity.   Each
lived in a world of his own, an unconscious transcen-
dentalist of the extreme party.   Another cage, another
world.   Let us contemplate a few of these extravagant
microcosms of the age.

CHAPTER VII.

THE GRAND EXPOSITION, WITH A SUPPLEMENT.

EACH of the visitors had in his hand a printed catalogue of the souls exhibited. Brilliant jets of gas illumined the broad passages and successive cages, which rather resembled the stages of a long line of diminutive theatres, than anything else I can think of.

Over the first cage was written, in crimson characters—

AN IRISH LANDLORD.

The interior resembled an apartment of a fashionable hotel in the utmost disorder and confusion. A tall and ghastly figure, in a torn shooting coat, with long, wiry, red whiskers and beard, strode irregularly up and down the apartment.

He appeared utterly unconscious of the presence of strangers, and continued to mutter half audible soliloquies, in a tone that vibrated between the most savage rage and the most overwhelming sentiment of remorse.

" It must be had—*must !*" he murmured, " at all costs, at all hazards. I must write to my agent. Ha! what does he mean by this delay ? Their rents are in in arrear ! Their crops have failed ! The old story. I know better. It is their infernal laziness ! They boil their potatoes, smoke their pipes, and care for nobody

temperament. Ran away at the end of two years with Captain of Infantry. Deserted by Captain, who was involved in debt, and unable to support her. Received into the ———— Asylum on the 14th day of March, 18—."

> " Es ist eine alte Geschichte
> Doch bleibt es ewig neu.
> 'Tis an oft repeated stor),
> And yet for ever new,"

murmured Basiline, as they quitted the distressing spectacle, to gaze upon another victim.

All, save Darian, Viridor, and Ignatius, started, as they read the title of the succeeding compartment—

AN EX-KING.

They beheld an old man with his hair white as the fleecy clouds of summer. His wrinkled visage revealed a dismal history of craft and toilsome cares. He appeared to enjoy a lucid interval—to enjoy, did I say? Alas! the wildest ravings of distracted oblivion were preferable to that old man's dread intervals of consciousness. He regarded the visitors with a sombre gaze of despair, whilst thus addressing them with a forced and hideous calmness—

" Look at me, children of earth, whoever you may be, and learn to profit by my deserved misfortunes! I was a king! I reigned by the choice of a nation, after years of exile and suffering, which did not teach me wisdom! I forgot that every magistrate is the servant of the people,—I forgot the crimes and punishments of my race,—I forgot my debt to the people, my master. I committed treason against my sovereigns,—I became

s

their corrupter and tyrant, who should have been their
benefactor and liberator; and I madly dreamed of opposing the laws of mental progress, and denying the authors
of my existence as a monarch; until one day I heard
the voice of my creator, like Adam after eating the forbidden fruit, and I fled in terror before the face of the
master I had robbed and outraged."

Full of solemn reflections on the sins and penalty of
this ancient man, the visitors continued their way to
discover that the fourth cage enclosed—

A MEDIOCRITY.

This room wore an official aspect. There were papers
tied with red tape, and files of reports and newspapers,
and chairs of impenetrable horsehair, strong in the legs,
and suited to bear the writhings of disappointment and
aggrieved mortality.

A small man, with pinched-up, insignificant features,
sat, with one leg crossed over the other, in an arm-
chair before a writing-table. His countenance yet
preserved an idiotic expression of *finesse*, as he muttered, with a hollow chuckle, " To delay—to say nothing,
with an air of profundity—to sustain hopes, and trust
to what may turn up—to steal the ideas and purchase
the labour of men of talent, behold the art of statesman-
ship summed up in a paragraph. Egad! I must make
some plausible reply to those confounded questions about
Ireland this evening, but as for the measure of Old
Bendigo, it must be suppressed at once. Only let us
push off business to the close of the session, and we shall
have the run of the house, like the younger brother at
his seniors."

Next in order came—

A DEMAGOGUE.

A man with coarse black hair, and a rubicund visage, sprang upon his legs at the appearance of our party, and burst extempore into a flood of oratory.

In a ferocious exordium he denounced everybody, and every party, as monsters of iniquity and far-seeing cruelty. He attributed to the ministry and aristocracy, designs of the most marvellous complication, which none but a madman could have conceived. He denounced the more calm and philosophical democrats, as luke-warm traitors, or "visionary theorists" (the old hackneyed phrase of fools of all parties). He preached the pike, the musket, and the sabre, and immediate insurrection, in spite of all odds against him and his supporters. He asked what they meant by giving the Queen a million a year to spend in sugar-plums? and the Prince Consort another fifty thousand for cigars? As for the national debt, why should the children pay what the fathers borrowed? why should they be taxed and ground to the dust, for the villanies of a man called Pitt, who, luckily for England, was dead and buried long ago. Take a sponge—make a clean wipe of it—and the thing was done. What they wanted was the Charter —no, there were six points—three cheers for every point—Hurrah!"

This man had been imprisoned for sedition, treated as a common felon, and eventually had been driven mad by poverty, and a wild consciousness of his own and the people's wrongs.

Little did he think that in the next apartment was the man to whom he was indebted for all his sufferings.

A GOVERNMENT SPY.

A low-browed, mean-looking creature, was rolling himself in a heap of straw on the floor of his cage. He gnashed his teeth with impotent fury, till the blood-stained foam dropped from the corners of his lips.

"A six months' voyage between me and England—here in the bush—in an Australian desert—with nothing stronger than tea to drink, and oxen for companions! Is this the fine position his pigmy lordship promised? Is this what I have sold myself to Hell for?—made myself a perjured, infamous, scouted wretch, at whose touch even murderers and burglars recoil! How well I recollect the day!—I was an informer before; but at least I had the law on my side. The peeler in plain clothes—he looked more of a gentleman, by G—, than Twaddle himself—took me to a house—I forget the street—we went in a cab. How polite the little Satan was! It was, 'Take a seat, Gruel,'—'don't be alarmed, Gruel,'—'a glass of wine, Gruel?' And how he lured me on, and twisted my thoughts inside out, and half made me believe that to be a lying, traitorous, heartless scoundrel, was next door to serving one's country, and getting statues on arches, like the Duke of Wellington! Oh, how his slippery gammon sickens me to think of, and to remember how I went among the poor, discontented fools, who waste their time in grumbling, instead of shooting down their rich, coldblooded tyrants, and firing their d——d houses! how I swore brotherhood with them, and encouraged them to talk treason over their beer, and to trust me with their papers, and——and all to get up in a box to swear black was white, to get them locked up and transported, killed off on the sly, for anything *I* know. I recollect how my head spun round, and my knees knocked together, as a prisoner came up, as quiet and easy as if he had been the judge himself, and looked at me. O God! shall I ever forget those looks of cold contempt and wondering pity. *They* did'nt care, they believed, at any rate, that they were right at bottom, and their friends called them martyrs. But I—I am branded, like Cain, with everlasting infamy. Go where I will, I dread recognition. And they have not even kept faith with me. They have sent me here, with a miserable hundred pounds in my pocket, and left me to get on as I can. How *can* I live in this quiet, country solitude? I, who have the memories of so many villanous lies, ingratitudes, and cowardly treacheries upon my conscience? I wish I had that little lordship by the throat—thus, thus—" and the poor wretch twisted a whisp of straw with furious excitement. "Die, die, dog of a lord," he yelled, " die, and let your knavish judges, who have no ears for the poor man, condemn me —ha! ha!—on my own oath—ha! ha! I have sworn to stronger things—die! die!" and the voice of the miserable *ci-devant* informer lapsed into inarticulate howlings, and threats of diabolical vengeance.

"He strangles the poor minister twenty times a day," said Viridor, "it would be an evil hour for the latter, if his cast-away tool were to break loose and encounter him alone!"

"It would perhaps be of more consequence to Twaddle,

than to the rest of the world," said Darian, with unusual bitterness. "A slippery, prevaricating, faithless chameleon of a Whig, is an object of far greater abhorrence to a Fire-worshipper, than the most obstinate Tory, or even the most rabid ecclesiastical bigot."

The horrified company passed on. They beheld in turn

A MAN OF FASHION.

Self love and vanity, excited to a fearful degree of sensitive suspicion, had turned his brain. He still amused himself with his toilette, and strutted, peacock-like, about his cage, despising mankind, as of old, without suspecting for an instant that two-thirds of them, in all probability, returned the compliment.

A JOURNALIST AND A BARRISTER,

Both driven mad by the confusion of their ideas, and their unprincipled mode of using them. The one had written, and the other had pleaded, half his life-time, in diametrical opposition to his real convictions, which, during the other moiety of his career, he had defended with consummate talent. At length they had both lost their hold on truth and moral certainty, and from many-headed monsters, degenerated into chaotic mysteries.

A SPECULATOR,

Who had robbed mankind without scruple—a sort of ex-king in miniature, who had become melancholy mad, from the utter want of social enjoyment, after being cut by all the world, on the detection of his frauds.

A RELIGIOUS FANATIC,

Whose soul was haunted by a phantom, which the poor idiot mistook for a God, and whose occupation, in the maniac's belief, was to make the creatures he had created utterly miserable on earth, and burn them after death to all eternity, if they did not thank him for their misery.

AN ARTIST,

The greatness of whose ideas necessitated canvasses fifteen feet by twelve, and figures eight feet high. He could not be persuaded that high art could exist without gigantic paintings. Moreover, he had a passion for painting very muscular men, and voluptuous-looking females, in a costume not recognised as presentable, save in the South Sea Islands. The greatness of his pictures, if not of his ideas, was the cause of his ruin. English architecture did not produce rooms large enough for his productions, and the state did not provide a national gallery for modern art. Thus he came to be exhibited in the Grand Exposition of All Nations, and drew charcoal cartoons upon the walls of his apartment.

A TOADY,

Who had so long flattered the whims of others, and sacrificed his own opinions to his patrons', that he had gone out of his mind altogether, and lost all consciousness of individual identity.

A DOCTOR,

Who had become *non compos mentis* from the number of patients he had dismissed to the shades in a long course of experiments upon the mysteries of man's bodily organisation. The dread of having poisoned an old lady by an extra dose of hydrocianic acid, and a coroner's inquest, destroyed what little sanity he had ever possessed.

A DRUNKARD,

Who had accustomed himself to drown his thoughts in wine so effectually, that no humane society could now recover them.

A POET,

Who had begun by adoring Tennyson, and ended by writing insane poems in an unknown tongue, formed of all the obsolete words in the dictionary, and complicated by so sublime a system of involution, that no mortal intellect but his own could unravel their mysteries. The world did not understand him. He did not awake and find himself famous, though he impoverished a poor and devoted mother to print his dismal lucubrations, whose utter failure brought him to his present climax. He amused himself by abusing the world in verse, for which he had abundant leisure.

A SOCIALIST PHILOSOPHER,

Who had taught despotism under the name of "Liberty, Equality, and Fraternity." Despairing of reducing society to a machine, and man to a numeral, he fell into a state of fanatic delirium, which qualified him for the Grand Exposition of all Nations.

These were a few of the vast gallery of souls, which had destroyed the fine balance of their nervous organs, by the violence of their passions or conceptions. At what vast expense and trouble they had been collected, it is of little import to narrate. Enough, that no phase of moral or intellectual aberration was without its representative in that marvellous and unexampled exhibition.

As for the virtuous and lofty intelligences, I must refer the reader to *the catalogue*, which may be seen at the British Museum, as soon as a certain *other* catalogue be printed for the information of the public.

*　　*　　*　　*　　*　　*

It was long past midnight, as Viridor descended from a cab at the gate of the Temple, and, thoroughly exhausted by the fatigues of the day and the excitement of the evening, hastened, on entering his chambers, to undress himself and prepare for repose.

Suddenly the appearance of his table struck him as changed from the condition in which he had left it. A quarto Viridor had been reading before leaving his chambers was open at a different page from that he had consulted. Although this circumstance might have arisen from his accidentally turning over a few pages, or even a draught of air in opening the door, it was sufficient to arouse all his old suspicions as to intrusion, during his absence, into his apartments.

Now, so far as Viridor knew, there was but one key to the door of his castle—for a man's chambers, if not his house, *are* his castle in England—and that key, Viridor had, as usual, carried with him in his pocket.

" I am afraid that old woman is a hypocrite after all," muttered the poet, " and yet I cannot help having faith in her round, honest, good-tempered face. Pshaw ! when once a man gets a fixed idea into his head—now

I could have sworn that I left that cupboard closed when I went out. No matter, I will try an experiment to-morrow, which will decide the question. I have not missed anything as yet. There is my purse, which I forgot to take with me, safe and untouched. No, it must be a mere fancy that haunts me. Last night, I thought I heard a noise, as of some animal breathing. It is very strange, and reminds me of some of the anecdotes of Burns' Anatomy of Sleep."

Thus meditating, Viridor entered his bed-room, placed the candle and lucifers, according to his custom, on a small table at his bed-side, and having completed his toilette for the night, betook himself to immediate repose.

Lying upon his right side, with his head supported on his hand, the young poet for some moments reflected on the strange Exposition which was to-morrow to be thrown open to the eagerly expectant metropolis—crowded, in consequence, with strangers from every state of the continent, the American republics, and even Egypt, Syria, and Persia.

During these reflections he pictured, with that involuntary play of fancy peculiar to excited nervous organisations, a variety of grotesque designs on the panels of the apartment—which latter was large, bare, and old-fashioned in its decorations. At length, extinguishing the candle, he turned round and endeavoured to compose himself to sleep.

Some considerable time elapsed, and distant clocks struck quarters, and halves, and three-quarters, and still Viridor lay awake, and planned, and turned, and combined, and changed his position, until, in the utter silence of the night, or rather of the morning, which began to break through the window-blinds faintly, as a beauty's smile upon a rival's triumph, Viridor distinctly heard the breathing which he had alluded to in his soliloquy, and which apparently proceeded from some place in the immediate vicinity.

Viridor rose, lighted the candle, and drawing part of the bed-clothes after him in his haste, by way of a robe, hastily examined every corner of both sitting-room and bed-room, first looking beneath the bed, which, indeed, was not a very probable locality, as, however deceptive sound may be, he could hardly have failed to detect so near a disturbance.

No place now remained unsearched but a large lumber-closet in the bed-room, which Viridor had not at first thought of searching, as, owing to its dilapidated condition, it had been, and still appeared to be, nailed up outside in a way that rendered it impossible of entry, without removing the nails.

But on minute inspection, Viridor discovered that several of the nails were missing, and that the others did not necessarily bite the interior woodwork.

The breathing had ceased, but nevertheless Viridor felt convinced that he was on the verge of some strange discovery. Such presentiments rarely deceive. He tore open the door, which offered no resistance, as he had anticipated, and entering the closet, which was of considerable size, he held up the flickering light, and cast a searching glance into the darkness before him.

Scarcely had he done so, than an object, which at first sight he mistook for a bundle of old clothes on the floor, started up, and displayed to his astonished gaze the

figure of a man, so ragged, so emaciated, and so wild
in its aspect, that he half mistook it for a spectre of
his own diseased imagination. Of a surety, no lunatic
exhibited in the Grand Exposition he had that evening
visited, could compete in horror with the wretch who
now confronted his gaze.

Viridor started back in horror, as the blood-shot eyes
of his unbidden guest glared upon him with a look which
his then tone of mind naturally interpreted as insanity.

"Who and what are you?" said the poet, sternly
motioning to the man to emerge from his place of con-
cealment.

"The most unfortunate of men," replied the ragged
stranger; "but I swear to you by my soul, that I came
not here to rob or injure you. Let me depart in peace,
my sufferings will soon be over."

For an instant Viridor, fatigued and irritated, was
about to give way to the suspicions natural under such
circumstances, and to rid himself of his unseemly visitor
as speedily as might be, leaving the secret of his entry,
whether by false key or unknown door, for after investigation.

But the sound of the stranger's voice, which was full of
unutterable sadness,—the study of his features, which
Viridor now observed to be of a singularly intellectual
cast,—above all, his own gentle heart, almost girlish in
its susceptibility, checked the unworthy impulse, and
caused him to assume a less severe aspect, as he briefly
demanded from the tenant of the closet an explanation
of his unaccountable conduct.

"Sir," replied the stranger, "I know you too well to
fear that you would seek to molest me for what I have

done, however dishonest or criminal it may appear in the eyes of vulgar persons. It is not very long since I tenanted these very chambers, like yourself. Unexpected misfortunes plunged me into utter poverty. I had no friends or relations to assist me, for I was left an orphan in my youth, and have never cultivated the acquaintance of men or women.

" My furniture was seized for rent, I was absolutely without resources at fifty years of age, and without possessing a single talent or science, by which I could earn a living. I had no choice but between starvation and beggary, when it suddenly occurred to me, that I had the key of my old chambers in my pocket.

" Impelled by I know not what design, I hovered about the house until I discovered that you were the new tenant. I then watched you out, and having seen you enter an omnibus for Kensington, I returned, and once more entered my old habitation.

" At first I merely intended to take a farewell look at my old apartments, dear to me from the many years I had occupied them. But happening to see some pages of manuscript lying on your table, I could not resist the temptation of trying to learn what sort of a man had become my substitute. The first words I read were these—I have repeated them so often that I cannot be mistaken in their tenor—' Life is more sacred than property. If society deny a man bread, society commands him to be a robber, for the law forbids suicide, and to rob a man of his property is a less crime than to rob him of his life. Therefore let the law deal more justly with those debtors and robbers, who, by poverty alone, are driven to such desperate resources.'

T

"It appeared to be a translation from an old Latin author, and was followed by annotations of your own, which deeply impressed me with respect for the benevolence and uprightness of your character.

"Seeing a loaf of bread upon the side-table, I proceeded to carry out the principles of the manuscript, by cutting a small piece in such a manner as to leave the loaf in appearance little changed, and—pardon my shameless audacity—from that time, now many weeks ago, I have, day after day, repeated my visits; feeding on the remnants of your breakfast, or robbing you of small slices of bread, cut in the same cunning manner; and amusing myself with the study of your books and manuscript, which I always endeavoured to replace with the nicest exactness. Often you were absent for whole days from the chambers, and I was left without food, or scarcely daring to touch what remained, for fear of exciting suspicion.

"At night, having no means of obtaining a lodging, I slept in the open air, under arch-ways, or other miserable shelter, until I found means to open that cupboard, which is, as you will observe, ventilated by a small opening near the ceiling; from that time I have been in the habit of listening for your footsteps (which I can distinguish from all others at the first sound of your tread), and then hastily creeping into my hiding-place, where I slept or meditated in silence, until I heard you again descend the staircase, and found myself at liberty to emerge from my confinement.

"And now farewell! do not regret that the crumbs from your table have fed a victim of the world's ignorance. I have lived too long to dream of human actions coinciding with human words. Nevertheless, go on as you have begun, preach justice, and when you have the power, practice charity."

So saying, the old man, placing the key—which was the key to the whole adventure—in the hands of his involuntary host, passed through the door with abrupt rapidity, leaving Viridor speechless with emotion at the recital of misery so abject. He was aroused from his reverie by the noise of a window-sash thrown violently open. He placed the candle on the ground, rushed into the adjoining room, and was barely in time to grasp the arm of the stranger, who strove desperately to throw himself headlong upon the sharp stones of the court below.

But though encumbered with the blankets, which left him one hand only at liberty, Viridor's youthful vigour was not to be resisted by the enfeebled frame of the stranger.

"Promise me not to make any new attempt upon your life, and I promise you, on my part, all the assistance you require," said the Grand Master of the Illuminati, with assuring kindness. "Oh, man of little faith! did you, then, ransack the repositories of my most secret thoughts, and yet doubt the unity of my doctrine with my life? Why did you not come to me, and tell me frankly your wants and sufferings? Each can but remedy the immediate suffering he encounters. Whatever my other errors, I have never allowed any motive, save imperative duty, to interfere with my sense of justice to the poor. For know, my friend, that to a philosophic mind, the duties of property, however limited, or extended, are its noblest rights. Base, indeed, in my eyes, is the man who, possessing a solitary loaf, allows his brother man to hunger at his side ! There will come a day when churches will be fewer, whilst school-houses are more abundant; when the cold charity of pseudo-Christians will be replaced by the living charity of their Master; when the heart will be thought worth educating as well as the head; and it will be no more to ask a passing stranger for a meal than for a direction to a street. Meanwhile, consider yourself my welcome guest. Repose upon that sofa for the night. To-morrow, you can, if it please you, inform me of the causes that have led to misfortunes which, until the contrary appear, I shall continue to believe unmerited."

The stranger pressed Viridor's hand between both his own, with a half incredulous gaze of delighted gratitude.

" O, my generous friend !" he exclaimed, " why did I doubt your greatness ? Life is indeed to me a burthen, yet I will live in the hope of proving to you my gratitude and my devotion."

It was already daylight, and the candle flickered with a pale and feeble light, as Viridor once more devoted himself to repose.

All slept in the great City of Jugglers, but it was the calm that foreboded the tempest.

END OF BOOK II.

BOOK III.

THE

PANIC IN THE SOUL MARKET.

CHAPTER I.

THE GIANT'S SHADOW.

A THINKING soul, owner of a leasehold property in an organic tenement of flesh, would as vainly strive to measure its relations to external entities, as to calculate the limit of a decimal repetend, or the varieties of combined forms and colors that may be produced by a kaleidoscope.

Every living spirit, like a celestial sun-god, emits in every direction, the radiating influence of its immeasurable power, and is finite only by comparison with a vaster Infinite.

This work,—this volcanic eruption of my soul, speech in the spiritual parliament of thought, sarcastic *repartee* to liars social, liars political, liars dialectic, analytic, and synthetic,—this mythical history, magnetic revelation, dream of poetic vanity, incomprehensible cartoon, or whatever else it turn out to be in the eyes of men or angels,—in a word, this volume, bound and illustrated, and to be had at circulating libraries, is now drawing to a rapid and inevitable conclusion.

My intercourse with you, my spirit-friends, must be interrupted. "I must pause for a reply;" and with so much unsaid, so little said, of the fiery-thought element which has swept me, as in a whirlwind, into publicity, I must await the cold judgment of the indifferent, the sharp invective of the hostile, and the rare praise of the sympathising reader. I must be patient—patient with the reflection that time, space, and I know not what other causes, have stood between me and the perfect realisation of my object. I have recorded the suggestions for measures which I was forbidden to develope in detail, though prepared and eager for the task; I have risked incurring the stigma of superficiality, for fear of being condemned as wearisome and pedantic, and in the dread of losing a season and an opportunity, for which I have so long sighed, I have written in a few weeks the history of spiritual combinations, which years of study have prepared, and at least as many months of artistic effort should have given form to.

Not that I demand indulgence from my political antagonists. Let them do their worst; I defy their enmity. It is from those only whose hearts beat in harmony with my own,—whose love for the people, and resolution to aid their progress from barbarism and misery, to civilisation and happiness, cause them to dread even an imperfect advocacy of their principles,—that I request consideration for having so rudely fulfilled a task which no other man has had the audacity to attempt.

Let the Viridors, and Darians, and Basilines of the age awake from their inactivity. I am but the sentinel of the night whose trumpet heralds the morning.

Yet, to resume the train of ideas with which this chapter began, how can the thinker, who once casts his treasures, real or fancied, into the gulph of print, that best telegraph of mind, how can he fix the circle of his readers, or say to what remote climes the commerce of the world may not bear his ghostly merchandize?

Who knows what Indian or Chinese philosopher, ambassador from Nepaul, or advanced Otaheitan speculator, may puzzle himself over this eccentric history?

I feel it truly difficult to convey to such remote intelligences, any adequate notion of the pitch to which Soul-dealing, and other similar speculations, had arrived in this metropolis, *par excellence* of jugglers!

Not only were Soul-agency offices multiplied, and soul-lists published, as described in the moneyarticles of the daily press, but the most singular schemes were started cotemporaneously, with a view to taking advantage of the public *cacoethes* of gambling.

One set of ingenious rascals had started an office as agents to all kings in Europe for the sale of titles. Patents of nobility were growing as common, and about as valuable, as protested bills in the market. Pedigrees were to be had with them, if required; and men sold their ancestors, and proclaimed themselves bastards, with the same coolness shewn in saddling their children with debt, to relieve themselves from taxation.

Even reputations were sold, and realised by advertisement. Blockheads, who never had an idea in their life, became known as poets of celebrity. Misers, who never gave anything but their names to a charity, were lauded, in all corners of the land, as noble-hearted philanthrophists. Statesmen, whose rental or family connexions had alone given them a chance of power, were credited with *bon mots* and sayings, which the seven wise Greeks might have envied.

But it was all a branch of the great soul-dealing system, and Ignatius Loyola Grey was unquestionably, at the moment, *the* man of his age. Unfortunately for him the age was on its last legs—and those were un-commonly black ones.

There was one good effect resulting from the soul-dealing mania, which has been already hinted at. It led people to think a little about their own spiritual natures. Psychology became a fashionable study, and Metapyhsics and Ontology were consequently much more generally patronised than of old. The sneerers at " philosophic mysticism, and all that sort of thing," disappeared daily. Academic retreats were founded. Neo-platonists had their lectures and meetings at one hall—Epicureans at another. The Pythagoreans, the Brahmins, the Con-fucians, were well-known philosophical debating clubs. Strange to say, Scepticism absolute was quite at a dis-count. The general rage was for knowledge, and what could be known by men who denied the existence of knowledge? In short, the general tendency of the age was decidedly towards intellectual development, at the moment that moral principle was at the lowest ebb in the country.

The cheap literature of the hour was marvellously changed, since Mysteries of London, and similar ultra-romantic productions, were the order of the day. An edition of Berkeley, in penny numbers, Kant's "Critique of Pure Reason," Hegel's "Logic" for the Million, and a cheap volume of Spinoza, had a prodigious sale. Swedenborg's visions were published in the "Parlour Library of Instruction," and a new system of Anthropology was continued through infinite numbers of the *Familiar Herald*, by the Editor, who was strongly suspected of some connexion with the Illuminati.

Darian, Viridor, and their united band of democrats,

watched every movement of the popular mind with intense interest. They knew that a terrible explosion was at hand, and prepared to ride upon the wave, which could not fail to overwhelm their blinded and unteachable antagonists.

Hollow murmurs of discontent already rolled sullenly over the surface of the country. With the exception of the great capitalists and landlords (a small band of huge harpies, who sit at all England's feasts, and taint, by their touch, the little remnants of the viands which they leave us), every class of society was involved in the most pitiful difficulty. There was no lack of enterprise or labour, and an actual plethora of capital, and yet everybody was embarrassed for money to meet his liabilities. The truth was that a set of ministers, utterly unequal to their solemn duties, had, from incapacity to understand, and want of energy to investigate, the nature of commerce, entirely neglected to make any provision for an adequate circulating medium; without which, a trading country cannot advance one step on the road of improvement.

To understand the currency question, requires a certain mathematical and philosophical genius. To discuss it radically, in the present work, is impossible. I shall therefore merely offer a few remarks, intelligible to a child, and perhaps, therefore, to a Lord John Twaddle and his followers.

In the first place, the inconvenience of everybody being in debt to everybody, and the trouble and complication introduced into trade by the utter impossibility of any approximation to a direct system of exchange on a cash basis, is too obvious to be disputed.

Secondly, nobody can for an instant deny the convenience of an abundant paper currency, representing solid capital ; or that the only objection to its adoption, is the danger of depreciation in value.

Thirdly, it is well known that the example of the French assignats (of which I have a dozen in my portfolio) is the great historical argument against paper money.

Fourthly, it is perfectly clear that that objection is utterly futile, applied to a country possessing institutions and credit such as those of England, where no anarchical or violent revolution is at all to be apprehended, unless the monopolists of political power become much madder than they are, which is an almost inconceivable prospect.

Fifthly, it is palpable that notes issued on the security of land, and payable as taxes, government salaries, &c., *cannot* sensibly depreciate, so long as the State itself do not become bankrupt.

I leave these suggestions to the consideration of political economists, bankers, merchants, and others, who ought to understand the matter, and revert to the thread of my narrative, with an apology for obtruding so dry a subject on my lady readers.

The discontent of the working classes arose partly from the difficulty of obtaining employment, owing greatly to the above embarrassment of their employers ; partly to a strong sense of long-inflicted injustice in depriving them of all voice in their own government, oppressing them with a most unequal share of taxes, and apathetically neglecting in legislation so many means of ameliorating and elevating their condition. These, they themselves began to discuss with a clearness, that proved them well worthy of the franchise, they at length demanded, in a voice, not to be stifled by gagging bills, suspended habeas corpus acts, or artificial temptations to riot and treason, constables' staves, soldiers' bayonets, or any other contemptible trickery of their rulers.

" Universal suffrage !" was their cry. " Mind before matter ! Reason above property ! The rights of nature above the usurped privileges of class ! Let the same justice annihilate the baron and the serf! Let us have no hereditary sages or idiots—no more cant about a stake in the country, when every man, with a soul to suffer and enjoy, is equally interested in the prosperity of his Fatherland ! We are all peers before God ! Let us abolish all Indo-Egyptian tradition of caste ! Let every man count as a man, and let the best man be the man to govern us ! "

Such was the cry of the people, which caused the House of Lords to tremble to its basis, and all Downing Street to turn pale with terror.

But a new impulse was about to be given to the movement.

The Grand Exposition of the Souls of all Nations had been opened. Thousands had visited it,—thousands had pondered in awe upon the irresistible conclusions it suggested. A great moral shock was given to the conscience of the age. Souls fell in the share-market, and a circumstance which just then occurred tended yet more strongly to arouse and stimulate the general popular excitement.

Entering the House of Peers in his ducal robes, with his coronet upon his head, Arthur Bolingbroke Darian, called Duke of St. George, deliberately proclaimed his resolution of renouncing for ever his title, his peerage,

U

and all its privileges.   Amid the dismayed looks of his colleagues, he cast his coronet to the ground, trampled upon it with contempt, and quitted the hall of legislators, amid a silence more ominous than the most stormy disapprobation.

The pale nobles looked at one another, like mariners expectant of shipwreck; and cold drops of perspiration oozed from beneath the wig of the chancellor.   The bishops were the first to recover themselves, and their anathemas were truly episcopal in their ferocity.

The people literally roared with exultation at this heroic initiation of their triumph; and the book of Viridor, which appeared on the following day, conspired to render the agitation yet more formidable to the aristocratic and plutocratic councils.

Viridor's book? what was it?—I will tell you. It was, to this present volume, what the sun is to a common gas lamp.   It said all that I have vainly striven to say; its sale was measured by tens of thousands, and its effects by—The Future.

So far is the ideal of the poet above the reality of the writer.

At the same time the whole Soul-Exchange was revolutionised by a placard posted on the base of Lord John Twaddle's brazen statue in the centre—

There   are   but   two   classes   of   Soul-Dealers— DUPES and SWINDLERS.

CHAPTER II.

A NON-POLITICAL PARTY.

IT is rather tantalising, at the close of an entertainment, to be introduced to a lovely girl one would wish to see a great deal of. Nevertheless, reader, I shall stand on no ceremony in introducing you, at this late chapter of my story, to Genevra Darian, the beautiful sister of the ex-ducal republican.

The day after Darian's resignation of his peerage, and Viridor's publication of his book, this charming lady issued invitations to about five hundred people for a grand democratic fête, for which preparations of unusual splendour were hinted at.

The eyes of all England, I might say Europe, were fixed upon the leaders of the Fire-worshippers, whose names were in everybody's mouth, and whose intentions were the subject of almost universal discussion.

It is not, therefore, to be wondered at, that the announcement of Genevra's fête caused intense excitement in every circle of the capital.

When the evening arrived the guests arrived also, with a punctuality which curiosity alone could have effected. Never before in ducal palace were assembled so heterogeneous a company. It is true that, at first glance, black coats, white linen, and shining boots, and varied dresses of silk, satin, and muslin were visible, much after the usual fashion. But on arriving at the grand suite of drawing-rooms, a transparency above the portal caused every guest to pause for an instant in admiration at the Dantesque inscription which its flaming characters presented :—

"YE WHO ENTER HERE LEAVE PREJUDICE BEHIND."

It was, indeed, necessary to do so ; for whether your next neighbour might be a marquis or a grocer, a man of letters or a mechanic, it was impossible to guess. Immense exertions had been made by Viridor, Darian, and their friends, to collect worthy representatives of every class, profession, trade, and calling in the metropolis.

Two or three brainless puppies of the " snob " genus, guardsmen, barristers, and clerical prigs, having posted themselves in a corner, amused their emptinesses by quizzically guessing at the position of their neighbours. Overhearing a venerable-looking old gentleman in spectacles discoursing on electricity, with a young man of remarkably graceful bearing, they set him down at once as the Secretary of the Royal Society, when, in fact, he was a respectable watchmaker from the city. The young man they determined to be a "counter-jumper." He proved to be the son of one of the oldest baronets in the kingdom.

A young lady whose air they considered as proof conclusive of high birth and breeding, turned out to be the daughter of a tailor, and an old woman they condemned as a vulgar cheesemonger's wife, proved a dowager marchioness before the evening was over.

A youth, with long hair, who was unmistakeably a painter, was found to be a medical student, and a prim-looking man, with a rather severe countenance, whom they stigmatised as an attorney's clerk, was, in reality an artist of considerable celebrity.

So variee were the elements of which Genevra's party consisted!

Nevertheless, everywhere reigned politeness and hilarity. The guests, whatever their station in life, felt bound to do their best to be agreeable. All conversed freely without introduction, and on every side were gay and animated groups. Nor did the daughters of the people, in their simple white muslin dresses, and flowers or ribbons tastefully arranged, yield in beauty to the proud ladies of the exclusive world, in their rustling satins and gaudy jewellery. With few exceptions, the members of less refined circles restrain their natural freedom to accord with the manners of their so-called superiors; whilst the latter adopted much of the unsophisticated ease which soon ceased to displease them in their new associates.

If the fashionable girls were amused by the timid admiration and exaggerated civility of their plebeian partners, the fair daughters of the trader and the mechanic were not the less disposed to smile at the *nonchalant* affectation of the sublime dandies.

As for the older men, it was wonderful how pleasantly they entered into conversation, with the most perfect ignorance of whom they were talking to.

Basiline, who had discarded her masculine attire, assisted Genevra to receive her motley guests, clad in a plain white robe of studied simplicity. A single white rose in her dark lustrous hair was her only ornament.

Genevra bore a great resemblance to Darian; also, in some degree, to Basiline; but her hair was of a deep chesnut colour, and her eyes much darker than even her brother's, or the Magyar's. Her form was perhaps a shade too slender for classic outline, but her look and smile were such as few could have resisted.

A little before supper, Viridor approached these two flowers of beauty, who, surrounded by a circle of admirers, were seated together on an ottoman in the farthest *salon*, and presented to them an old gentleman of deeply-interesting aspect. His brow was one of singular expanse, and an appearance of severe ill-health added greatly to the interest of his appearance.

"Who is he?" said Basiline, rising, and taking Viridor's arm, whilst the old gentleman remained amid the crowd in conversation with Genevra. "I am sure that there is something strange in the history of your friend, by his looks and manner; pray gratify my woman's curiosity?"

"I am glad you condescend to own yourself a woman, for the sake of my friend Darian," replied Viridor, gaily. "As for the old man you have seen, his story is soon told. Having been left an orphan at an early age, with a small fortune, he devoted himself to the profoundest study of the natural sciences, with a view solely to making discoveries and inventions, calculated to benefit mankind. He has spent his whole substance in experiments and models; and has really contrived some extraordinary machines for lessening human labour, and performing operations hitherto tedious and expensive, in the simplest and most economical manner. His great idea is, that the world is to be regenerated by mechanical contrivances, and chemical and electric agencies. For more than twenty years of gross neglect, and too often grosser injustice, on the part of those, whose assistance he claimed, he has struggled nobly to carry out, and perfect his inventions. His unpublished treatises are of a most valuable character, especially one entitled "The Philosophy of Motion," which I have placed already in the hands of a printer on my own hazard. Some of his sanitary contrivances are especially suited for practical adoption. Taken altogether, he is a man of genius, and a representative spirit of his age. He may yet live to achieve the most brilliant reputation."

It was the strange guest of Viridor's chambers, whose history he thus briefly indicated. The misfortunes of the stranger are not without parallels in the memory of many of my readers.

At this moment there was a general move towards the supper-room, which had been constructed temporarily in the garden, to accommodate the whole company in the most luxurious manner.

" I shall grow jealous if you have so many *tête-a-têtes*," said Darian, smiling, as he suddenly appeared before Viridor and Basiline, and drew the arm of the latter through his own, whilst he pressed her hand with lover-like intelligence.

" I will soon relieve you of your doubts," rejoined Viridor, with a mysterious significance, and disappearing in the crowd, he returned in a few minutes with a young creature, of such dream-like beauty, on his arm, that both Darian and Basiline started in amazement. They had, strangely enough for people of their penetrating minds, given Viridor credit for utter absorption in his political aims, and indifference to all the sweets of sexual sympathy. They little dreamed that love was the only

passion to which Viridor was capable of sacrificing—
even—well, it must be written, for I scorn to overrate
the virtues of my dearest friends—even his country.

Luckily, Grace demanded no such sacrifice.

" What an angelic countenance!" whispered Basiline
to Darian.

" How very, very beautiful she is!" said Grace Morton
to Viridor.

And they passed on to the supper-room.

CHAPTER III.

THE STRIKE OF THE PRESS.

" Vox populi, vox Dei."

THE sun rose on the morrow of the Lady Genevra Darian's party ; it pursued its westerly course,—it paused in the zenith, and the whole City of Jugglers appeared yet to sleep, so great was their amazement.

Not one morning paper had appeared.

Had the world reached its final moment ? Was the trumpet of the resurrection about to sound ?

The juggler citizens were seized by sudden qualms of conscience. They deserted their places of business,— haunts of pleasure,—or late breakfast tables, and hovered anxiously about the offices of the absent journals. All was dismay and confusion in those centres of intelligence. To all its inquiries, the public received vague and unsatisfactory replies, and looks of consternation equal to their own. The life of the great city appeared to stagnate,—its blood to cease flowing—its heart to pulsate feebly, as a dying man's. What could this awful silence mean ? Where were the stinging, the indignant, the thundering leaders ?—where were the last night's debates ? — where were the "foreign correspondent's articles," the "state of Europe," the "latest news from France, by electric telegraph ?" where even the account of the Lady Genevra's party, which everybody was eager to read ?

All was silent. The *Timeserver*, the *Morning Ghost*, the *Cobbler*, the *Humbug*, the *Staggerer*, even the *Daily Nous* gave no signs of vitality.

The streets near their offices were crowded with wondering citizens. With a dire presentiment of some hideous catastrophe, they gazed in one another's pale faces, and suggested that, after all, a journal, despite its regal assumption of the *we*, and sustained semblance of personal identity, was neither an animal, nor a machine. They reflected that it must be printed by printers, and edited by editors; that reporters must report, and translators translate; and in fine, many real, living, two-legged mammals, of the order *bimana, genus homo,* be employed in its production.

Where, then, *were* these workmen of the hand and head, and why was not their work done that day?

The compositors were there, and the pressmen, and the printers' devils; but the writers, where were they? Echo answered " where?"

At last the truth became known, and oozed out to the public. The journalists of all grades, editors, sub-editors, compilers, financiers, reporters, and even penny-a-liners, had broken out into open rebellion against their tyrants.

THEY HAD STRUCK FOR FAME.

The capitalists, proprietors of the journals, were in a state of fury and despair. Literature had asserted its dignity. No literary man would be the puppet of a stupider man than himself any longer. Either they would sign their names to all they wrote, and write their real convictions in all they signed, or—no more " copy " from them for organs soon to become organs of public opinion, as they had hitherto been expressions of private interests.

In vain the despairing capitalists offered increased salaries, diminished labour, luxurious accommodations, alternate relief from night-work, and whatever other temptations they could devise—the journalists gave but one answer :—

" Our names to our articles, the position in society to which our respective talents entitle us, the political independence and influence which our reputation must secure us. Keep your gold, squeeze more from our brains, if it please you, but leave us our dignity as men. We will be vague phantoms and blind instruments no longer. We are sick of the masks we have worn so long, we are sick of falling into old age and decrepitude unknown and unhonoured. We are weary of seeing our inferiors in the lighter walks of literature gain fame and money by a few trifling efforts ; whilst we, who grapple daily with the toughest questions of the age, may at any moment be cast aside like worn-out gloves, by our masters ; and in case of distress have not even a claim upon that last of all resources to literary desperation."*

---

* The Literary Fund assists only the authors of books. To avoid all misconstruction, I here take the liberty of stating, that deeply as I sympathise with and honour journalism. as the great lever of progress, I never yet had any connexion whatever with any newspaper. Profoundly reflecting for many years on the nature of journalism, I am now firmly persuaded that the anonymous system is utterly unworthy of an age of enlightenment and honesty. What weight has anonymous writing with any sensible person? None. It protects falsehood, cowardice, and ignoble ideas ; as for its protecting the journalist, as a man, against personal attacks, if he write truth, he requires no such protection. When, even as a boy, I wrote my burlesque of the Young England folly, I gave my publisher strict orders

It may readily be imagined that Darian and Viridor were at the bottom of this glorious conspiracy of talent against capital. It was at Genevra's party that the plot had been thoroughly developed. Not a little had the eloquent look of their hostess, and Basiline, and even Grace, who had learned to impassion herself for all Viridor's aims, contributed to decide the future representatives of the people, in favour of the bold course they adopted. Viridor proved to them how glorious would be their position, if once they would assert their individual dignity as thinkers ; and Darian entreated them to lay aside all pecuniary apprehensions ; as he was prepared to advance any sums, to start journals of their own upon the new system, which might be requisite.

The soldiers of the press, seeing suddenly opened before them, a vista of honourable ambition, which led to the highest offices in the state, parted in high spirits from their entertainers, at an early hour, in a large number of vehicles, expressly provided, for Richmond. There, giving themselves up to festivity, they awaited, in passive strength, the submission of their quondam masters.

The *Timeserver* alone, by its immensely extended resources, contrived to replace the whole of its staff, in

to give my name and address to all enquirers; and at the house of Mr. M—— G——n, the member for M——r, I caused myself to be pointed out to the Young England leader, that he might have every opportunity of demanding satisfaction of any kind he pleased. I look upon a blow as a barbarism, and a duel as insanity ; but of all vices cowardice is the meanest and most contemptible I can imagine. Sir Edward Bulwer Lytton, in his " England and the English," long a 1 denounced the anonymous system. I will never cease to denounce it, whilst I can find a publisher, or pay a printer, to give my thoughts to the public.

time to appear on the morning following the catastrophe.

All the other journals were revolutionized, and, what was most extraordinary, turned out to be all advocates of the liberal interest, so soon as the writers, by appending their signatures, became impressed with the solemn responsibility of their duties to their fellow men.

But it was not long before Viridor and Darian started, themselves, a new journal, to which almost every author of talent and celebrity contributed, and before which even the sale of the leviathan *Timeserver* began gradually to diminish.

It was evident now, that the great political battle was to be fought between the House of Commons and the Press; it was also a matter of easy prophecy, that the Press would soon be the victor in the struggle. For the Press was the voice and parliament of the whole people, and the House of Commons was but the complot of a fractional part of the community, to retain all power in their own hands.

The Press, too, was becoming daily more united, whilst the Commons became hourly more divided—and a house divided against itself cannot stand; neither can Satan; and what is the peerage but a satanic delusion, soon to be dissipated by the breath of liberty and reason?

Lord John Twaddle now shuddered at the very names of Darian and Viridor; the sight of Cordian, Viziers, or Might, the free-traders, and the manly tone of their voices, made his heart turn sick with despair. Robert the Devil had withdrawn into retirement and inactivity. Ben Sidonia rose only to give a semblance of existence

x

to his disheartened and expiring party. At length, Twaddle, overwhelmed by the terror and embarrassment of an agitation, which he could neither crush by brute force, nor restrain by any devices of his intellect, fell suddenly sick, even to political death, and to the astonishment of the country, resigned office, and accepted the Chiltern Hundreds, although actually in possession of a clear majority of seven ! !

A Whig resign office with a majority ! it was enough to revive the popular faith in miracles, and sink Hume's essay to perdition !

King John having abdicated, who was to succeed him? There was a stormy interregnum of a whole month, during which time everything went on as usual, and a fresh election for the City of Jugglers took place.

Viridor was the democratic candidate. He was opposed by uncounted gold, and some human pretence to senatorial honors, whose name has escaped me. The struggle was hot and close. Every voice was raised in favour of Viridor; but, thanks to our Landocracy's repudiation of the ballot, for all purposes but their own club elections, every five-pound note was in favour of the Plutocrat. Nevertheless, there was a spirit walking the streets of the great city which whispered to the hearts and consciences of men as it passed, that the days of soul-dealing were passing away; and that Truth and Justice were, after all, the interest of rich as well as poor. Viridor was elected—elected by a majority of nine, the number of the muses.

Not a single bribe had been given by his friends, on any pretence, or under any disguise. All he had done was to print an address, which was distributed to every elector.

His speech on the hustings concluded with these pointed words—

"My countrymen! I thank you for the trust you place in my charge. I hope few months will elapse before I shall again appeal to your support, when no limited constituency, no household extension of suffrage, no pitiful half measure of justice, in any way, will prevent *any* one of the thousands I now see before me from exercising his natural rights as a man, a thinker, and a citizen! Your election makes me the representative of a class, my own principles make me a representative of the whole people!"

Then burst from the panting crowd, upon whose hearts the words of Viridor descended like drops of liquid fire, one mighty, heartspoken shout for equal rights as men, which swelled and swelled upon the air, until even at Westminster, its magnetic shock caused trees to wave, and the souls of oligarchs to tremble.

The people asked for justice. Woe to the foolish crew that yet delayed their answer! Will history teach nothing to such men? It taught no wisdom to Louis Philippe, none to Guizot. Are the Twaddles, and the Chicory* Woodenheads, and the Grubs, and their adherents, more obstinate than Louis, more ignorant than Guizot?

The sequel will teach us.

* A Chancellor of the Exchequer, who advocates the fraudulent adulteration of coffee with a vile and noxious root called chicory.

CHAPTER IV.

THE PANIC—THE BEGINNING OF THE END.

LIKE thoughts of vengeance upon the soul of an exiled patriot, night descended upon the great City of Jugglers. A sea of men rushed, and surged, and recoiled, in the principal thoroughfares of the capital. Hoarse cries, sombre rumblings, and murmurings of the agitated crowd fell with dreadful distinctness upon the assembled senators at St. Stephen's. It was known that the military were all under arms, but the moral sentiment was wanting to the hearts of the fragmentary, and, as it were, provisional ministry. Their courage was at zero, their energies were paralysed, and all their words and counsels indicated deplorable weakness and indecision.

"The Franchise for ever!" shouted the mob, and the greater number of the middle classes joined, either openly or secretly, in the cry. It seemed as if all London had descended into the streets. Every effort of the police was utterly ineffectual. It was no Kennington-common meeting, but a unanimous rising of the working classes—a demonstration of their strength, and an assertion of their rights. All the youth of the metropolis joined enthusiastically in the cry—every voteless lodger, whatever his station in life, involuntarily sympathised in the movement.

It was proposed to order the military to charge the populace; many members of the House of Commons, which had become, in the extremity of the supposed danger, the centre of executive as well as administrative power, supported the proposition.

Viridor rose from the seat he had just taken amid the few Fire-worshippers in the assembly. " If you shed blood—only one drop of blood—this night," he said solemnly, "your lives are not worth three hours' purchase. The people are in earnest. It is no partial rising. A single musket fired is the signal of a terrific conflict, of a civil war from one end of the country to the other. Rather let us mount horse ourselves, and sally forth to harangue the people. I will give notice of a bill for extension of suffrage to all adults tomorrow; to-night we must give the people hope—or await the crisis of their despair."

At such moments the strongest mind invariably takes the lead. The hated Viridor's advice was immediately acted upon. That a word from him or Darian would decide the conduct of the people, no one for an instant doubted. In reality, the two theoretical Republicans had as little control over the outbreak and its leaders as any of their colleagues; but their names were all-powerful at the moment.

Accordingly Viridor and Darian, who was in the gallery of the House at the time, mounted two horses, which they procured with difficulty, and alternately addressing the crowd, by degrees made their way down Parliament Street, and along the Strand, until a vivid brightness, reflected on the eastern sky, announced that some building had been fired by the rioters.

The same prophetic thought struck both Darian and Viridor at the same moment.

"It is the *Timeserver* office !" exclaimed the latter.

"I fear so," replied Darian, "But see, what is that? They are dragging a man along with some ferocious intent—"

"Away with the rascally Soul Agent," cried the surrounding mob, and Viridor, dashing forwards, beheld, by the gleam of a lamp, the livid features of Ignatius, who, with torn garments, and a rope about his neck, was, doubtless, on the verge of expiating his moral iniquities by a summary condemnation and execution at the hands of the people he had despised and degraded.

Viridor seized the Soul Agent by the arm, and, by an almost superhuman exertion of strength, released him from the hands of the two men who held him. Then Darian, having dismounted from his horse, half dragged, half carried the exhausted and terrified Ignatius through the crowd, to an adjoining tavern. His gigantic stature and great bodily vigour enabled him to effect this object by a prodigious effort, whilst Viridor appealed to all the better feelings of the people, and entreated them to communicate to their friends the immediate prospect of a legal recognition of their rights, and, at length, by a happy and audacious suggestion, was the means of restoring tranquillity, and averting the threatening tempest.

"Let us form ourselves," he cried, "into a human telegraph, and immediately transmit the good news to the whole body of the patriots. My name is Bernard Viridor, my friend is Arthur Darian ; we pledge ourselves that justice shall be done you if you will refrain from all brutal violence, unworthy of your sacred cause."

The people hailed the suggestion with acclamations; and as their immediate objects were indefinite, and their leaders undecided, soon began to disperse, and seek their homes and suppers. A shower of rain accelerated this movement, and thus the danger of an insurrection was, for the moment, removed.

But Robert Russel Brown, the stout partner of the dark speculator, who stood in the shadow of the Duke's statue in our first chapter (like many things as mean that flourish in the shadow of military power), had the misfortune to be hanged from a lamp-post on Blackfriars Bridge, where he was found in the morning by the police, who cut him down, and carried him to the nearest station-house.

We must now pass rapidly over the few events yet to be recorded in these pages. The day arrived for the third reading of Viridor's bill. It was carried in defiance of the most violent opposition. It had fifty thousand supporters outside, whose choral eloquence did much for its success.

The franchise was extended to every male in the kingdom having attained the age of twenty-one years. A dissolution of parliament was expected. The people were in ecstacies of triumph. Viridor was sent for by the Queen. He declined office. Malignant rumour said that he was too stern a republican to serve a monarch— in his eyes an extravagant superfluity.

Meanwhile, the panic in the Soul Market had reached its climax. The devil himself would not have bought souls at so grievous a discount. The Soul Exchange was shut up, and the beadle was its only tenant. The Exeter Arcade was not more desolate.

Ignatius had migrated to America, with a view to slave-dealing. He could not make up his mind to relinquish his old trade. The tribe of *Nut*—to quote Hindostanee from the "Wanderings of a Pilgrim," a recent work on India, by a lady of remarkable talent—the race of high-caste jugglers had lost the brightest star of their benighted firmament. Peace be to his victims!

Darian and Basiline were married.

"We have won the prize!" said Darian; "we have a right to happiness,—let us have not one, but twelve honeymoons, and then——"

"There is an Austrian empire to destroy!" said the beautiful Hungarian, sudden fire lighting up the languishing eyes, with which she gazed upon her husband, as their carriage, drawn by snorting steeds of iron, was borne swiftly away from the great City of Jugglers.

The same night, Viridor returned home to his chambers, after sharing the festivities at Darian's palace. He had no dread of intruders now; for he had had a new patent lock put upon his door, in case his second self-installed guest should chance to be of a less eligible character than the first. And yet, strange and unaccountable spectacle! the first thing he beheld on entering his sitting-room was Grace Morton, seated in his armchair, her head thrown back, her fair face pale as a marble portrait, her lips slightly parted, her arms pendant at her sides, her bosom heaving occasionally with deep sighs, as in a dream of passionate sorrow. She slept. Viridor approached her, and moved the candle which was burning upon the table, in such a manner as to relieve her eyelids from its glare. A sense of remorse came over him. For three days he had not seen Grace; he had forgotten her existence, or postponed all thoughts of love, to the overwhelming pressure of political activity. How many audiences had he given—how many visits had he received—how many letters had he written —what stirring articles had he composed, in that brief interval!

But what cared Grace for politics! Like an exquisite flower, she had taken root on one spot, and that spot was Viridor's heart. Not hearing from him, she had called again and again at his chambers, without finding him at home. At length, that evening she found the door open. Viridor had failed to turn the key, going out hastily that morning.

There she had waited, hour after hour, a prey to the bitterest anxiety. At length, utterly exhausted by the tumult of her feelings, she had fallen asleep, as described, in the great arm-chair, with the candle, which she had found means to light, burning on the table.

Never had she appeared so beautiful to Viridor, as at that moment. He felt quite a criminal, for causing her so much pain, as he now well divined. He took her hand and pressed it in his own. She woke, and gazed upon him, at first, as in a dream. Then suddenly becoming conscious of his presence, she murmured in a tone of gentle reproach, that brought tears in the eyes of the repentant poet—

" O, Bernard, Bernard! had you *quite* forgotten me?"

"My own dearest girl ! my sweet, beautiful Grace ! Never, by all my eternal hopes I swear it, never did I truly love woman until I saw you ! Oh ! let us part no more in life, my adored, my eternal bride !"

And Viridor, kneeling by the side of Grace, kissed the taper fingers of her small white hands.

This is the beginning of the history I have hoped would find some few kindred souls to sympathise with its mysteries. The beginning, did I say? Yes, the beginning, indeed; however contradictory may seem the conventional necessity which compels me, at the same moment, to acknowledge with regret that it is

THE END.

JUST PUBLISHED,

T Y P E E ;

OR,

A RESIDENCE IN THE MARQUESAS

BY

Herman Melville.

With an Engraving on Copper by F. H. T. Bellew.

Price 2s. 6d.

" A companion after our own hearts."—*Times.*

" This book is excellent—quite first-rate.—*Blackwood.*

" A narrative of singular beauty—a second Robinson Crusoe."—
John Bull.

This is the **only cheap Unabridged
Edition** extant—all others being more or
less curtailed. The volume just issued is a
verbatim reprint of the original work, without
addition or diminution.

H. J. GIBBS, 4, TAVISTOCK-STREET, STRAND.

CHARACTERISTICS

OF

THE THREE KINGDOMS:

CONSISTING OF

THREE ETCHINGS,

By F. H. T. Bellew,

WITH

DESCRIPTIVE LETTER-PRESS, by Captain Bellew.

Price 2s. 6d.

Also Now Ready, price 6d.,

THE COCKNEY IN SCOTLAND,

BY F. H. T. BELLEW

(Junius Javelin),

With Numerous Illustrations on Wood and Copper, by the Author.

London:—H. J. GIBBS, 4, TAVISTOCK STREET.
Edinburgh:—HUGH PATON, ADAM SQUARE.